JOURNEYS TO THE EDGE OF WONDER

A Novel of Spiritual Adventure

Jack Byrd

Introduction by Alan Cohen

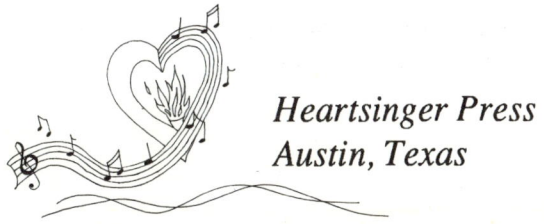

Heartsinger Press
Austin, Texas

JOURNEYS TO THE EDGE OF WONDER
A Novel of Spiritual Adventure

© 1992 By Jack Byrd

Cover Art: *Enlightenment* © 1978
By Robert Venosa

All rights reserved. No part of this book may be reproduced or utilized in any form or by any means, electronic or mechanical, including photocopying, recording in any information storage and retrieval system, without permission in writing from the Publisher.

Library of Congress Catalog Number: 92-73804

ISBN: 0-9633982-0-2

To order additional copies of this book:
please send check or money order in the amount of $9.95 per copy (sales tax included) + $2.00 postage & handling for the first copy and $0.50 postage & handling for each additional copy *(if 5 or more copies are ordered, postage & handling is free!)* to:

Heartsinger Press
2021 Guadalupe St., Suite 100-56
Austin, Texas 78705

Please address all comments and inquiries to the above address.

Printed in the United States of America
at Morgan Printing in Austin, Texas

To my mother—
for her unceasing love and support.

And to my father—
who lies buried near a small West Texas town
and is not forgotten by his son.

ACKNOWLEDGMENTS

Many hands and hearts contributed to the creation and publication of this book. I am grateful to everyone who assisted me in even the smallest way. Special thanks go to:

- Deborah Morin, for her many valuable suggestions and continued support,

- Alan Cohen, for his heart-felt and beautiful introduction,

- Olympia Koutsoudas, for her superb editorial suggestions,

- Robert Venosa, for his generosity regarding use of his magnificent painting, *Enlightenment*, for the cover of this book,

- Sara Gill, for her beautifully crafted special art work,

- the staff at Morgan Printing, for their friendly and professional assistance,

- and especially Donna Morris. Donna, you lent a much-needed ear as this book evolved. You understood its scope and intent and offered valuable insights. You supported this book—and me—in a way no one else could. You were a true friend. For this I will always be grateful.

INTRODUCTION

We are living during an amazing time. Lives are changing more quickly than ever. The challenges that face us as individuals and a planet are more pressing and crucial than ever. People at every strata of life are questioning the values under which we were trained. The world into which we were born is not the one we are living in, nor is it the one we will pass on to the next generation.

It is clear that if we are to survive as people and a planet, we are going to have to discover a new way of living, beginning with a new consciousness. In short, we need to do something radically different, we need to do it quickly, and we need new models for living in harmony with the purpose Spirit intended for us.

Journeys is a magnificent, poetic, and heartfelt vision of the possibilities for reclaiming the heaven we have lost. In his noble, eloquent, and yet personal style Jack Byrd takes us through an amazing journey of inner transformation. From almost paralyzing pain and confusion to the ultimate glory of ascension, we find a map of the adventure in consciousness that all of us ultimately traverse.

It did not take me long, as I wended my way through these sometimes frightening, always stimulating passages, to realize that it was my own story that I was reading. Spirit has an awesome way of placing personal lessons before us, and *Journeys* is certainly a mirror of my own life, from the darkest fears to the brightest possibilities. Perhaps you will discover the same.

Perhaps the most important understanding which this book illuminated for me, even in the early pages, is that there is a wave of energy that has flooded the Earth plane, for our awakening. This energy has affected all of us in many ways, often dramatically. Feelings of inner explosiveness, fear, elation, tension, frustration, ecstasy, confusion, and intense excitement are but a few of the manifestations of the quickening that is now happening. If you have experienced such feelings, or at least have had a sense of confusion about your purpose on the planet, then take heart. *Journeys* offers us an exciting and promising roadmap for the translation of our lives from hardship to divinity. The changes are good, and we must flow with them to be lifted to our next stage of evolution.

As William Sherrill, through whose eyes we discover beauties, declares, "We are not helpless victims whose fate has been cast... I know that I belong to another race that represents evolution consciously entering into time and directing its own destiny."

The book you are holding in your hands offers divine principles, some of which may be far ahead of the day when they will be accepted and practiced commonly. In this sense, *Journeys*, may be a premonition of a world yet to come. That world will come through you and me.

And yet the principles upon which the new world is based are as familiar as the teachings of Jesus and the other great ones throughout the ages. "Forgive... and replace your withered, stifled, confined, tormented self with the unlimited freedom and joy of knowing that comes with the knowledge of ourselves as God's children."

Is *Journeys* a true story? I believe it is possible. I believe that there is a plan and an evolution that is moving within us and around us that goes far beyond any understanding we may surmise based on the life we have seen until now. I do know that the life toward which we are moving is far more magnificent and wondrous than the one we have known.

        Alan Cohen
        August 1992

JOURNEYS TO THE EDGE OF WONDER

A Novel of Spiritual Adventure

Jack Byrd

"Someday, after mastering the winds, the waves, the tide, and gravity, we shall harness for God the energies of love: and then—for the second time in the history of the world man will have discovered fire."
—Teilhard de Chardin

"Life is but a dream dreamed by God. The beautiful thing about it is that it is we who awaken from it."
—Ancient Saying

PROLOG

My name is Victor Holliday. I am a publisher of books. The one you are holding now was written by a man I met only once, and then just briefly. The manuscript came into my hands six months ago, with such an urgency of purpose that I had to set aside all other projects in favor of it.

I met William Sherrill at a party given by a mutual friend. We spoke only in passing, making polite conversation about nothing of consequence. Though my attention was elsewhere that night, I do remember the striking, unusual look he had about him. It was the expression in his face, mostly—a kind of tension and softness mated together, a strange combination of intensity struggling to be controlled and a degree of sincerity I'd never seen before. And there was a sadness, a sadness as deep as the ocean and distant as the stars. I saw it. I knew what it was. He couldn't hide it, though he seemed unconsciously to be trying to.

After reading the manuscript this man produced, I wished to God I had spent time trying to understand who he was—*what* he was. But my attention had been focused on our hostess, Mindy L. Since the party, I had not heard from her until six months ago, at which time she came to me with the manuscript. She said she was frightened and very confused. She had read it twice in the past week and had felt her world was spinning away beneath her feet. William had sent the manuscript in the mail to her with specific instructions to read it and then show it to me in the hope I would publish it.

I read the manuscript far into the night. The urgency alluded to in its latter pages was clear. Yet it was not just the clear call for action that kept me turning the pages. No, it was more than that. It was the sheer *beauty* of it all, the sheer rapture I felt with its author as the pages fell before the probing of my eyes like wheat before the scythe. This was clearly no mere diary of a man teetering on the brink of insanity as it had first appeared. This was the story of a mighty soul's unfolding into something beyond our wildest dreams and beliefs. His hopes, his fears, his confusion—all these were present. And underlying these was a courage and a raw strength of will rarely seen in the world today.

I wish I had known William Sherrill. I'm convinced by his book that he was a courageous explorer of uncharted and sometimes frightening territories—and a great man. I salute him, wherever he may be in that vast expanse of reality he learned to roam through at will. If any of the entries set forth in the coming pages can be believed (and the words he used are made of iron and fire), each of us needs to take a very long, hard look at ourselves and our picture of the world—and the underpinnings we believe so securely hold that picture in place. If the urgency expressed in the latter part of the book has even a grain of truth in it, we may not have much time. You must decide for yourself.

Beginnings

January 22

Sunset pales the sky in deepening shades of lavender, red, blue. The first stars wink into view. The crystal silence is broken by the shrill call of a night bird, then effortlessly reassembled. The moon is a gourd of light. Twilight.

The sun has fallen below the horizon. It is like a hammer beating down the earth, pulling a veil of darkness behind it. Shapes and shadows dance in the subtle breeze. Tall trees stand like silent sentries in the night. I am alone.

It's happening again. I can feel it. A shiver is going up my spine—a tingling sensation running throughout my body. And a 'whoosh' sound like night winds rushing through a just-opened door is rising in my head. Louder. Louder. I am afraid.

The fourth time in as many nights. Each attack has been stronger than the one before. Dear God, what's happening to me? The sound in my head is growing louder and stronger, like a freight train coming closer and closer. I can't stop it. I can't stop it! Dear God, I'm going to die! The pain! Aaaaagggggghhhhh!

* * *

It's over now. I can relax a little. A sense of relief, euphoria even, has settled over my body and mind. Slowly I open my eyes. I had shut them when the light, a beautiful golden light, flashed in my mind. The light had gradually faded to the pitch black darkness I'm used to and comfortable with. I seem to be all right. But, oh, God! My hand! What's happening to my hand! Sweet Jesus!

* * *

Wave upon wave of a nameless fear crashed against my spirit. I watched helplessly as my left hand grew brighter and brighter by small degrees. A pins-and-needles sensation shot through my hand; otherwise, it felt undamaged. I trembled with apprehension. My fear was not so much because my hand seemed surrounded by an ever increasingly intense golden light as because it was seeming to dissolve *into* that light, was *becoming* that light.

My panic eased in a few moments, though, as the brightness around my hand began to fade and lessen, just as the brightness that flashed inside my mind had faded quietly into darkness. Soon I felt completely normal—no lights, no sounds, no strange rising sensations.

January 23

I have thought of calling a doctor, a friend, a minister—anybody. But what could they tell me? That I have been having delusions and need rest? That I am mentally ill? I know they would find nothing wrong with me physically. I feel fine. In fact, I have never felt better in my whole life—even back in my college days when I was running five miles a day. An exhilaration similar to what I felt back then after a hard run of several miles swept over me, enveloped me as the eerie light surrounded me. But what I feel now is more than just an unusual brand of 'runners high,' much more.

I am troubled. I know I did not imagine the experience. But what did it mean? The first time something similar had occurred—a couple of weeks ago—I had simply been awakened by a shrill sound like that of a tea kettle whistling in my head. The sound was accompanied by a mild sense of giddiness and the feeling that I was rising a couple of feet into the air. Nothing too unusual. Nothing to worry about. A strange, unusually lucid dream perhaps, or a bizarre, disorienting state of mind brought on by too much wine earlier.

A more dramatic attack occurred the next night. I was awakened by what I thought was thunder. Drawing back the drapes over my bedroom window, I saw nothing but twinkling stars, a cloudless night. I laughed at myself and went back to bed. Just after settling back in, I heard an electric hiss, a crackle that seemed to come from inside my head, and saw a flash of light so brilliant I jumped up with a start. For over an hour I felt dazed and restless. No reason for alarm, I thought. Too much stress lately. Not enough sleep or good food.

Nothing else happened for a couple of days and I began to relax a little. But a few nights later the sensations returned, with greater force than before. I became genuinely concerned for my health and about my sanity. I called a close friend for support, understanding, anything she could offer; but she was too busy to speak to me. "In a hurry...can't talk now.... Can it wait?" "No, it can't," I said to myself." *"No it can't!"* I said something to her—I don't remember what—and hung up the phone. It didn't matter. I knew by the tone of her voice that she wouldn't understand, wouldn't be able to give me the comfort and reassurance I so desperately needed.

At this point I feel I can't speak to anyone about these strange episodes. It is no longer a case of needing to be reassured they are not hallucinatory or harmful. The light around my hand changed all that. I *know* the episodes are real and I feel they must be harmful. I also know that no authority on Earth can tell me exactly what has happened or what the end of it all might be. I am alone in this.

January 27
My hand seems perfectly normal today, though it still tingles as though a mild electrical charge is constantly racing through it. But I can't get over the frightening certainty that it had not been merely *surrounded* by light but had actually *dissolved* into light, had *become* light.

This morning as I stared at that hand a new fear seized me, one that caused my eyes to blink in disbelief and my entire body to shudder. The tiny scar just below the little finger of that hand—the scar I had gotten last summer when a frightened cat scratched me—it was gone! It was gone!

February 4
I rose early and watched the morning sun burst through the clouds in shades of gold and vermillion. I squinted through my bedroom window at the new day with weariness instead of excitement. I hadn't slept much or well—hardly at all, in fact. The experiences of the past month or so have raised many questions I can't answer, many fears I dare not voice. When I stared in the mirror, I saw a haggard, troubled face. I stayed up late last night, trying to understand what has been happening to me, which is why I started keeping this journal; but the stress was due to something more than tiredness. My face looks as

though it was a battleground where thoughts and feelings had waged a huge battle against fear—and been soundly beaten.

Mindy will be back in town soon. Perhaps she, of all people, will understand how I feel. At least she can give me some comfort. I hope so.

February 7

It happened again last night. Dear God, I'm afraid! Like an alcoholic quickly losing himself to a bottle, I seem to be losing myself to this thing. But I don't *want* this bottle. I didn't seek it out; I didn't ask for it.

I remember going through today in a kind of reverie, like a somnambulist. Thank God it's Saturday—no monotonous drive into the city to a dull job. I took several short naps to catch up on the sleep I missed last night, but my rest was troubled—if, indeed, it could be called rest at all. Once I woke up and forgot where I was, what time of day it was. I felt drugged. I know I am only trying to use sleep to forget the turbulence and fear those strange, psychotic experiences stir up in me. They weigh on me like a heavy slab of wrought iron.

The numbness ended a couple of hours ago. Fear crashed through it like a huge iron ball hurtling through an old brick building, crashed through my confused, troubled mind as it happened again. But this time something new was added: in addition to my left hand once again glowing with a bright, golden blaze, my right leg and three fingers of my right hand began to glow also. Once again I feared that my entire body was losing itself to something alien and horrible. In silent, helpless terror, I felt a numbing, electric sensation spread until it engulfed both of my arms and legs.

I have searched my mind for some philosophy, some scrap of religious belief that could explain this terrifying event or that could comfort me with some truth, something that could make me feel that things would turn out all right. But nothing I have learned in all my thirty years offers a single shred of comfort to me. I have become painfully aware of how shallowly most of us go through life, accepting as the truth of existence the first systems of thought and religious belief given us by our parents and teachers and ministers. And now I see each of these initial models of life, with few exceptions, as just a thin veneer—a single coat of flat paint masking for a moment the alternating sheens of terror and trembling wonder at being alive that lie just underneath. And now some unknown force is altering my life, a force that cares nothing for religions or philosophies—a cold, dispassionate, alien principle that is slowly, methodically making me over in its image. All my beliefs in goodness and love and immortality melted away, when the flesh and bone of my body dissolved into...what? Into what?

February 8

I awoke this morning and saw the sun peeking its reddish face over the top layer of gray-silver clouds. For a moment I thought what I had experienced last night was a nightmare. But as the cobwebs of sleep were brushed from my mind, I knew I had not been dreaming. My arms and legs now looked normal; but I could not rid myself of the thought, of the *certainty*, that for a short period of time they had vanished like melting snow, had ceased to be flesh and blood, and had dissolved into something else.... They had melted out of existence and gone to some alien place, only to return *in better condition than before.*

This time, two more scars and a blemish had mysteriously disappeared from my limbs, along with the stiffness in my left elbow—an old football injury. I felt good physically, exhilarated really. For the first time I wondered if these experiences were good rather than evil in nature, as I had first assumed. Perhaps they were the prelude to something wonderful and beautiful.

But I felt within myself that nothing so frightening—so alien—could be good. And if these changes *were* good in nature, if they were but the prelude to some miraculous transformation all humanity would one day go through—just as all caterpillars will one day go through the mysterious change into butterflies—why were they happening to me? Why not to a saint, a mystic, a minister—to someone holy, someone deserving, someone who still believed in the God of religions?

If my experiences were indeed good and natural events, like puberty, blueprinted and programmed into the cellular structure of my body to take place at a particular time, why were they not happening all around me to people older, wiser, or simply more spiritual than I? No, I thought, these are not holy events to be cherished and coveted. They can't be. I've done nothing to be worthy of them. They *can't* be. And as I gazed at the mirror on the wall of my seaside cottage, the flesh seemed to melt away from my face. Shivering in fear, I stared through the empty sockets of a cold, lifeless structure of bone.

February 19

I quit my job this morning, withdrew my savings from the bank. I can find no meaning or joy in my work anymore. Life has no color. My fear of dissolving completely into that spreading light haunts me constantly, steals all my thoughts, seeps into all my actions. It's been four weeks since the strange and frightening experiences began. They have not returned since the night of the 7th. I hope and pray to whatever gods there might be that this was the last of them. I want no more of the loneliness, the fear of disintegration evoked during those times.

Perhaps the episodes are over. But their work is done. I can never be the same. The physical scars that vanished are painful reminders that I did not dream or imagine the experiences, and the scars left on my beliefs about the world are like ugly, infected sores that will not heal. I've lost interest in the few friends I had and the few activities I used to enjoy. Superficial—all of it. I find myself becoming cynical and lazy and apathetic. I do little but sleep and think. I no longer am joyous when seeing and doing simple things. I am alone, even in crowds. There is nothing—no one—to comfort me. I won't call Mindy. There's no point any longer. She means well, but what can she say or do? There is a hunger in me—a thirst—for what, I do not know. I need time, and I need help to sort all this out. But who can I trust? Who can I turn to? Who?

March 12

Weeks have passed, and though no more frightening experiences have come to me, still I feel the anguish at what has gone before, feel the growing fear that something is very different about me, is very wrong with me. I feel more and more that I am losing control of myself—of my body and my thoughts. Something alien and possibly evil is changing me into something other than human and there is nothing I can do to stop this change from happening...no one I can turn to for help and reassurance.

Never in all my life have I felt so terribly alone. This feeling is not just the aloneness one feels when others aren't around or don't seem to care. It is an aloneness that reflects the isolation of all humanity from the rest of the universe. It is a symbol of the sterile, antiseptic and analytical separation from nature that reached full flower with the scientific revolution and the coming of technology. As I gaze out at the structures of metal and brick and steel that one cannot escape even this far away from the city, I feel a loathing for them. They have no life. They are artificial and hollow, an insult to whatever powers created the trees and the rocks and the seas.

A great sadness is sweeping over me. It is a sadness born of the knowledge so clear to me now that men and women have taken the beauty and goodness of spirit entrusted to them and bartered it for material things, losing themselves and spoiling the earth in the process. I am beginning to see the story of Adam and Eve in the Garden of Eden in a new light. I see it now as more than just a myth. In a way I cannot explain, I know the story to be a true reflection of how the consciousness of men and women fell with the abuse of self-consciousness and the creative principle. The mistake is in seeing it as a myth or a single story happening on a particular day. It is a record of the rise and fall of the consciousness of humanity over an immense period of time. I *know* this. And I don't know how I know this.

I've never had such feelings before; and as I ponder these thoughts, a series of questions takes hold of me. Can these new insights and feelings be a result of internal changes heralded, or even caused, by those five frightening experiences? Is this conclusion just another step in the process of isolation and alienation from the world that began with that rushing sound in my head? Is this sense of aloneness as purely negative as I have assumed it to be? For even with the pain and the fear, a curious sense of joy and knowingness is spreading over me, a mixed feeling akin to the pain and joy I have felt when my heart has been broken. I am confused.

March 14

No clear answers have come to the questions put forth in my last entry, but a growing sense of wonder is gradually replacing the fear that sought to envelop me. Though I no longer view this new way of looking at the world as evil, it *is* confusing and seems to alienate me further from others. I feel I have been swept away in a small boat, far away from other people playing in the sand and shallows of the shoreline, with only a twig for a paddle. It now seems evident that the price of science and technology has been too great. In its quest for power and control humankind has lost its innocence and true purpose—whatever that might be—along with the joy of just living, of just being. My spirit aches for simpler times, aches to run barefoot through lush forests unblemished by the hand of man, to live in a wild and beautiful world of unknown wonders and adventures. I yearn to live in the world as it must have been when it was young.

March 29

I have begun to rise early and greet the morning sun. I take time to walk through the brush and along the beach. I bathe in the ocean at night under a kiln of ivory stars. I am beginning to feel alive again, and with this renewed joy in simple living comes a peace I've never known before. I am beginning to care less and less what brought about these changes in me or where they might be leading me. I am learning to be content with the joy of each day, each moment, and to not worry what tomorrow will bring. The fears and anxieties brought on by the mysterious experiences a few weeks ago are slowly vanishing, without a fuss, like mist on open air.

April 19

It's been weeks since my last entry. The questions regarding my sanity remain, yet I feel much less fear than I did during those early days. I am growing more and more convinced that the nature of what happened to me—and continues to happen—is good. I hope to God it is. I am unsettled by the lack of control and direction I have, as well as a lack of clear understanding. But a calmness, an inner reserve of peace that I am unable to explain, has begun to settle over me.

I've had no more of the explosive experiences, but that strange and frightening process has set in motion a series of transformations I am unable to stop, if indeed I wanted to. The loneliness, the isolation, the alienation from others even while in their presence continues; but I no longer see this as a solely negative experience. It has given me a chance to reevaluate my life, to examine it bit by bit from the ground up. Things that once seemed important have a shallow, metallic look to them now. In fact, most of my life up to this point seems to have been filled with meaningless actions and thoughts that I've called 'living.' And therein lies one of the keys to the fear those early experiences engendered. They were giving me my first real look at what a jest my life had been to that point, at how little I had settled for and been contented with, at how quickly and cheaply I had bartered my potential as a human being.

I shouldn't be so unkind toward myself and others for the way we've lived our lives. We just didn't know there was a better way. We just didn't *know*. Oh, there have always been those who knew of a better was and tried to show it to others, but fear and ignorance are great slave-masters; and the cold, barren prison walls of the narrow, limited world we've made for ourselves are all we've known. The way we live our lives is not really anyone's fault; but it's a tragedy that leaves me weeping like a child. The irony is that I am now able to see the triviality of my life, yet unable to find a meaningful path.

I have a hunger, an insatiable desire, to find the path to deeper meaning in my life. There is also a fear that this process within me will suddenly stop, leaving me trapped between two states of consciousness—one I can no longer go back to; one I cannot go forward in. I must be contented to let this process unfold as it will; I must trust it. Perhaps in so doing I will learn the true meaning of faith. Something was ripped away from me those few weeks ago, and for a reason I've yet to learn. That I will never be the same is clear to me. But perhaps those experiences hold the key, the answer, to my dilemma. I only hope I can survive the changes.

April 30

Sadness washes over me, permeates my being. I can't help thinking of how life seems to have denied or mistreated me. This self-absorption is an indulgence. I know that. But sometimes I choose to give reign to that part of myself.

The light of the evening sun is playing through the branches of a beautiful old tree filled to near-bursting with countless green leaves. A gentle wind is blowing through the upper branches, causing the leaves to shake back and forth vigorously. They are dancing for me, and at the same time, like mischievous little fairies, *laughing* at me, at my self pity, my fear, my confusion. They know better than I the humor and joy of life. They know better than I how to surrender to each moment's perfection. I still can't surrender. I'm still afraid for myself, for what has happened and may continue to happen to me.

* * *

Twilight has silently stolen upon me. I must have spent at least a couple of hours absorbed in myself. I watch as the pastel blue bowl of evening turns, by seamless shades, into a deepening blue sky. I see the Big Dipper, Ursa Major. The huge ladle of the cup portion, I notice, is held at the exact angle a cup of water offered to a thirsty traveler would be. I am that thirsty traveler. My throat is parched with the fears I have swallowed in the desire to control my life, to understand what is happening to me. *Oh, God, I'm afraid of losing my dreams.* I imagine that Jesus, the Jesus I loved as a child and denied as an adult, is offering that cup of stars to me—offering me life and an end to all thirst from that ladle of wonder and beauty and immense magnitude. My soul is not large enough, not important enough to hold what those endless stars are offering. I am not worthy—just as I am not worthy of the transformation taking place in my body and soul. I look in the Savior's eyes, look deep into those eyes...eyes that have no end to them, eyes I could lose myself in. I feel a sense of peace. Those eyes tell me I *am* worthy. I *am* loved. I breathe those seven stars into my heart and feel less lonely than I have in a very long time.

May 4

I look out across the rolling sea before me. I turn around and gaze at the mountains behind me. I ponder my reasons for being in this cottage, in this place. I've always been a loner, even as a child. I enjoy family and friends but have felt somehow distant from them all, felt that I didn't fit in, didn't belong. My dream was to own my own place facing the ocean, backed by the mountains. In this way I thought to get the best of all possible worlds. I'd have the excitement and mystery of the ever-changing sea to my front; the strength, solidity, and permanence of the rocks and hills to my back. It was a way to escape my feelings of being different—separate. It was a place for my solitude to unfold itself, a place for whatever creativity lay within me to come to fruition. What a joke! Any creativity I might have has lain fallow all these years, clouded over by laziness, blocked by apathy and lack of direction.

I tried to paint for a while and littered my closets with unfinished portraits of the sea, the sunsets, the mountains, the stars; but the pictures never really satisfied that ache within me to give something of myself to the world. None of them satisfied my desire to create something I would be proud to share with others. None of them was worth a damn! I finally stopped trying; and a part of me started drying up, atrophying, dying. I now see that the perfect environment for me to live and create in has very little to do with the outside world. I'd have been unsuccessful and unhappy wherever I went.

My unhappiness has had to do with the environment I've created within myself, I think. For, yes—it's now clear that I've created my own internal reality all these years. The external world, my family, my friends—they are not responsible for my view of the world. When I found no happiness or fulfillment in my world, I blamed those around me, blamed life. I never knew.... But something is changing inside of me. A part that was empty is slowly becoming filled, drop by drop.

I would never have been happy in the life I lived before. I was spending all my time and energies running away from life, hiding in what I called the 'desire for solitude.' But I was running away even from solitude. I never even took the time to enjoy the aloneness possible here—never ran along the beach reveling in the joy of life. I never even hiked to the top of these small mountains behind me.

I've lied to myself—so thoroughly I never even suspected what I was up to. I've been afraid of life and have used every opportunity I could to justify my anger and loneliness and frustration. Yes. Yes! But now something has changed. Something wonderful has happened. A gleam of golden light has settled around the edges of the dismal picture I've painted of my life, and as the gleam grows brighter I see that the fear of the past few months is not of losing the life I've known thus far. No, that's not it. There's been so little to lose. It's the trembling fear of losing myself to wonder, to something greater than myself, greater than the known....

A storm is coming soon—I can feel it—a mighty wind that will swallow up the last of my security, the last of my faith and trust in the old ways. The end of the world is coming for me, the end of the only world I've known. And there will be no little corner left to hide in.

May 16

A light flashed on in my head last night, a burst like a thousand fireworks displays rocketing through my brain. Once more the wind rushed through my head, the way it had on that first night, so long ago, when my transformation began. But this time it was much stronger, much wilder—a mighty wind raging through my mind with all the primeval force of hurricanes and tornadoes, earthquakes and erupting volcanoes. And this time I was not afraid.

The golden glow grew within me until my entire head seemed made of light. Then it spread through my arms and chest and legs until my entire body seemed filled with it—filled like a bottle with a warm, thick, fluid light. I felt my body vanish into that warm effulgence, cease to exist. I cared not if I were dying, nor if I would ever be able to return to the world of flesh and blood, so exhilarated did I feel. A veil of darkness lifted from me then, and all my fears vanished into that golden radiance—slid from me like smooth stones down an icy slope. I felt weightless, free, ecstatic.

Rising lightly into the gold-tinged air, I passed right through the roof of my cottage. With but a single thought I was miles over the ocean, staring at the frothy white-capped waves far beneath me. Suddenly I plunged into the ocean. To my amazement I could see through the murky blackness, could see the fish and rocks and undersea currents. Not only did I know which fish were harmful and which were not, but I also did not need to breathe or concern myself with temperature or pressure. I had never felt so free in all my life!

The sense of freedom I felt is not one that can be easily described. The joy of discovery was there, along with an ecstasy of release from bodily tensions and confinement. But what I felt most in those few moments was a profound sense of *aliveness*—an aliveness so intense words fail me. If an experience such as mine were within the domain of common experience, there would be words that would communicate what I felt; but language can only be useful when it incorporates *shared* images, experiences, meanings, and feelings that everyone has known. Language evolves from common experience. I am beginning to understand why the mystics of old had such trouble communicating what they had seen or felt during a vision or other profound mystical experience. To try to communicate what there were no words for was hopeless, yet because of the love that is also present at such elevated times, they had to try—as I now have to try.

A deep love has come on the wings of my recent sojourn out of my body, a love so great it doesn't matter that others will not understand or will think me crazy or foolish. I *must* try to communicate what is happening to me during this transformative process. I *must*.... I now believe I am having a brush with the divine.

When I felt myself flying over the sea, I was in a state of mind I've never known before, except dimly in dreams. How can I explain it? Imagine the excitement you have when a summer storm starts rolling in. The sky begins to darken, thunder begins to roll, and what had been a boring, hot and sticky afternoon is suddenly transformed into a magical twilight. The air tastes fresh and clean, the wind rises and feels cool as it whips at your clothing. As the dark clouds roll in and dump their liquid burden in great drops, everything is intensely alive and unpredictable. All the petty cares and worries, all the mundane aspects of living by routines in the day-to-day world melt away like fish sliding into the sea. Now imagine that feeling of excitement magnified a thousand times. Add to it the feeling you had as a very young child at Christmas, or some other wonder-filled holiday, with all the excitement and love and joy also magnified a thousand times. Then you will have some idea of the magnificent joy I felt while flying through the air, reversing the laws of the world and the firm beliefs of humanity about the limitations of the mind and body, and then plunging into the ocean and viewing, without fear or effort, things no human eyes have beheld before. That experience was better by far than it would have been if I had done these things within my ordinary state of mind and being. Oh, yes! For that was the key to the experience's trembling beauty and greatness. In a dream we may perform an amazing feat such as flying, then wake up and lament that we cannot accomplish the same thing in waking consciousness. But were we able to do so, we would soon let it become as mundane as other events in our lives, for our *consciousness* has not altered. I remember looking forward to my first plane ride. I was overwhelmed by the thought that I would soon be soaring above the clouds, realizing a dream most of humanity had never known. The plane ride *was* exciting, but not as exciting as I had expected. After an hour or so of looking out the window, I grew a little bored and settled back in my seat, amazed at technology but not awed or filled with the wonder I had so wanted and expected. The more flights I took in my life, the more commonplace the experience became until flight became little more than an ordinary occurrence—convenient, yes; magical, no.

    A great sadness wells up inside of me as I become aware of how small a part of our divinity, how little of our true freedom, we know and experience. I remember with fondness, and with pain, the words of the great visionary poet, Wordsworth, when he says in "Ode on the Intimations of Immortality"

> Heaven lies about us in our infancy!
> Shades of the prison house begin to close
>   Upon the growing Boy,

> But He beholds the light, and whence it flows,
>   He sees it in his joy;
> The Youth, who daily farther from the east
>   Must travel, still is Nature's Priest,
>   And by the vision splendid
>   Is on his way attended;
> At length the Man perceives it die away,
> And fade into the light of common day.

I enjoyed the poem in my teenage years and understood its truth; but most of my enjoyment came from the secure knowledge that I would never fall prey to the traps of the world, would never lose my sense of divinity and magic. Now, despite all I thought I had done to retain my innocence and child-like wonder, I realize that I have sunk as deeply into the prison house as the others I so passionately wished to avoid becoming like. At the same time I also feel a deep wonder and strangeness as I make this entry, for the transformation occurring within me may well be an attempt to reverse that process of identifying with the world, a way to break the prison walls I've felt closing in so tightly around me most of my life. It may be that I did *not* dream in vain during those early years, that I was *not* living in a world of fantasy only but holding instead onto the only real thing in my life, though I saw it in glimpses only. Could this be why these experiences have come to me now? Could it?

I have gotten a little off track. It's understandable in light of the deep feelings evoked when I recall that otherworldly episode into the air and the sea. I don't know if it happened in another body or in the flesh and blood one I've always called home. It doesn't matter. All I know is that my body became filled with light and seemed alien and remote from anything flesh and blood. Yet it was still me, a 'me' more vital and free than I've ever known before, even in my dreams. As I rose into the air I knew an exhilaration I can't describe. I felt I had taken my first true breath of air, of life. I rose without effort into the sky and saw colors and hues I'd never seen before. There were yellows and blues and reds, of course; but they seemed to be born not of this world or the senses of man. A part of me marveled at this; another part knew it to be perfectly normal—the natural state of things. I looked at the sea far below me and wanted to plunge into its murky depths. I did so and was amazed that I did not need to breathe. And it wasn't just that I didn't need to breathe oxygen; I didn't need to breathe at all. Life was breathing *me*. It did not matter where I found myself going. I was safe, and I was unlimited. All my fears melted from me—slipped away as smoothly and easily as I had slipped away from the heavy matter of my body.

September 11

It's been a long time since I last made a serious entry—almost four months. This lapse has not been due to lack of interest on my part, just to a lack of anything I could deem as important enough to record. No more transformative episodes have occurred, though I've desperately wanted them. I've begged whatever gods or presences there are not to leave me half-formed, half-awakened; but they have been silent. The notes I scribbled to myself during the past several weeks can largely be ignored, for they mainly consist of the kind of doubts and fears and anger expressed in the first pages of this journal. The content of those notes may have been slightly different because the truth finally dawned on me that I am not the plaything of some dark, alien principle or the butt of a joke from some fiendish cosmic prankster. Nonetheless, I've let my ego-self rule my thoughts during most of the interim. I feel a little like the Israelites during the time of Moses. Even though they had been delivered from the bondage of the Egyptians and seen great miracles from God, still their faith fell from them like water through a sieve at the first sight of further trouble or discomfort. They begged for new gods to worship and fell away from a glory that had manifested before their own eyes.

I am like those Israelites for I have doubted the meaning and validity of my experiences on many occasions. I have let doubt and fear cloud my judgment. I have begged for new gods to worship because the old ones seemed to have forsaken me. Foolishness really. The ramblings of a spoiled child. It is for this reason I have destroyed those self-absorbed whinings.

In the past couple of months I have come to realize that I have not been forsaken, or abandoned, or forgotten. A wisdom far greater than mine has been guiding me, allowing me time to integrate my earlier experiences with the light, allowing me to bring up and release the remaining vestiges of fear and anger and littleness, just as one who is fasting requires time for the built-up poisons to be released from the body. It may be also that those experiences taxed my fragile mind and body to the limits they were capable of withstanding, and time had to pass before more such episodes could occur. I am hopeful this is the case and that like a circuit that has been overloaded by too much electricity flowing through it at one time I haven't blown a fuse in the process.

In any case, I now believe that these past few months of inactivity were a necessary part of my transformative process. I believe that like an unborn child I've needed a period of time to fully form, to give my body time to adapt to the new matrix of consciousness that has been sweeping over me like a huge wave for lo, these many months. Perhaps I've been in the eye of that storm the past few months—a time necessary to prepare for the coming of the next part of the storm. The possibilities are many and I can only guess what will actually happen. I have no one to talk with about such things. I've tried to communicate some of what's happened to me but even Mindy, my dear friend, Mindy, isn't able to help or understand. But I know that she loves me, the way a mother still loves the child who comes to her with a math problem she can't solve or even understand. Knowing that she loves me does make a difference; though like that child, my questions still remain.

July 14

Almost a year has passed since my last entry. Part of me feels I've failed myself in letting this journal go unattended for so long. This time, however, it's not because I had nothing to report or even that I succumbed to laziness or lack of discipline. On the contrary, so *many* things have happened. Yet I put off recording those happenings until now because I needed time for clear insights to form. I wanted time to develop a perspective out of all the confusion I was experiencing. Now I have it. Now I'm ready to write.

During these past several months I've been consumed by a passion for books. I've always loved reading books but had lost that joy five or six years ago, had grown tired of learning of someone else's triumphs and failures, loves and losses. Diving into the ocean of another person's mind and soul had become too painful. My own world had grown too narrow and brittle. But now that has changed, for *I* have changed; and books have again become the exciting adventures they were for me as a very young child.

Eight months ago I began to read books on the great religions of the world and soon discovered that behind every great religion there has also been, like a shadow mirror-image, a secretive, mystical counterpart. Those few individuals that belonged to these less public societies were those who wished to know the truth behind the dogma of their religion, who wished to know first-hand what others accepted through blind faith in second-hand sources, however holy or well-intentioned those sources may have been. My favorites were the Sufis, those God-intoxicated ones who, seeing beyond the ritual of Islamic traditions in their knowledge of themselves as God, whirled and sang their way to ecstasy.

In studying the religious traditions of the world, I came upon a curious phenomenon most people are aware of yet have never questioned: the brilliant halo of golden light around the head and sometimes the entire bodies of the saints of all religions. I had known of the human aura from the studies done in Kirilian photography and knew that it was an electrical or magnetic field of energy surrounding the body. I had always felt that since it was not visible to the human eye except in the rare case of true psychics, the presence of the aura around saints and other holy persons was but a symbolic representation of their holiness and not something actually seen or present. When I recalled the light I had seen bursting in my mind and then surrounding my own body, a delicious wisdom began to dawn upon me. Clearly, what I and at least some saints had experienced had been a heightened energy running through our bodies, an energy that had generated a much more powerful aura, so powerful, in fact, that it really *had* been visible! The electrical and magnetic 'charge' had been increased to the point of visibility in the same way that energy around a powerful generator is visible. But the question still remained: How had those saints learned to 'step up' that energy current? Had they learned to maintain that heightened level of intensity all the time or did the energy occur only during rare holy experiences? Had it had harmful side effects? Were my experiences similar to theirs in nature and meaning or had I merely stumbled onto something a relative few before me had developed through great effort and desire? I had to know.

I began to read everything I could find about psychic and spiritual transformations, those sought for and those that had burst forth mysteriously and unbidden. The main thrust of my studies was centered around the Christian saints since my early training had been in that tradition. I spent almost every waking moment at the library or at home reading these books. The few acquaintances I made during this time thought I was a little crazy or at least eccentric. I didn't care. I was on fire with excitement, with understanding. I was passionate in my interest—fanatical, driven. I knew that this delightful, all-consuming passion must be akin to what great scientists and artists and musicians down through the centuries have felt. Had I tapped into a great secret of creativity? Of genius? It didn't matter. The joy I was feeling was enough.

What I didn't notice at the time was that my energy levels changed dramatically. I slept far less than ever before and seemed much clearer of mind. I found myself taking long walks along the beach once more. My breathing deepened and air began to have a fresh, clean taste to it instead of the stuffy, enervating quality I had always known. Maybe this new enjoyment of breathing was due to the excitement of discovery I was experiencing. Perhaps it was from the increased physical activity I was engaging in. Probably it was from both. I had a slightly wild-eyed look which probably frightened more than a few people. But I didn't care because I was excited. Lord, but I was excited! What I was finding out from those books was shedding new light on my own experiences, was clearing out the last remaining doubts and fears I had about the validity and goodness of them. Now that I was beginning to understand that I was not the only one who had had them, I began to thirst for more of them.

I read the books of Gopi Krishna and saw how, through a process that nearly killed him, he released the Kundalini serpent-fire that lies coiled at the base of the spine. I read about Buddha and how enlightenment had come after three days of hellish battles with the demons of his mind and ego-self under the Bodhi tree. I read about Jesus and his temptation by the devil for forty days and nights. And I read Carlos Castaneda and of his journeys through terror and wonder with the Yaqui Indian sorcerer and holy man Don Juan. I began to feel a great kinship with those noble and courageous individuals for I had concluded that my experiences had been holy encounters and not mad delusions or psychotic episodes. At least I chose to believe they were. Nothing else made any sense or gave me any peace of mind. Small pieces were falling into place in this great puzzle that my life had become, and the biggest pieces were yet to come.

The Christian saints evoked in me a deep sympathy and communion for the goodness they believed in and lived, even though in many cases the saints seemed illiterate and ignorant of the world and sometimes even of the rituals and basic teachings of the Church. It was the goodness of their hearts that struck me most. It seemed that the purity and resolve of purpose found in their hearts was enough to carry them into legend as well as heaven. I read of Joan of Arc and her 'voices' and how they had led this simple, French, peasant girl to do mighty deeds for her country and the Church. I studied St. Francis of Assisi and read about how a change had come over this revelrous son of a wealthy merchant in Italy upon leaving the Crusades and being sick with fever almost unto death. I read about St. Bernadette Soubirous, the humble 14-year-old girl who had seen the Virgin Mary in a city dump and stepped into legend with her innocence, simplicity, and purity of heart and spirit. I read also about St. Anselm of Canterbury and St. Augustine and Thomas Aquinas, those mighty souls who stormed the gates of heaven through their intellect and single-minded desire to know and to serve God. I read of St. Theresa of Avila and St. John of the Cross. I read about the self-flagellating saints and the saints tortured in body by their fellow man or in mind by their own desires and fears. I searched through numerous biographies and autobiographies for a clue, a shred of information that would relate to the experiences I had had only a few months earlier.

I loved the saints and felt a deep sense of understanding and oneness with them. At times felt I *became* them, so strong and clear was my empathy and sense of communion with them. Wave upon wave of a quality of beauty and feeling I cannot describe would sweep over me without warning, would engulf me. I would see pictures of other times, other lives. My soul would fill with sights and sounds and *feelings* that seemed to come from those earlier times, straight from the hearts and minds of those I had grown to love so deeply. It was as though I were literally climbing inside the souls of the saints and seeing the world through their minds and hearts. At such times I would not feel so alone anymore.

Often I wept with sorrow at the beauty of those magnificent souls. I felt unworthy to be in the presence of such beings. I wept with the knowledge of the great pain they had endured for their beliefs, for the loneliness they must have felt from being around others who did not and could not understand them. I wished with all my heart that I could have been there with them, that I could have served them or aided them in some way. I wished I could have lived with them, loved them, died in their place—for with them I felt I had found a true family. It was not that I felt worthy of them, really. Oh, no—it was more that I now knew enough to fully appreciate *their* worth. I felt a little like Salieri must have initially felt toward Mozart. He was said to have been brilliant enough to appreciate and assist the genius of

Mozart but not gifted enough to be great himself. I hoped it would not be so with me, that I would not have been blessed with an understanding of the saints' greatness but denied the ability to achieve some measure of that greatness myself. I did not wish to be half-formed, to remain in that strange in-between state Salieri must have been doomed to live his life in. I did not want to fall prey to feelings of hatred and anger and jealousy toward the ones I loved most. But for now, understanding the saints was enough, though I would have loved to have made a difference in their lives in the way they had made a difference for me.

In my research, I found a few reports of strange experiences of these holy men and women—for example: having fire put to their hands but feeling no pain and suffering no injury, of bleeding in the same areas of their bodies where Jesus had been nailed to the cross, and so on. But it was not until I found *The Incorruptibles* that I began to fit the larger pieces into the puzzle. This wonderful book by Joan Carroll Cruz chronicles in tiny, thumbnail sketches the lives of some three hundred saints, whose bodies, or parts of them, did not exhibit the corruption and decay of the flesh common to all life. The astonishing thing was that in many cases the bodies of these saints remained in an uncorrupted state for *centuries* after their death. I could read only small parts of these accounts at one time, so powerful was their impact on me.

Something was beginning to click inside my mind—answers to questions as yet unformed were seeping into my consciousness. I felt the dawning of something wonderful and precious. Soon I also came upon reports that in addition to any number of unusual occurrences such as a sweetness in the air around them and healings effected in their presence surrounding the death of these great saints, there often was a *light* around them near the time of their death or shortly thereafter. Sometimes the light was so brilliant it could be seen to surround the house where they were laid to rest for miles around. It was clear to me that the light spoken of in those passages was the same pure light I had experienced around *my* body—a light that was not around my body at all but into which my body had dissolved, a light so holy no imperfection could withstand it. I remember with both a shudder of fear and a trembling of joy the scars and stiffness that vanished into that sacred light. Perhaps I was not holy, as these men and women had been, but I knew I was not crazy either. My experiences were *real* and the beginning of something so wonderful that my mind whirled with the thought of it.

* * *

I swam in the beauty that was coming into my mind and heart. Though I was not having the kind of experiences I so wanted, I began to recognize that my transformation was most definitely continuing. It was now manifesting primarily in my *mind* rather than my body. The groundwork had been laid in my body more than a year ago, to prepare it to receive the influx of insights that were constantly bombarding my consciousness like marble-sized hail on a tin roof. It became obvious to me that had I not had those earlier episodes, those experiences that ripped me away from the fragile, fearful, mundane existence I knew, I never would have allowed or been able to withstand the beauty and power of these new insights, some of which arrived full-blown in my mind as an 'Ah Ha!' experience that did not require rational thought to be understood. It was during the time of these new insights that I became aware of a gentle and loving inner presence that loved me and blessed me and taught me if I but listened to it. I knew that it had been there with me even when I had been frightened and full of despair and when I had been angry at all the gods that ever were, and when I had doubted everything I could not see or touch. I knew also that it would never forsake me—had never forsaken me. And for the first time in my life I felt truly loved.

* * *

I read more and more about the saints, particularly the ones whose bodies had not corrupted upon their passing. At first, of course, I doubted such a thing was possible, but there were so many reports that before long I could not doubt their authenticity. Part of me knew the truth, even as I knew that the body was the key to the transformative process—a door, a gate, an opening to another dimension. The body was a vehicle through which many worlds could be known. The secret to unlocking this 'door,' I thought, was to circumvent the programming placed in us all from a very early age. Yes, circumvent the conditioning, the fears, the programmed responses that keep us bound generation after generation to seeing and feeling things in the same way. We limit ourselves and our experiences because at some time in dim antiquity someone decided certain things were impossible, certain things were necessary, certain things 'had always been that way,' until each of us now is little more than an automaton playing out the limited instructions passed along to us generation after generation. We are like Pavlovian dogs salivating on cue each time the bell of our conditioning rings. No wonder we are so limited and unhappy! We claim to despise slavery and bondage; yet we have, without giving so much as a thought, lived our entire *lives* in bondage of the worse kind—bondage to a way of thinking and living that allows little of our true heritage to come through. Amazingly, it is *we* who have been our own taskmasters and jailers. We have *begged* to keep our chains tight about us lest we face the wonder and terror of true freedom, of taking our places beside God. And we have done so without even a whimper. It is so clear to me now. How could I have been so blind before? How could *anyone* be so blind? When the tyranny of the ego-mind has ended, then only can the true work of transformation begin. It is no longer surprising to me that the saints had transformations that extended to their bodies as well as their minds and spirits. In devoting themselves so purely and completely to God, they had replaced their conditioning with a new agenda, one that allowed great energies to pass unobstructed through them. They were no longer fettered with limiting thoughts or selfish motives. They wanted only to *know* and to *serve*. And to *love*.

Having bodies that were so devoted to God that enormous spiritual energies were able to pass through them, energies that had been used to heal and teach and serve, had allowed the bodies of certain saints to remain free from the corruption of the flesh. Even so, this seemed but a single step, albeit a giant one, toward what I have come to refer to as translation or ascension—the transformation of the body into pure light.

In my readings I came across the book *Ye Are Gods* by Annalee Skarin, a Christian woman writing in the middle of this century. To say that she was inspired by God does not begin to do her justice. The woman was *consumed* by God, was *on fire* with a sense of the sacred and the desire to serve. It's obvious. The words burn from the pages.

I remember being about half way through Skarin's book when I chanced to read a small statement on one of the front pages. I had missed it initially, so anxious was I to get to the heart of the book. Now it struck me like the slap of a cold, wet hand. In a few simple words it reported that the body of Annalee Skarin had never been found. It was believed that she had gone through that mysterious process known as 'translation.' My mouth dropped open wide. Could this be true? In this day and age? I vaguely remembered mention in the Bible of how the prophet Elijah had been carried to heaven on a whirlwind without experiencing death. I also recalled mention of the city of Enoch and its mysterious removal to heaven. I had glossed over those reports as symbolic writings or exaggerations at best. Now I could barely breathe, my excitement and shock were so great. *This* was the missing puzzle piece I had been searching for. These accounts explained what might be happening to me. Those saints whose bodies had not corrupted at death had simply not completed the process begun in their bodies—a process aimed not only at the transformation and preservation of the body through the power of light, but also toward the actual *translation* of that body *into* light! It was still not clear why, if this is indeed what has been happening to me, I had been chosen, but all these accounts did give me the final sigh of relief that I was not alone in my experiences. I had a strong sense that there had been in the past and probably were today people with experiences similar to mine. Besides, the 'whys' of the world are often like vultures picking at our flesh in the hot desert or leeches sucking our blood. They should not hold us back from trusting the light of understanding to make itself known at the proper time and boldly moving forward in our lives.

What I noticed in the writings of Annalee Skarin was that she possessed an intensity I had never encountered before. The strength of her conviction and inner knowing leaped from the pages and did not seek for my agreement or my thoughts. She gave no quarter with her truth. She stated it for all to see. Her truth was not open to analysis or debate or question. It was simply stated as truth by one who believed it singlemindedly. I began to sense that by completely giving herself over to one purpose—knowing and serving God—she had stormed the gates of heaven with the laser-like focus of her consciousness. She had drawn to herself greater energies by her willingness to be a receptacle for wisdom and sacredness, and she had been able to handle those higher currents of energy by removing all obstructions, all resistances to them. She had been a perfect electrical energy conduit, with nothing left of her humanness to block the flow of pure spirit through her.

I, through some fluke of fate, had also become a conduit for those energies of the divine, was like the saints for brief moments. My fear and pain had come not from the experiences themselves but from my *resistance* to them! The saints had focused their lives completely on God and taken *all* experiences—both those of joy and those of pain—as coming from God and therefore good in nature. When their transformations began, they put themselves into God's hands and thus avoided much of the fear, confusion, and pain I had initially experienced through my resistance. I still did not know why those divine energies had come to me, but now I knew that more than anything else I wanted them to return. They had begun to teach me, somehow to *love* me, to give direction to my life; and I wanted to follow the path they led me down, even if it cost me my life.

* * *

    Through extensive research I found more accounts of ascensions. I soon realized that ascension was not as rare an event as I had first imagined. Though I still did not feel worthy of such a holy event, I tried to weed out petty fears and limiting thoughts that still formed so much of my life's automatic operating system. I began to observe my mental processes. I saw how I limited and sabotaged myself with thoughts such as, "This is too good to be true," "I can't believe my good fortune," "I'll just *die* if that happens," "What else could go wrong today?" and a hundred others. I began to catch those slippery saboteurs, those harmful thoughts, before they slithered into my conscious mind. I found that I could stop them and change them into more positive thoughts that issued forth as healing and nourishing ideas and words. Soon I began to catch them before they were fully formed and stop them, causing them to perish before they could take a single poisonous breath.

    I resumed my practice of running along the beach at night, of exercising regularly, of eating nourishing foods, and being aware of my breath and breathing more deeply. These efforts, together with the powerful focus I was developing from knowing what my life was about, of having my life truly *mean* something, began to change my feelings and state of being. I felt much lighter in my body and mind and had less need for sleep or the kind of mind-numbing entertainment that I had spent so much of my life pursuing. I stopped feeling so lonely. I monitored my thoughts constantly, continually weeding the garden of my mind. And I began to meditate. I had toyed with that practice many times in the past in much the same way that a child picks at a plate of food he's convinced he doesn't like. Now, however, I plunged into meditation, prayed and gave thanks for the sense of direction and purpose and understanding that was coming to me.

* * *

The question of why the bodies of some of the saints had remained untouched by physical decay at death and some had not continued to haunt me. I wondered why none seemed to have achieved the translation or ascension that Annalee Skarin, who was never proclaimed or hailed as a saint, had perhaps accomplished. For a time I fenced with the question on a purely mental level and tried to best it on that battlefield; but no answers came. I continued to read the accounts of saints and noted that some of the most popular ones or the ones deemed most holy were not among those elite few who had left an imperishable body behind. St. Francis of Assisi, one of the most beloved saints of all, died and left a body as subject to decay as that of any other man, though his life had been devoted to God's work and praise. St. Therese of Lisieux, 'The Little Flower of Jesus,' second in fame and popularity in her native France only to St. Joan of Arc (whose body could not withstand the flames), had a normal death and decay of the body. In fact, this young saint-to-be was once asked if she would like her body to remain free of the stain of corruption as had that of some of the saints before her. With an almost horrified look on her face Therese had replied, "Oh, no! I *don't want* that to happen! I just want to be like everyone else." And her wish was granted.

It is also interesting to note that some of the imperishable bodies of saints *did* in fact eventually decay—perhaps a hundred years after death; perhaps several centuries later. Sometimes the whole body decayed, but sometimes a part or parts of the body were preserved. Why? Did some energy suffusing their form and protecting it from deteriorating lessen as time went on until it was spent and could no longer preserve the body from the ravages of decay? Had the amount or intensity of the energies sustaining their lifeless bodies been directly related to their degree of spiritual purity?

My questions remained unanswered until one day I meditated on truth. Taking a break from all my reading and intense searching, I had played along the beach until twilight and felt relaxed and refreshed both in mind and body. After taking several of the deep breaths that had become so much a part of my daily routine, I centered myself in the darkness and quiet of my bedroom closet, as I had accustomed myself to doing in the late evenings. I relaxed my body and mind further until I reached a state of peace I had not known for several weeks. I was in a very subtle state of consciousness, as though several coarse layers had been shed; and I no longer had to fight my body's demands for attention or my mind's tricks and endless chatter. Understanding life's deepest secrets seemed so easy from the filmy strand of awareness I lived on in such moments. In my mind's eye I 'saw' the questions I wanted so badly to know the answer to—witnessed them being clearly asked—easily, lucidly, effortlessly. No logical or rational thought process was involved, only the intent to know. The circuits of the mind that deal with logic were circumvented. As I waited silently, patiently in the dark, answers formed. They came like tiny seeds borne by the wind, like ecstatic little explosions of light dancing in my mind—insights arriving full-blown in my consciousness.

What I understood in those leaping flames of awareness was that the bodies of only the most holy and pure saints remained preserved after they died. The degree of purity and love allowed to flow unhampered through their bodies determined the length of time those bodies remained free of stain and corruption. I also saw that many good men and women hailed as saints had left this world with stains of darkness in their souls, perhaps from some doubt or fear, or a remnant of fleshly ways—and this blemish had kept the light from flowing freely through them, thereby preventing bodily transformation. Though these great saints left behind bodies as subject to decay as those of normal people, their work was no less remarkable. The value of their work was unaffected by their retained human weaknesses and conflicts because their hearts were pure and full of love and inner strength. Moreover, those like 'The Little Flower,' who seemed destined to leave a preserved body behind, perhaps *chose* not to, withdrawing energy from their bodies that they might give them back to the earth. Like a shining dew drop slipping into the sea, they would leave no trace, no remnant of themselves save their love and wisdom.

I understood that few saints, or perhaps none, had achieved the translation of the physical body into light known as ascension because the purity of heart that extended to the body was not enough. This saintly purity of heart was but an interim step, though a necessary and powerful one, between the normal bodily decay and ascension, a halfway marker of consciousness. In the beauty of their purity and love, the holy ones did not have the power of wisdom and will; they had given their lives to God in innocence and simplicity and gentleness but had not the fullness of wisdom and understanding that makes one whole. They had seen no need for such wisdom and understanding; all they wished was to love God and His creatures, and to bathe in the eternal simplicity of His will. Such a beautiful thing it was. And yet...and yet.... The words of the scripture flashed forth in my mind: "Be ye wise as serpents and gentle as doves." Those great saints had not been on *fire* with holy wisdom; they had smoldered quietly with holy love. *That* was why Annalee Skarin had, I believed, stopped not at a body so filled with light and love that it would last a thousand years beyond her death but instead had transformed that body *itself* into light and given it back not to the earth but to heaven.

* * *

I rose from meditation and busied myself around the house. I hadn't realized how long I'd been meditating until I pulled the drapes. Ivory stars had given way to morning's twilight. I watched as the sun's first fiery rays leaped from the horizon and formed a path of golden light, a shimmering, other-worldly light—a fairy gleam beckoning me to walk across it. In the intoxication of the moment I felt almost as though I could, that this magical pathway of golden light might lead to an undreamed of world of wonder and beauty such as I had never before imagined. People ought always to greet the morning with just such a sense of wonder, magic, and adventure, I thought.

Though I had been up all night meditating, I felt rested and refreshed. I spent the whole morning climbing hills and running along the beach. It was such a blessing to be living alone with the wild, ever-changing ocean on one side and the quiet, stable, hills on the other. Such a perfect balance of nature, I thought. I began to see these two extremes as symbols of my life. There was the part of me that was in constant flux, constant change, going wherever the moment carried me; and there was the part that always seemed the same, that resisted change, that seemed immensely old and wise and unshakeable. Just as both elements were compatible in nature, so were they becoming in me, though for much of my life they had been at war with each other, pitting their primal strengths against each other in a clash of confusion and destruction. Now those two elements seemed calm within me, calm and settled, so that conflict seemed a thing of my distant past, fear but an illusion based on clouded perception.

During the next few days I began to notice dramatic changes in my body and mind. My body felt alive and unconflicted as a sense of wholeness spread through every part of me. I moved with the grace and unwasted movement of a cat, and my mind was clear and untroubled. I felt that for most of my life my mind had been like an obstructed drainpipe, clogged with conflict and fear and inertia. Now the obstructions were vanishing, permitting a free flow of energy and vitality and aliveness. I felt like a small airplane that had always had the brake on, so that even though the engine revved up, it could do no more than vibrate and rock from side to side and front to back with the strain—or a runner confined by lead weights who had just had them removed.

August 9

As is often my habit these days I arose early this morning. Out my kitchen window a streak of rich orange light cut through the dark, heavy layer of clouds in the east and lay like a huge, heated sword, a monstrous blade balanced perfectly on the edge of the distant landscape. It hung there like a fiery weapon mighty enough to cleave the whole world asunder, yet gentle enough to disturb not even the slumber of a tiny bird.

And so my day began, with a hint of excitement, the thrill of clarity and peace of mind, and of ease in my body, and no sadness. I was sitting in my wooden chair watching the day peacefully unfold when I was shaken by the sound of thunder. A storm rolling in, I thought. Going outside to have a look, I saw no evidence of a storm—just a few dark clouds along the horizon, too far away to account for the sharp cracks of thunder I'd just heard. Strange. But there *was* a difference in the air—not the fresh quality I love so much when a storm is on its way but something I'd never known before. There was a *sweetness* to the air, a honey-like quality I could not account for. I puzzled at this smell for a moment; but before I could understand it, a series of three loud thunderclaps broke the silence and

I saw a brilliant flash of light. For a moment I thought I had been struck by lightning, for a powerful current shot through my body, causing me to fall to the ground. And then I *knew*...I knew that the thunder and lightning I sensed were not phenomena of the outside world but were *inside* of me. It was happening again....

This time I was not afraid. For a brief instant all my previous fears and apprehensions fell upon me like a bomb bursting wide open and seeking to engulf me, to destroy my heart and mind with their force. But that moment quickly passed as the strength and knowing and joy of the past year and a half rose strong within me, shattering my fears into tiny shards of shrapnel, deflecting them harmlessly to the ground like spent sparkles. Because I did not fight my fears or resist them as I had in the early days, pain and panic vanished. I let the experience unfold, whatever it might be.

The sound in my head surged with a mighty intensity until it sounded like a boiling tea kettle the size of a house. Other sounds like that of an approaching tornado were barely audible in what seemed to be a distance. Though I trembled slightly I breathed evenly as I lay on the ground where I had fallen and watched first my hands then my feet turn into light—to glow, then shimmer, then fade, then wink out, only to be replaced by a brilliant golden glow. I felt an electric sensation passing through me, as if each cell in my body were flaring up in an explosion of raw energy then dissolving away to light.

Then my whole body was filled with light, a holy radiance that must have been what those few saints had known. I heard music, music so sweet and sublime it must have come from angel-breath. The hauntingly beautiful strains, notes that were both beautiful and painful at the same time, chords that seemed to hint at another world, beckoned me.

Feeling light and unfettered, I rose from the ground without effort as if answering the music's call. Indeed, effort would have been necessary if I had tried to remain earthbound. I was no longer aware of having a body, even one of light. I seemed to be but a point of consciousness free of the laws of the world. I moved solely by the power of my thoughts. In a moment I was gliding over the sea. With but another thought, I was over the Himalayas, reveling in the snowy glory of those majestic peaks. I soared closer and saw monasteries hidden in small niches of the mountains, saw ancient caves long hidden from the prying eyes of men wherein lay vast storehouses of ancient wisdom and objects of beauty and devotion. Nothing escaped my all-seeing eye. For that was what I seemed to be—a vast, single, all-seeing eye. In a flash I saw the Biblical statement: "Lest your eye be single and your body filled with light...." How simple it all was! How well-known. In those early days I had thought that no one had ever had the kind of experiences I was having. Yet now I understood that sacred literature from all religious traditions was full of such references for those with eyes to see. As I shot like a lightning bolt to Peru and Ireland and Greenland, I felt a kinship with the other explorers of the mind and spirit before me.

In each place I journeyed, my awareness was drawn to places of mystery and wisdom, places unknown to the masses of humanity who went about their day to day lives with no belief in magic and wonder. And these places were all right *here*, waiting to be explored and cherished! This was the true adventure! *This* was what life should be! I was carried along on waves of joy.

I have no idea how long that wondrous journey lasted. I only remember a jolt going through me, as if someone had slapped me, then dizziness, then an awareness of my physical body as it lay on the ground. It seemed so stiff and coarse compared to the freedom I had just known that I almost wept. A thin gloss of gray-black clouds had drifted in from the north, slowly drawing a dark veil over the delicate blue face of the evening sky. A thick haze of orange light, blazing like an enormous torch burning in the twilight, lit the distant hills.

Looking up at the sky, I rested for a couple of hours on the ground where I lay, then pulled myself to my feet and went inside to write this down. My thoughts are clear now and its best to write when an event is clear in one's mind. It's important that I keep a careful record of what is happening to me. I understand that now. Now I am unconflicted. My true life, of which the old had been merely a shadow-image, without substance and without direction, has now begun. It is time for me to claim my destiny.

August 13

For the past few days my body has had a pleasant tingle, no doubt a remnant of that powerful experience on the 9th. My body feels vibrant and 'tingly,' more so than ever, and this electric 'tickle' leads me to believe that a bodily transformation is going on—will continue to go on—even when I am not having one of my 'beauties,' as I have come to call my non-ordinary, otherworldly episodes. It's interesting how I decided to use 'beauties' to describe my experiences. The last episode had felt as though I were taking my first step, or my first breath. Yes, perhaps that would be an accurate description of how I felt. After being jolted back to physical awareness my first thought was, "Beauty. I've been filled with a *beauty*...an absolute and sublime beauty." Now the only word that comes to mind when I think of that experience or of any of those before it is beauty. Those precious, ecstatic experiences of mine are beauties coming from the inner edge of wonder. With joy in my heart for the grace that has been bestowed on me I recall the words of the ancient saying: "Life is but a dream dreamed by God. The beautiful thing about it is that it is *we* who awaken from it." Yes, beauty.

August 16

In the past few days I've felt an occasional rumble of thunder within me or seen a brief flash of light but no beauties came to me until last night. I was lying in bed when the rumblings began. The sounds grew louder until a sharp, electrical 'crackle' shot across the dark sky of my consciousness, lighting up the inner landscape like a bolt of lightning. I felt myself growing lighter in both mind and body. The by now familiar process of my body changing to light continued until I could see myself as a sphere of rich golden light with the shape of my body, then as but a blur of formless energy. No words can describe the incredible freedom and exhilaration I felt in those moments. The joy, the wonder, the beauty of it all! It was at this time that I became aware once more of the gentle presence within me, brushing against me like the gossamer touch of angel-wings, bidding me follow its promptings. The love I felt from this presence, which seemed neither masculine nor feminine, was overwhelming and unshakeable. I went where it willed me to go, saw what it instructed me to see. This time I did not look upon the wonders of the world but instead dove into the very innards of the earth. An eerie silver-gold phosphorescence lit my way as I viewed the inner parts of the world from just beneath the surface to the fiery interior itself. I saw wonders never before seen by man. I saw evidence of immensely old past civilizations, some primitive and some advanced beyond our own, buried under hundreds or thousands of feet of dirt and rock. Some were old even when the land was young. I knew that some of these had come from the distant stars, others from pockets within the earth itself, shut away from the ordinary stream of evolution that had led to my own race and civilization. The remnants of other civilizations were simply grim and tragic reminders that several times a race of men and women had risen to dominance on Earth only to fall prey to the destruction born of the evil in their hearts. Archaeologists have uncovered many old civilizations, yet there are undiscovered *hundreds* I was privileged to see the ruins of as, led by the voice of the presence within me, I skimmed along the inside rim of the earth. I dove farther and farther into the earth until I came to its molten center, the fiery heart of the planet itself. I felt the flames, and imagined myself to be Joan of Arc, though this inferno was many times greater than the fire which had consumed the Maid of Orleans. I imagined that the purpose of my being in that place of immense heat and pressure was one of purification, that I needed to give myself to the flames, to burn off the dross of impurities that still clung to my life in a physical body. I wanted, as Saint Joan had done in her moment of fire, to shout, "Blessed Jesus!" Whether or not it was necessary to shout this phrase, I was pleased to see it as such. For this was my christening, literally my baptism by fire into a life of spirit and light that I had always secretly longed for. A life I had feared was not real. I had therefore hidden the hope for such a life until the desire was like a festering wound, so deep within me that I was never aware of it as more than a dull, gnawing pain.

This baptism was my new birth, my new and shining entry into life, the fulfillment of my childhood dreams for true adventure. Like the pain of unrequited love, such had the longings for mystical adventure been. Now the pain was at an end. I was at the center of the earth! And I was fully *conscious* of being there. It was no dream, no delusion, no vain imagining. I was *there*! And I stood long in those fierce, orange and yellow, molten flames and did not burn.

August 22

I've had no more beauties since that ecstatic cleansing in the liquid, living fire at Earth's core; but the ecstasy of that experience and the one only days before was great enough to last for many, many days. I've let the past few days be ones of reflection and thanksgiving, for I feel incredibly blessed—and excited. The expectation of further adventures sends fire through my veins and chills up my spine. Recording these beauties is easier now than in the early days of my transformation because I feel so free of conflict now. Before, part of me was constantly looking over my shoulder, half expecting to see the shadow of fear and doubt and limitation following me; such is no longer case. I'm beginning to see that a life without fear really *is* possible.

For the past few days a curious image has been forming in my mind, the image of a woman I'm sure I've never met. Her face first appeared to me at the height of a deep meditation. I thought it was perhaps the symbolic representation of that sweet presence living within me, guiding me. But when I asked if this were so, I received a very definite "no," and the image faded away. It appeared again the next day, this time in a cloud that floated overhead—a perfect pencil-etching of that face—the dark hair and eyes, the pale complexion. Later the image formed in the trees, the rocks, the ocean spray—even in the woodgrain of my bedroom door. At first I enjoyed the little game my mind seemed to be creating for me; but after the fourth or fifth appearance of the strange countenance, I began seriously to consider its significance. It *meant* something, but I did not know what. Then, as quickly as the process of seeing the face had begun, it ended. Even when I tried to see the face, I could not. Strange.

September 1

Last night, I was sitting on my front porch, the irregular droning of insects passing by bringing me back to consciousness each time I nodded off. A beautiful sunset was forming in the west. The pink tinge of the setting sun was floating on a sea of white clouds. I sat entranced as I watched twilight creep in on cat's feet, then gradually leave. Finally night fell before my unhurried sight, as a pastel orange light rose up to meet the vaulted sky. As I stared at the deepening colors of night, a powerful realization dawned upon me. Clearly, my time for reading books was at an end. Just as the sunset and twilight are different each day, so is each person a unique individual, different from day to day. I realized that all great men and women found truth within themselves and not in another's teachings, however beautiful those teachings may be. Those teachings are but fingers pointing at the moon. The time for examining more fingers was ended. I needed to seek the moon directly.

I read somewhere that above the entrance to a monastery in the Far East are inscribed the words: "A thousand monks, a thousand religions." How true this now seems to me! For how could anyone, no matter how holy or well intentioned, know the truth for another human being? All we can do is live our lives with as much integrity as possible, forgive as much as possible, love ourselves and others and the source of our lives with all our strength and mind and heart and spirit, and share as much as we are able with those who wish to receive, without concern as to the outcome of that sharing. Such have I come to know from the gentle presence within me.

But perhaps I was a little premature when I thought the time for reading books was at an end. Behind each book stands a man or woman—his or her hopes and dreams, knowledge and beliefs. And often there is a genuine desire to give something to the world. This desire to share must always be honored and cherished. Viewed in this light, all books are worth reading. It would be more accurate, then, to say that I realized while sitting on that porch that the time for seeking answers outside of myself was ended. It was so very clear that outward seeking is not the answer, just as pictures of cakes in a magazine cannot satisfy one's hunger. Truth cannot come from others. The truth can only come from within ourselves—from those inner 'knowings' that have a rightness about them, that pluck the strings of our heart and vibrate in harmony with our innermost selves. I wanted to dance, to shout with joy with the understanding that, contained within each of us is a repository of—or an open channel, a conduit to—all the wisdom in the universe! We are, each one of us, a laboratory of transformation completely equipped with all the instructions, tools, and raw materials necessary to perform that great alchemy of the soul, the changing of matter into light.

It is into this great laboratory of transformation that I unknowingly stumbled those many months ago. And it is there I must go to understand that strange and beautiful phenomenon known as ascension.

The Light Begins to Dawn

September 10

This morning I went shopping and realized some things about myself. As I drove to town, the beauty of the clouds and behind them the deep blue luster of the morning sky moved me. I would have liked to spend more time enjoying the scene, but soon the slowly moving freeway traffic demanded my attention. Traffic speed was gradually reduced to a crawl, and my attention wandered to the people in the other cars. I realized that I had never really *noticed* them before. I had always been busy getting someplace, usually in a hurry. More often than I cared to remember, my destination was to a job I did not like, a job that didn't use my skills or kindle a desire to learn, a job that did not serve me. So I noticed very little during such times, times that seem now like a distant dream. But today I felt no hurry, no pressing need to be anywhere. I was content to be in my car, driving down the freeway, heading toward a shopping center a few miles away. It was Monday and I was caught in morning rush-hour traffic. Looking at the faces of those other drivers I knew what for many of them the day was to be: work, a couple of beers, and loneliness, whether with someone or not—then the sweet oblivion of sleep before the cycle repeated itself the next morning. I felt a deep sadness for them, wanted to tell them what I knew and was discovering more of daily: our thoughts create our reality. We are not helpless victims whose fate has been cast. We are unlimited beings destined for greatness and joy.

I looked at the other drivers with fondness and knew that I was not like them, not like other humans in general. I realized that I belonged to another race of men and women, a race that represented evolution consciously entering into time and directing its own destiny.

As I watched the clouds drift by then fade away, I realized that the old world was fading away for me, slipping through my fingers like fine grains of sand. My roots were the same, but the flowering taking place within me was separating me from my own species. I did not feel pompous about this difference, and I did not feel lonely in the usual sense. It was simply a realization of the truth, and a willingness to accept it. I *was* escaping the bonds of my species, and that change was bringing me into much greater unity with *all* of life. And there was the paradox. The more separate I felt from others, the more kinship I felt with them also, for each of us had come from the same immensely beautiful, humble beginnings. I felt an intense desire building within me to extend myself to others, to experience the full range of my humanness, but at the same I felt a hesitancy to do so.

All my life I had tried to fit in, to be as others were, but without much success. The simple comforts and pleasures other people seemed to care about had never interested me, really. Oh, I'd indulged in them and imagined they made me happy, but those kinds of pleasures never lasted, never truly satisfied me. It was clear that I now had little in common with other people any more, if indeed I ever did. I now felt isolated, removed from the ordinary stream of life, in a remote, desolate land. I knew this feeling of isolation had been in my consciousness all my life but had hidden in the shadows of my mind. But with the beauties I'd experienced recently, the sense of aloneness had no longer been trailing me like a faint shadow-image but had been very much in front of me, demanding attention like a spoiled or needy child. It was not the kind of loneliness born of self indulgence or fear or need; it was more a pang of recognition that so few have opened themselves in the way that I had, a pang of sadness that I had no one to talk with about my experiences, no one to compare notes with or gain understanding from. I felt blessed to have that gentle presence guiding me through challenging times; yet I did miss having friends, people to talk with. I seemed to have grown apart from the few friends I had.

And so I felt rather sad and a little lonely as I drove down that road, but also happy in a way I had never been while growing up. A sense of peacefulness—serenity—now underlay the sadness and loneliness. That peacefulness emerged as a calmness that was as strong as an oak tree, flowering forth as a deep and sturdy joy. Whereas what I had before imagined to be happiness was like a leaf blowing in a stiff breeze, vulnerable, fragile, flittering in whatever way the wind chose to cast it. A tear and a smile while driving down the highway.

September 17

Like a faint mist of illumination descending quietly into my mind, a profound insight came to me recently. It was that, like certain foods that are very rich, beauty can only be taken in small amounts. Too much beauty at one time overwhelms us, momentarily threatens to overthrow our ego-mind structure—that part of us that believes that we are only what is confined inside our skin, that we will die, that there is not enough love or money or pleasure to go around, that we are separate from each other, separate from God, and doomed to time. We therefore resist beauty in its many forms by distracting ourselves endlessly with the superficial, perishable things in life. We make rules and laws and regulations so that we don't have to think for ourselves or listen within to the voice of guidance and intuition. In so doing we give up spontaneity and wonder. We no longer feel we have to take responsibility for our actions, our thoughts, our lives. So firmly embedded are those rules and regulations which automate our lives that we live only on the surface, afraid to dive beneath the outer skin of things into the unknown face of existence. We are afraid to surrender ourselves to the terror and wonder of facing what we truly are. We don't have the courage to embrace the crushing force of beauty, of pure, sublime beauty. The ego fears only when we look inward; so all of our attention is directed outward. We distract ourselves with a world we've made real by our thoughts, a world we've folded into three dimensions and imprisoned in linear time for our convenience. Time is no longer the tool for transformation and sharing it was intended to be but a haven away from God, a hiding place, a smoke-filled room with loud music and alcohol, a refuge that beckons us to forget the love within us and the glory of humanity. Even those who seek more in their lives, who strive for a way out of the prison house, a way into the light of holiness, seek God in books and teachers and groups of fellow-seekers, focusing their attention on something outside themselves, even when they are deep in meditation. Even when they appear to be looking within, they focus on external offerings. They do not understand that what they are searching *for* is what they are searching *with*.

What we settle for and love are the little brushes with beauty that we experience through movies and television and top-40 music. We settle for them because they are safe and make us feel good and keep our prison bars securely in place, like the 'safe' tour of Lion Country Safari as opposed to the wildness and unpredictability of the jungle. We carefully avoid true beauty and thus true love because we are afraid that our fragile ego-selves can't survive the tidal waves of meaning and naked, unveiled, unleashed beauty. And we're right. But it's our *ego-self* that can't survive, not our true self. We fear the death of the ego-self. We fear losing ourselves to wonder, to plunging headlong into God. I know. I speak from experience. Our fear of letting go of our ego-self and surrendering ourselves fully to life is also why we avoid depth in relationships.

No one is to be blamed for shunning beauty, really. We are all aware on some level that inside our mighty armor we are fragile beings, easily bruised and broken. The key then is to create a structure strong enough to withstand the ecstatic force of pure beauty and wonder. For yes, wonder and beauty are harbingers of the divine, come straight from heaven, and the sheer glory of them in their pure form can overwhelm an unprepared soul. Each of my beauties taxed my spirit to its limits; and in each experience I could have easily lost myself to the world, roaring off to infinity, lost in a world of madness, drifting like a rudderless boat through dark, uncharted seas. When the necessary internal structure is created, however, a transformation into the higher life each of us is destined for is possible. Just as we shift from one gear to another in a car, we must be bold enough to leave first gear behind, though it does function to get us around. I have had a taste of the higher 'gears,' experienced great speed, felt the wind whipping through my hair and face. Now I can settle for nothing less. I have seen the world from the butterfly's perspective, have soared high into the air on gossamer wings, have tasted the sublime freedom of flight and unboundedness—and I will never be able to go back to being a caterpillar again. All of my previous attempts to soar above the mundane things in life have been but the attempt to put wings on the caterpillar I was, to move more quickly, to see more; but the bulky, limited perspective and consciousness of the caterpillar is not enough. Now I *know*...the only way to soar like a butterfly, is to *become* one. That is what is happening to me, and I now know everyone has this potential. It is coded into the body to unfold at its proper time as surely as puberty is. It was programmed into the entire race of man to collectively be triggered at some time in the far future. But I also know that it can be triggered at *any time* by individuals bold enough to unleash the program themselves or fortunate enough for an accident, or a fluke, or an outpouring of unfathomable grace to do it for them, thereby setting their feet on the path of wonder.

September 22

I knew instinctively the search for truth was within all the time but like everyone else I was afraid...afraid I'd lack the courage needed for the seeking, afraid I'd actually *find* what I was looking for, afraid of the change my life would then go through. I've spent a lot of my life looking for truth in places I knew it would not be found, but there was safety and comfort in exploring well-lit places. I was afraid of the uncertainty, of the loneliness and of the fear I might experience if I looked deeply within myself for answers. But now I have found the pathway to truth; it was within myself all the time. I smile at how life leads us on merry chases, knowing full well that we will never achieve the prize, never find the hidden treasure, until we tire of the game of looking outside ourselves for answers and, resting exhausted, discover that the treasure was hidden in our pockets all the time.

September 25

I saw the face again—that image of a woman I've never met—but this time something different happened, something I don't yet understand but which I know is significant. The image formed itself in the evening shadows cast through my living room window onto the wall. There it was, a perfect picture, down even to the most intricate detail, formed of the silhouetted contrast of light and shadow and woodgrain on the wall—a two-dimensional image transformed by a miraculous blending of light and dark into a three-dimensional face. Even the eyes had substance to them. As I stared at the face, more real and detailed than I had ever seen it before, I felt an emotion I couldn't put a name to. It was not love, or even longing, though certainly the face was lovely. It was not even awe or curiosity or wonder. There was something about that face that was immensely old, though in years it appeared to be about twenty-five. It spoke of an understanding that was deep and aged and quiet, like an unfathomably old chunk of rock lying at the bottom of the sea, far removed from the ravages of man and even of time, a splinter of mountain that had seen civilizations rise and tumble while it remained unmoved. This sense of great age coupled with youth was the feeling I had as I gazed at that face, that shadow-portrait on my wall.

Suddenly, like a shot, I was jolted out of my trance-like state, so abruptly that I stumbled backward and hit my head on a cabinet door. I collapsed in a heap and fell to the floor. When I recovered a few moments later, the image on the door was nothing more than a patch of shadow. What had shocked me so explosively was that the face, the face I had come so accustomed to viewing in this passive, studious way, this time at that last moment *had looked back at me.*

October 2
I haven't been able to get the image of that face out of my mind though it hasn't appeared since my last entry. I admit I've been hesitant to fix my eyes on anything for other than a cursory glance for fear of seeing the face and being jolted again. It's a little silly, I know, but even though it seems to represent no threat of any kind to me, I still feel uneasy. 'Spooky' might be the best word to describe my feelings about it. And yet part of me secretly wants it to reappear, wants to understand what it means. Thus far no hint of its meaning has come to me, no scrap or thread or clue to go on. At times like this I can only be patient and trust that the answers will come at the proper time, but that it is somehow connected to—important to—the transformation going on within me seems clear.

October 7
As I mentioned a while back, I believe the key to the proper unfoldment and integration of the experiences I've been having lies in creating a structure strong enough to withstand the heightened energies required for the transformative process. This is true not only on the physical level but on the emotional and mental levels of consciousness as well. I recognize that part of the reason I had so much trouble with these heightened energies in the beginning was that I was *afraid* of them; therefore, I resisted them. The confusion I felt, the anger, the fear, all served to create blocks to the energies, so that as they rushed through me they could not flow freely and were somewhat distorted, giving way to disoriented or limited experiences. This resulted in still more confusion and fear, which in turn created more concern and more distortion. The resistance to the free flow of those vast energies caused great physical pain. I thought this pain was due to the experiences themselves; but now I see that it was my *resistance* to them, my refusal to let the transformative experience unfold, that caused it, not the experiences themselves. As these

energies coursed through me more and more, they began to 'remake' me, 'rewire' me, as it were, so that my physical form could withstand them better; and as that process continued, the blockages began to disappear for I no longer felt the need to resist them as I had before. That's when I began to experience joy when those beauties came and began to long for them when they did not.

October 10
Last night I sat on my porch and watched the sun gently ease itself down below the distant hills. The sky was a beautiful pastel blue with a hint of iron gray. A delicate splash of yellow trailed the sun's fiery path. I looked at my hand, the one that had first begun to burn with that holy light so long ago that it now seemed like centuries, looked at it, turned it, twisted it a dozen different ways, saw it from a hundred different perspectives. I was impressed with what an intricate and efficient mechanism the hand is, what a marvelous feat of engineering. I wondered as I held it there in front of my face, wondered what secrets it could tell me, what secrets my entire body could tell me. Indeed it was becoming clear to me that my body, that laboratory of transformation and power, was a microcosm of the entire universe, that it was but a reflection on a tiny scale of all the wonder and power and complex beauty to be found in the infinite reaches of space. Even the elements of which my body was composed were born in the fiery heart of an exploding sun eons upon eons ago, so that no matter how wretched or unloved I might feel, I could always hold my head high, knowing that I was made of the stuff of stars.

As I continued to muse about my hand and life and the universe, a series of questions took hold of me; the answers came so quickly that they hardly seemed questions at all. It was more that the entire dialog arrived full-blown—questions and answers together—in my mind. The questions were: If my body is but a tiny reflection of the vast macrocosm of the universe, could it be that the transformation that is happening within me could also be happening—or intended to happen—on a gigantic scale with the entire universe as well? Is the universe a 'God machine,' wherein all things are evolving toward God through quantum-leap transformations into higher and higher matrices of order and being? Am I but one of many harbingers before me signaling the process that will eventually occur not only to all people but to all life, to all matter, as well? Is the entire universe destined to 'ascend,' to be transformed ultimately to light, to rest forever in the bosom of God *as* God? An answer to my probing came neatly wrapped in the same package as the questions. It was a feeling of resounding *yes!* My mind swam with this new insight into the purpose and destiny of the universe. Even if this new awareness were only partly correct, I was on the trail of the most beautiful understanding imaginable. And though my body was tired, I could not fall asleep until the shining light of day beckoned my singing soul.

October 15

The preoccupation I've felt with my body lately led to a marvelous experience this morning. I was again staring at my left hand, musing about the nature of flesh and blood and matter, about how transitory and plastic physical life is, when a howling sound like the wind moaning through a partially opened door wrested my attention away. To my amazement, a great wind then began rushing through my body. I had always experienced wind as pushing *against* my body, not as rushing *through* it; and though I did not resist this unfamiliar sensation, the gale-like winds made me dizzy with their intensity and I started losing consciousness.

My consciousness was brought back, however, by the distant sound of sweet music that grew closer and closer until it, too, was within me. Though the music was very gentle and soft, it replaced the rising fury of the wind rushing through me, leaving only a faint echo of the storm.

Like a beautiful seductress, the sweet music beckoned me, lured me, enticed me to follow it wherever it might lead. I became a point of consciousness once more and followed the siren-music right into my body.

The colors were dazzling and radiant as I beheld with spell-bound eyes the marvelous machine that was my body. I had, of course, learned some of the basic workings of the human body in biology and physiology classes, had seen pictures and read articles; but nothing had prepared me for the wonders that lay before me. Lit by a dazzling violet glow, the interior of the body was such a complex yet simple mechanism that I was shocked that our greatest minds knew so little about it.

As I followed the enchanting melodies I saw the body unfold before me in a descending order like notes on a music scale. First I saw whole systems at work—skeletal, circulatory, muscular, and nervous. Then I viewed the individual elements composing these vast and intricate systems. The liver, the kidneys, the spleen, and other organs lay before me like shimmering islands as I moved through my body, a body I had never really known or loved. These organs pulsed with life and vitality in different rhythms that combined with the rhythms of other organs and systems to form a magnificent symphony. My body was *singing* to me!

Each system worked in perfect harmony, each had its own distinct color and brightness and melody. Each was its own sovereign yet needed the others to exist. Each organ was subservient to its system, yet this was no master-slave relationship or one of levels of importance. Each system and each organ needed all the others to function properly; each depended on the others. It was a marvelous display of true community, true family, true teamwork.

A pinkish-gold glow, more beautiful than any other color I had yet seen on this fantastic journey through my body, leapt into my vision. The color moved to the thunderous pulsating rhythms that had underlain all the other sounds. My mind danced with delight as the focus of my vision sharpened and I beheld my heart. As a machine it was a marvelous thing with precise workings, like a fine Swiss watch; but as an object of beauty it was still more marvelous for it powered the entire body, supplying it with energy and sustenance. It was no surprise to me that feelings of love have always been thought to reside within the heart, for an outpouring of love that can't be named was springing from that heart with each beat, with the opening and closing of each chamber, with each outbreath and inbreath of that marvelous organ. I cried with the love I felt coming from this miraculous organ, for it *cared* so much for every atom and cell of my body, no part being too small, too insignificant to be beyond the reach of its uncompromising, unconditional love. And I cried for the shame I felt in knowing that I had always neglected and resented this magnificent body, including the heart, which I had blamed for the pain I felt when I tried to love and was hurt or rejected. My heart worked constantly and tirelessly to give life to each part of my body down to the very smallest. It had cared for my body, nourished it, loved it more deeply than a mother loves her child, even when I had not.

Neither the heart nor any of the other organs or whole systems needed conscious direction to perform their magnificent, relentless work. Theirs was truly a labor of love directed by an intelligence I could not yet name.

I was absorbed for what seemed like hours in the beauty of my own heart. I would have remained longer but was jolted by the flash of a bright golden light. I snapped out of my reverie and found myself moving once again. This time, though, the movement was so fast I had no time to revel in the beauty and wonder of individual systems and organs.

It was straight to the brain I went. A lovely golden sheen suffused that mighty organ of thought as it pulsed and hummed to the beat of the heart. My eyes became more finely attuned to the brain's function and movement, and I witnessed the countless millions of processes going on with every beat. If each of the other organs were individual instruments playing in harmony with each other, then surely the brain was the orchestra's leader—a marvelous conductor who knew perfectly the function of each orchestra piece, knew the score so well that even the slightest variance in beat or melody was noticed. This was one of the major functions of the brain—to ensure the proper functioning of the individual systems and organs and their interrelations. And yet, and yet.... There was more to the brain than that—much more. As I watched further and let my consciousness sink deeper into the mysteries of my own brain, I saw the place where thoughts are born. All input from each part of this magnificent body poured in through the neuronal pathways to more concentrated nerve bundles. But as of yet there was no sight of the mechanism the brain uses to interpret and give meaning to the countless bits of information constantly arriving via these pathways.

At this point I felt the presence of a power and a joy I had not known before. A delicate silver glow sprinkled with a continuous shower of sparks from the golden electrical flares produced by the constantly firing neurons filled my vision. It was like the magical cold-fire display of countless fireflies on a moonlit night. The sight was magnificent.

I knew that the silver radiance came not from the brain itself, that the brain was but a receiving station for it. The radiance came through a vortex in the back of the head, a whirl of energy so powerful it caused the hair nearest it to swirl. When that silver radiance mixed with the information from the body in the form of incoming input from each physical part and from the access pathways to past memories and experiences, a thought was born—a pure, original idea not reproduced in that exact way anywhere else in the universe or at any time in all the history of life.

I also saw that when the silver essence was absent from the neuronal flickers, a thought based only on past understandings and habits was produced—a caricature, a mockery of the true thought I had just seen created. I saw how very easy it was to block the intermingling of the silver essence, how simple it was to shut it off, denying it access into the inner workings of the brain, to leave it like a starving, unwanted orphan on the doorstep outside the mind.

The secrets of creativity, of psychic phenomena, and of spirituality were all locked up in this marvelous symbiosis of energy that was unfolding before me. But like a mysterious, veiled dancer, the deeper answers flitted sensually around my consciousness, teased and excited my understanding, then slipped, fully-veiled away. I was sure that the answer to the experiences I had been having lay locked somehow within the processes I had been observing. I knew that with a deeper plunge into those processes of mind I could fully understand the mysterious process within me that had begun almost two years ago and which had begun shaping my life into something I still could not fathom.

Another flash of golden light shot across my vision as I bathed, momentarily lost in abstraction, in the beauty of my own brain. The images I had seen flickered and changed in the twinkling of an eye; and now I was moving through individual arteries and veins, taking a roller coaster ride through the body. The blood vessels narrowed; and I transferred to smaller and smaller ones until I rode the crimson waves of the tiniest of all, the capillaries. I felt a little like a commuter in a large city riding the transit system to various parts of the city, to the well-traveled places and the side streets as well. It was a grand tour of the body's circulatory system.

The golden light flickered again, and this time I saw individual cells, huge and radiant, looming before me. Inside each of these luminous, multi-colored spheres was a mass of a jelly-like substance, and at its center, the nucleus. The ethereal music continued to play but now in muted tones.

The supernal gold light once more exploded into my field of vision. With that flash, I entered one of those cells and began swirling around, lost in a vortex of light and color and sound. When my movement slowed, I could see the long, twisted strands of individual chromosomes. As I fine-tuned my attention, the chromosomes dissolved away, revealing the genes themselves, those basic building blocks of life. I saw the double helical strands that had eluded the understanding of scientists for so long and was overjoyed as I saw the incredibly intricate combinations of the four elements that code all genetics and heredity. I saw what no man or woman before me had seen, glimpsed the inner workings of the basic blueprint of life, of *my* life. A fantastic golden light permeated the scene, gave life to it in a way I could not understand, nourished it, intermingled with it, gave it substance—a vast golden sea on which floated all of life. A sweet melody was playing in all its purity from these four elements as they danced along the double helical strands. It wasn't that music was playing *around* these elements; it was more that it was coming *from* them, that it *was* them. In some incomprehensible way they *were* music! It became clear to me as I watched this dance of life at its most basic level that our bodies literally are musical instruments, down even to the genetic coding, that music is as fundamental to our nature, as much a part of our being, as is light. No, *more*. Each element was a note being played by some cosmic musician—pure, simple, beautiful music rising from an ocean of light. With great humility and even greater awe I realized that that musician was *me*.

* * *

I came back to human awareness like one waking from a dream separated from consciousness by the thinnest of films. The transition was gentle. But I had not been dreaming. I spent the next couple of days really noticing my body, watching it, observing how it moved, how it felt, how it thought. Trying to become conscious of as many events occurring within my body as possible, I tried to follow its natural processes. How little time I had spent getting to know my body before! I would often break out in great sobs of sadness that such a splendid thing as our bodies generally went so unloved and unknown. It was as unacknowledged as the cameraman behind the scenes or the orchestra in the pit during an opera, or the costume designer or choreographer of a magnificent ballet. Untiringly performing their labors of love, all these background helpers work solely to benefit the actors. For the actors we batter our hands with praise, but we never even think of those unknown, unsung, and unseen workers.

I wept in shame for the lack of love and acknowledgement I had given to my body, my earthly home. I wept for the love I had felt while exploring my body's depths, for my body's tireless effort to support and nourish and teach me. I vowed I would never, never forsake it again. A sadness came when I thought of the preoccupation so many people have with the body—not with loving it and understanding its wonders but with using it as a tool to gain power over others while avoiding looking at their mortality. I saw how we are often ashamed of our bodies, of our mortality, and use those bodies as altars for our guilt and our anger; we sacrifice our innocence and our love of life on these altars. I saw also that most relationships are an unholy wedding of our fear and isolation with our anger and our guilt. I knew that it did not matter if one had a body that was obese or old or short or unattractive in the eyes of the world, that the body was such a marvelous piece of living art and beauty that such considerations are not even worthy of mention. How could we be so blind to the majesty of this magnificent shrine? How could the color of one body or the size or sex or features of another have significance when viewing a person's worth?

October 22

This morning I woke up with a song in my heart. Twilight had barely faded as I stepped outside my house to greet the morning. It was one of those rare days when everything seems unblemished and new. A soft yellow glow lit the cloud flecks floating on the horizon, transforming them into nuggets of gold. The morning sounds of insects buzzing, small animals scurrying around, and birds singing were like music to me, a cacophony of melodies. I felt good.

As was my usual habit these days, I had a small breakfast of fruit and grains and sat on the porch, content and in love with my life. Then *she* appeared—this time not just as a disembodied face but as a whole woman. At first I thought the sun was playing tricks on me. Golden flickers of sunlight, little fairy-gleams forming magical impressions on my eyes, were stealing through the spaces in the tree next to my porch. But then, in their merry little dance those little sparks of light began to join together and the outline of a woman began to emerge. I blinked out of habit and disbelief, but the outline was still there. As I watched with amazement, the misty image took form before me, became as solid to look at as the tree itself through the intricate blending of light and shadow. Before me stood the woman whose face had so startled and intrigued me on several occasions.

I don't know if another person would have seen anything more than a play of light and shadow, but it was clear to me that she was real—a soft, ghostly presence that stared at me with the loveliest brown eyes I'd ever seen. Her mouth moved as if she were trying to speak to me, yet she could not. When she realized no words were coming out, she ceased her efforts and let her eyes speak for her. Her body swayed slightly as though she were light as a feather and might be blown away by the gentle breeze at any moment, but her arms and legs did not move of themselves.

Staring back at her with curiosity and astonishment in my face, I searched her face for a clue to her identity and purpose. I thought for a moment she might be the disembodied spirit of a person who had passed from this world. Then I dismissed the idea. This lady, whoever she might be, had no look of death about her. On the contrary, in those features, which were both youthful yet ancient as the mountains, was a force of life, a vitality, an essence coming through more powerfully than any I'd ever felt from another living thing. She implored me with her eyes, beckoned me...where? Then, as quickly as she had appeared before my eyes, she vanished. And once more I was staring at nothing more than a play of light and shadow.

October 25

Casting a soft pink blush over the distant hills, the morning sun rose over the horizon. A beautiful patch of lemon-yellow sky gently lay over a band of pastel peach, separated only by a thin wisp of gray clouds. I had just roused myself from a peaceful sleep, a sleep in which I dreamed of the lady I had seen so clearly the day before, and was entranced by the colors of morning. The colors and textures were so lovely I found myself wishing very much to share them with someone, anyone. I even fantasized that the lady would mysteriously appear again and watch this glorious sunrise with me. Alas, she did not. But something—or someone—did appear. Something inside me that was starting to grow like a newly-formed fetus was beginning to share my experiences with me, almost like a separate entity. Perhaps it was the gentle and loving presence I had felt within me on several occasions. But no...this something was definitely feminine in nature, whereas the presence I had felt previously seemed neither masculine nor feminine.

It may seem a little silly, but I was so filled with joy that I went outside and threw my arms around the old tree next to my porch and hugged it as though it were a long-lost lover. I didn't care if I looked silly anymore. I laughed and laughed.

As I laughed, a curious sensation came over me. A *strangeness* that was not uncomfortable—just unfamiliar—began to fill me, to send eerie feelings through my body. At the same time, images began to form in my mind, images so clear I had trouble distinguishing them from those my senses were reporting from the world around me. I saw the sky change colors from China blue to steel gray, to pitch black and back again to brilliant blue. I felt the wind rise and fall, rise and fall. I grew stiff in my joints and slow in my movements till not even a single finger moved. An awareness slowly dawned on me that I was seeing, actually *seeing*, what that tree had 'seen' in its life. I was *becoming* the tree! For a moment there was a twinge of fear, and I felt constricted and claustrophobic; but as I relaxed into the sensation, those feelings ceased. What I saw was the world as seen by the dim, dream-like consciousness of a tree; yet, my awareness as a man was not far removed from me. It was still there, observing what was happening but from a detached, greatly withdrawn position—much as a coach of a great tennis star remains detached and observant during a championship match.

Images and colors without form or boundary flooded my field of vision. Dull sensations of need arose and were fulfilled by water coursing through intricate root systems, by sunlight dancing on unfurled leaves. And there was the dull pang of winter chills on barren branches, over and over again throughout the years.

I sensed the growth that tree had gone through in its hundred and fifty or so years. I saw it grow thinner as each cycle of winter came and passed until it was but a tiny sapling only a few feet high and a few inches thick. Then it was but a tiny shoot, then a tiny green sprout barely out of the ground, and finally, but a seed waiting to burst forth onto the land. There was a sense not only of the individual life of this tree but of the life that was going on around it during the span of its existence. I saw no images of people or things but was dimly aware of *feelings* that seemed to hang in the air, like musty smells in an old attic, feelings that spoke of lives that had been lived nearby during that century and a half this tree had been alive. These vortices of energy gave me an overwhelming sense of nostalgia for those who lived during that time, a time that was gone, a time I would never see. I wept and wept.

I was still weeping when I came to myself, still hugging that old tree. It had stood silent, rarely noticed, for so many years; yet it had been witness to so much. I walked slowly to the porch and sat down. The sun was now high in the sky and several clouds now covered the sheet-of-glass sky, covered it like a patchwork quilt. I was stiff and a little weary, but I didn't care. I had seen and felt what I never thought possible—the consciousness and life of a tree.

November 3

I went outside this morning to greet the rising sun. I often do so. It gives me a sense of renewed strength and new beginnings to watch the sky turn from dark black to cobalt blue to the pale indigo of early morning. I love to watch the splashes of color that silently explode onto the horizon as the sun comes up like a golden hot air balloon rising in slow motion over the distant hills. The day is too young for weariness to be in my heart or mind. Dreams of the night have left a trail of wonder and untold beauty in my soul, an excitement the magic of morning twilight—a time when logic has had no time to raise its rigid head—serves only to nourish and enhance.

I once read that the American Indians made a ritual of greeting the morning sun. They felt they gained strength and renewal from its healing rays. A people very close to the earth, they saw little separation between themselves, the earth, and the Great Spirit. I yearn for a time when others will view life in the same way. Though I am often filled with great beauty and awe these days, a part is missing—the *sharing* of that beauty with others who can understand it. I am often so overcome by the knowledge of what's happening inside me that I feel I'll burst if that joy and love is not turned outward into the world. But as of yet I have no sense of how to do that, other than through the keeping of this journal. I know of no one who could understand—or even believe—the transformation that is happening within me. I know of no one who would not think me severely ill or delusionary if I tried to explain to them what has been happening to me.

The vision of the lady who appeared to me has evoked feelings of great longing, has brought me literally face to face with an aspect of my life that has been missing all these years. I've had brief relationships with women, nothing that filled more than a momentary need for companionship or physical pleasure. Like cheap paint that for a moment gave a semblance of beauty and endurance, those relationships quickly cracked or faded. Like shadows fading at the break of dawn, those moments of pleasure and companionship vanished, leaving me with greater doubt, greater confusion, greater longing and loneliness than before. Yet I kept pursuing women, knowing deep inside that relationships were not just illusions, that they represented something that was real, though I never in my life truly experienced it. And now this lady, whether real or created by my own desires, was telling me with her eyes—was showing me with the noble, elegant way she held her head—that it *was* possible to have a relationship born of love, integrity, and mutual respect, that did not fade with time but instead grew stronger, calmer, deeper, like the great oak tree in my front yard.

As I mused on these thoughts, I picked up a small rock and prepared to throw it at a fallen branch fifty feet distant. It was nothing special, just a small piece of sandstone common to this locale. Just as I was ready to let go of the rock, several images flashed into my mind, and I let the hand clutching the rock fall at my side.

Still holding the rock, I saw images of the land I was standing on covered with water. The sky went blurry, then pitch black; and I had a sense of being several feet beneath the ground. The feeling was similar to the one I had several months ago when I rose from my earthly body and dove to the bottom of the sea. The difference was that I had the sense not only of being at the bottom of the sea but also of *being* the bit of stone I was holding as well, and of being in another time. Currents and swirls of energy moved through my consciousness, making me dizzy. Then there was stillness, a more complete stillness than I had ever known—a darkness, a silence, a stillness that flesh and blood cannot know. In that moment I *was* the rock, was living the rock's life, in much the same way I had done with the tree. The complete lack of hurry or the need to *do* anything, moved me. I simply *was*. The only recollection I have in my experience as a human being that even comes close to that pervading sense of just *being* is the dim memory I have of my life before I was born. I remember a sense of peace that needed no name, no category, no subject-object reflection for its existence—a beingness that was *not* nothingness. It was a consciousness completely at rest that knew nothing of fear or existence or desire. While holding that rock I experienced a state that perfectly represents the Buddhist idea of nirvana, which is not the nothingness many have misunderstood it to be but the cessation of all desire and activity as consciousness melts back into the sacred ground of being out of which all things come. The state was like the snuffing out of a candle, and the seed of knowing came that the goal of all religions, all the heavens and nirvanas and samadhis, must first have been born of the dim remembrance of, and the longing for, the state I was blessed to be living during that timeless moment I was holding the rock.

The waters began to recede and a dim, muddy blob of light appeared. It steadily grew brighter and more defined until I was gazing once again at the sun. I was on the shore once more—once more a piece of sandstone rudely awakened from slumber at the bottom of the sea by time and receding waters. And then I was a flesh and blood man again, still clutching that rock, clutching it as though it were the most precious stone in the world, my fingers tense and sore with the effort. I ran to the ocean then, ran till the water was up to my knees. I threw the rock as far as I could...seeking to return it to the peace and stillness and freedom it had once known and which I, for a precious moment, had been privileged to share.

November 10

The experiences I had with the tree and the rock excited me, gave me a sense of adventure and awe. It was not just the power of the visual images that thrilled and ignited me. Far more enrapturing were the *feelings* I had received from those objects, an indescribable set of feelings that were not merely nostalgia. There was a very real feeling of having lived during the years that rushed through me during those two experiences, of having tasted the joys and sorrows of not just the objects whose consciousness I had entered but of the collective wave of feelings of those who had lived during those times. I have no matrix of past experience to compare these experiences with. It would be like people blind all their lives suddenly being gifted with perfect vision. How would they describe a horse, a person, a sunset? How would they describe this new and alien faculty by which they *knew* the object was there but not by hearing or tasting or touching or smelling it?

I read recently that the ability to hold an object and see or feel its history is called psychometry, another term scoffed at by science but recognized for centuries in psychic and mystical circles. It is becoming clear that I must reevaluate everything I thought I knew—

everything the world has accepted and taught as the truth—in the light of my new experiences. *Everything* must now be questioned. I can no longer scoff at an idea simply because it doesn't make sense within my personal framework of reality. I can no longer accept the opinions or truths of others as the truth for myself solely on the basis of others' experience. As my transformation continues, my old framework of reality is giving way, is being shown to be built on shifting sand. A new foundation for living is being constructed within me now, a foundation I suspect will be so solid it will support a structure that can reach all the way to the stars.

With the opening that has occurred in me since my transformation began, many new abilities such as psychometry are also being unfolded in me. With those first experiences a channel opened that now allows the energy to flow largely unimpeded. What direction it takes is usually a surprise to me, and a pleasant one at that. Not being certain where these experiences will lead me, when they will occur, or what form they will take no longer gives cause for alarm and anxiety, as they did in the beginning. Instead, I look forward to them, as though they are the only true way to live. Now I understand what true adventure is. I'm living it.

November 14

I went to a shop where crystals and jewelry are sold and was fascinated by the exquisiteness and variety of crystals. I had never really paid much attention to them before. They looked pretty when light shone through them but otherwise held little interest for me. But today was different. I noticed recently that all of my senses seemed to be heightened, but in the crystal shop they seemed to be multiplied a hundred fold. What I noticed first was the high-pitched tones resonating from each of the crystals—the higher tones coming from the more purely cut ones. I also noticed that the ones that had been artificially manufactured had only a vague, dull tone. A bright glow surrounded the natural crystals, which resonated with power; whereas no glow or only a dim, muddy radiance emanated from the artificial ones, no matter how intricate or finely cut they appeared to be.

I had heard that crystals could be used in healing but had always dismissed the notion as but another bit of 'New Age' quackery. In view of my recent experiences and the falling away of many things I had always believed without question to be true, however, I looked at the crystals with an open mind. I began to see that there might, in fact, be some truth to the claims.

I listened to the crystals sing in high-pitched harmonic tones, vibrating at incredible rates. With my new sight, I saw them blaze like tiny, many-faceted suns. I was awed by the vast amounts of energy the crystals contained. I held one in my hand and felt something like heat building up in that hand. It wasn't heat, really. It was more of a tingling sensation, a sense of the movement of particles and energy, of vibration and life coursing through that crystal and into my hand. Images of heat and pressure and loneliness, of light and music and symmetry, began to fill my mind. I began to lose myself to the crystal and must have looked a little dazed. Someone touched me on the shoulder and asked if I was all right. I snapped out of my reverie for a moment and was about to look for a quiet, hidden spot in the shop to continue this new psychometric adventure—so beautiful were the images that had started coming—when I spied a little display featuring tiny bits of a meteorite. A card said they were small pieces of a large meteorite found in Arizona by a man who wished to share his find with others. He had first displayed the entire rock but later decided to cut it up in tiny pieces so that others could purchase them and share a part of his find. For some reason I was drawn to the display and put the crystal back in its proper place. I then picked up a piece of the black meteorite, shiny and smooth on the one side, dull and rough on the other. It had a good feel to it, a solid, ancient feel. I rolled it around in my hand a few times. It had a strangeness about it I can't describe. This enigmatic piece of rock had a power beyond anything the crystals possessed. I could *feel* it; yet it did not put out heat or sound or vibration of any kind. I decided that rather than risk an experiment with it there I would buy it and take it home with me. My experiment with the crystal would have to wait.

I had stayed late at the crystal shop; the final fingers of light were streaming from the setting sun as I left. Twilight was pulling its cobalt-blue mantle lit with milk-white stars across the colors of the day in a sweet, nurturing caress all mothers would envy. I loved watching the stars.

When I got home I took the tiny bit of meteorite with me to the beach. Flecks of foam lit silver by the pearly white stars danced as the surf rushed in, then fell back. The sky was still and clear and lovely. I lay down just out of reach of the ever-grasping fingers of water, the black stone held firmly in my right hand. I felt young under this fresh sky—young and alive. I breathed in the ocean spray and gave thanks.

I closed my eyes for a few moments and began to focus on the meteorite. Images began to cross my mind, but they were too blurred or fleeting for me to understand. I tried to will them to slow down, to express themselves in ways I could understand; but they did not. An anxiety began to build up in my heart. Pressure began to fill my mind; and I had the sensation of being dropped down a dark well whose sides I could not touch, whose depth I could not gauge. It was an uncomfortable, helpless feeling. Then, with a loud bang, it stopped.

I shook my head and opened my eyes, blinking several times as I did. Then I felt a terror so great I knew it could not be borne by flesh and blood. No structure made of physical matter could have withstood the shock. *There was no ground beneath me, no ocean beside me. I was adrift in a sea of stars—alone, I knew not where.* I felt a sense of panic a thousand times greater than a fear of heights, for the *world* had vanished, life had vanished...all I knew had vanished from me. And I just drifted.

As I gradually gained control of myself I noticed that the stars were not the ones I had known on Earth. There were no familiar constellations, no bright points by which I could gain a sense of direction or position. Instead, I was looking at a totally alien sky with patches of stars in brilliant hues of red and blue. To the side there was a large gap where no stars shown—a void, a reach of sky so remote even stars had not taken root there. I turned around and my heart leaped up. There before me, floating in all that alien blackness was a galaxy of stars, a white-gold blur of muted light shaped like a Mexican sombrero, as large to my sight as my outstretched hand. Upon seeing this image, all traces of fear vanished as though they had never been. In their place was a sense of the glorious and sublime. I no longer cared if I lived, if this was a dream, or if I would cease to exist. None of that mattered. All I wanted was to gaze at the sublime, absolute beauty hovering in the darkness before me.

Because I had no reference points, the beauty in the darkness, the glory that was before me now, seemed to be a delicious fruit I could reach out and grasp with my hand—a brilliant, dazzling jewel that could be mine for the taking. A deep reverence filled me, for I knew that in each moment I was witnessing more beauty and meaning and glory than a thousand people could know in a lifetime of bodily existence. It was clear that no 'body' could withstand the current of this much glory, just as nothing physical could have withstood the shock of fear I had known in those first few moments. It was the kind of absolute terror a person might experience upon waking from a pleasant sleep only to find himself miles above the earth with no means of support. Only pure spirit unencumbered by matter could sustain the shock of it.

Substance materialized under my feet, a jagged landscape appeared before me, and I was aware of being on a small planet or moon. I looked around and was moved by the utter barrenness surrounding me, the utter remoteness. A great sadness like a heavy fog over a large seaboard city lay over this place. There was no color or movement or life, only endless flat wastes broken here and there by tall, thin formations that resembled twisted trees of rock, columns of dark stone, or lighthouses—lonely sentinels on the remotest outpost in the universe.

Tears came to my eyes as the barrenness and remoteness of this planet moved through me. In that dark, purple-tinged sky, in the shape and beckoning loneliness of that galaxy, was more beauty than I'd ever known before. Then I *knew*, I knew that the tiny piece of black rock had come from this small, barren world—had somehow broken away or been knocked away from its home by some unknown force and raced at some fantastically high speed through space for an eternity before crossing the path of Earth. The man who found it had thought it was only a passing bit of cosmic rubble, a curiosity to be shared for its novelty. But this 'novelty' was a hundred million times older than he, older even than Earth itself. It had left the beauty of that galaxy and drifted, drifted for ever so long—a message in a bottle adrift in a sea of stars, a piece of bread cast upon infinite waters with little chance of ever being found, much less of being known. No one knew of it or its place of origin. No one knew the beauty of the galaxy that lit its nights. No one had known that galaxy as other than an obscure point of light through the largest of telescopes or a string of numbers and letters in a thick, dusty book. Yet there the two objects were—a smudge of light a hundred billion times larger and more glorious than our own sun, and a tiny, dead world, old when the earth was young. Only *I* knew about all this.

I came to myself with a gentle sigh. Familiar stars lit the sky, and the comforting lap of the seashore filled my ears with the joys of sound, a pleasure alien to the place I had so recently come from. I dug my hands into the soft, wet sand and breathed the sweet air. I lay there a few minutes more before rising to go home. I was in no hurry. I would put the tiny meteorite fragment on a shelf in my living room. It would be a constant reminder that there was no limit on how far, how long, or against what odds life with even the dim consciousness of a rock would travel in order that its life and beauty might be revealed.

December 2
Life is changing in such kind and gentle ways. I've had no more beauties since the experience with the tiny chunk of star-stone a couple of weeks ago—nothing dramatic or overly exciting. But there *has* been a constant seepage into my being of what I could only describe as 'grace,' an effortless gentleness and a calm, inner knowing that have given me a profoundly deep sense of peace and a glow of warmth I can sometimes see radiating from my body as a faint light in the darkness, a ray of hope that not all the darkness in the world can overcome.

December 12
As I watch the sunlight fade into twilight and the silent, gray clouds gather shades of pink and violet and blue, I wonder what the true meaning of this panorama is for me. I...I who have known such joy and beauty and freedom in the past few months still yearn to know how my life fits into this tremendous scheme of things, how I am to serve that mysterious and beautiful force of life that has begun to teach me, to love me.
    I often see a glimpse of that purpose just before my consciousness slips the bonds of waking life, boards a schooner of fairy-light and sails on seas of dreams. I glimpse something lying just beyond the edge of my vision, something just past the margin of my knowing, that beckons me then is gone. I know that it is what lies beyond this margin of knowing, this edge of wonder, that I must one day come to understand.
    It's calm now and cool and quiet, very unlike the noisy activity of the day. The tall trees stand guard over my rare sense of peace. A cool gentle breeze helps me forget the heat of harsher days. At such times as now I feel most alive, most able to reflect without distortion the beauty God shines on my spirit. (A thought just came that I

should have said "the beauty God shines *through* my spirit or, perhaps even more accurately, *as* my spirit.")

Once I believed that heaven's gate had to be fought for or stormed or earned in a thousand painful or frightening ways, ways only a chosen few had the strength, courage, or understanding to accomplish. Now I am growing more and more convinced that this is not so, that it is in stillness—in quiet actions and gentle thoughts—that heaven's prize is gained, that a smile and a kind word are mightier in God's kingdom than all the booming voices and intricate minds that speak of salvation or enlightenment.

Once I believed I had failed or that I simply did not belong to the world of drugs, loud stereos, endless parties, and insensitive people I seemed constantly surrounded by. If I had written a book during that time, a fitting title might have been *The Light that Failed*, to characterize the frustration, depression, and futility I so often experienced as I saw the light of my spirit continually engulfed by waves of confusion and sorrow. The dreams of my youth, the innocence I remember so well as a child, all seem to have withered and died like some delicate flower thirsting in the desert. And yet, I now know it is not so, that there is a radiant dawn after even the darkest night, a calm after even the most violent storm. I know that my dreams and joys can never die so long as I can feel the inner rapture a sunset brings or know the quiet beauty of the trees, the stars, the mountains—so long as I can see the beauty and glory of humanity and life mirrored back to me in the eyes of a beautiful woman.

December 22

Christ was born in the heart of winter, the season of heavy snows and icy winds, during a time when hopes and dreams seemed barren and forgotten in the hearts of men. Perhaps it is best that miracles occur when least expected and in ways not predicted or logical.

The winds are brisk and cool tonight. I sat, cold but revitalized, on the beach for an hour this evening and enjoyed the invigorating weather. I watched the waves rush to shore in their never ending quest to engulf the land. Those waves were doomed to continually fail, like Sisyphus pushing the rock up the hill only to have it roll back down each time just before the summit was reached. I have felt a little bit like those waves lately—constantly reaching for something that eludes my grasp just as it seems within reach. The incredible experiences I've had with the tree, the rock, and the meteorite are like precious jewels glittering in the vault of my heart. They can never grow dim or be stolen from me. And yet, there is something *more* to be experienced, something I see in fleeting glimpses yet have no words to describe. These images flash into my consciousness for the tiniest fraction of a moment then are gone, like a flash of lightning, leaving only a thunderclap of confusion and longing behind. I know this longing has to do with both the hauntingly beautiful shadow lady and the idea of ascension. I feel the need to engage myself once more in the inner search for meaning I began a few months ago when I found myself exploring my body all the way down to the cellular level and beyond. I am growing more and more convinced that all problems, all questions will be resolved simultaneously, when I unravel the secret and meaning of ascension.

True Adventure

December 27

The light has come! Oh, the joy of it all! For I now *know* the secret of ascension, at least in part. And more! And more! My fingers are trembling as I try to put on paper what has happened to me.

It seems like months have passed, so much has taken place since that last entry just before Christmas. My fingers are trembling—not from fear but joy—joy at the wonder and sublimity of life and the rare beauties I have been privileged to experience and be part of.

Preoccupied with rejoining the inner search I hoped would provide more pieces to the puzzle of my life, I had spent the better part of two days in deep meditation, seeking to once again be drawn into my body to finer and finer levels of organization down to the cellular level and perhaps even to the building blocks of life itself, the basic elements that make up the double helix of DNA. I tried every technique I knew to induce the experience—visualization, chanting, deep breathing, and one-pointed focusing—but nothing worked. In frustration, I finally gave up and lay down to rest, mollified by the knowledge that I was pushing too hard, was trying to force an experience to occur that must happen of itself. Shortly after I lay down I heard a mighty sound like a strong wind rushing through a partially open door followed by a sound like the crack of a rifle blast going off in my head. The suddenness of the noises brought me from a state of drowsiness to full alert; but in order to focus on the sounds I lay still. I began to drift then, like a boat loosed from its moorings, and was gently lulled by a sweet, gentle melody wafting through the ethers I had already started to float through. As in my previous experience, my mind was filled with brilliant colors and dazzling shapes as I began to enter and explore my body once more. This time, however, I willed myself straight to the brain, for surely if the secret of ascension lay in the body, it must be in the brain. With that assumption, I was immediately in the midst of that magnificent organ of thought. My previous adventure there had left no doubt that the greatest mysteries were to be found and, hopefully, solved in that marvelous transmitter and receiver of subtle energies.

With a flash of blinding radiance, I was in the midst of my own brain, that precious dispatcher of thought, superb transformer of energies. I saw once more the splendid workings of the neuronal passageways and the connecting synapses. This time, however, I was aware not only of the beauty and splendor of that intricate mechanism but also of the incredible *power* it housed. My consciousness reeled from the sheer strength and fury unloosed by the processes going on. A storm was brewing—a gale of hurricane proportions. I wondered if this is why we instinctively love the wildness and naked power of storms—because one is going on within us all the time. To imagine the force of mind unleashed at this level by the fully engaged processes of a genius like Einstein was beyond me.

As I willed that I go to still deeper levels of my brain in search of the elusive secrets of ascension, the storm of mind subsided. The golden light suffusing the brain engulfed my consciousness. The light became almost white in its intensity as it began to cover my field of vision like a blanket of fresh fallen snow. Then it fell away, all by itself, and left me once more surrounded by a sweet, rapturous music and the double helix of life. I stared in awe at the building blocks of my physical self and listened as they sang their sweet, sad song to me. I was reminded of the mournful, yet deeply beautiful songs of the humpback whales, songs said to reflect the history and memories of the ages over a distance of up to five hundred miles. Those whale songs were sent out like messages in bottles hurled into the blackness of the oceans. How lonely those songs were; but the song I now heard had only dim echoes of loneliness in it. It was a composition of joy and of life and vitality. The intricacy of science and mathematics was in it, as well as the beauty and mystery of art. I would have stayed in this magnificence for a very long time had I not seen the bright gleam of light and color once again burst upon me like the flash of a camera.

I was jolted out of my reverie by sights I had not yet seen in all my journeys, all my beauties. When I traveled through my body before, I thought the journey was over when I reached the level of

DNA; but now I knew it was not so, that it was possible to go even *farther* than that—down, down to the atomic structure itself! There before me, floating in an ocean of golden light, I saw the pulses—felt the energies—of the very atoms that made up my physical form.

How can I describe the exquisite beauty I experienced in that moment? The sheer intensity of awe? I know now that the reason I could not go to this level previously was that I was unable to withstand this much glory bombarding my soul. Much had happened between my two sojourns into the body, however, and like a rock constantly battered by incoming tides, so my consciousness had been weathered, had been hollowed out by that crashing spray of beauty and understanding. I now had a greater capacity for experience than before. With this greater capacity for experience came a greater compassion toward others and a greater desire to share the joy of my journeys with them.

I wondered if the strain I felt in trying to contain the beauty and wonder crashing into my spirit was how it had been for Jesus...wondered if the sheer glory surrounding his pristine spirit had constantly threatened to overwhelm his earthly self. I knew in a moment of bliss that it was so and that it is as difficult to bear glory as it is to bear pain. Jesus' apparent suffering was not solely from the torment of abused flesh and misunderstood teachings but also from the sheer anguish of funneling the unthinkable beauty and love of God through an individual consciousness. The strain on that mind and body must have been *enormous*. And he had done it all for *us*!

A strong mixture of both joy and sadness washed over me as I thought about the life of Jesus. A fine line had to be walked; and had the great energies surrounding him not been able to run through cleansed, unimpeded conduits, his body and mind would not have been able to survive the strain. To walk the path leading to ascension is like performing a highwire act. It is difficult and requires the greatest intensity of focus, balance, and intent. Yet when the necessary skills are mastered, it gives the greatest feeling of aliveness that can be known, a glorious exaltation of the human body, unfettered by lack and limitation, living neither in the past nor projecting that past forward as the future, but living right *now*! Now, which is eternity.

Lost in the rapture of being at the very atomic level of my brain, I bathed in that sea of golden wonder for what seemed to be a long time. A dim shadow cast over the muted golden radiance reminded me of the shadows cast by the full moon on rocks lit by its silvery luminescence. I needed nothing; I wanted nothing. And I lived a long life there.

Suddenly, the pulses of energy I had observed earlier increased and swirls and eddies began to form in this ebullient sea, a sea of energy within my own *brain*. Waves I had gently bobbed up and down with now crashed against me, whipping me this way, then that. Soon I was in the midst of a raging storm as the pulses of energy increased and the swirling motions began to whip the ocean into circular globules of motion and throbbing light. Spaces formed between the points of pulsating light, and the ocean now looked as if it had been unevenly whipped by a giant mixer so that what remained were globs of concentrated light connected by a filmy golden tissue. It looked much like the web of a golden spider against a background of fog at night. And I knew that the sea had not actually changed—I had. I had descended into it at the call of that directing presence, that sweet, gentle presence inside myself, and was seeing in finer and finer detail. I was becoming smaller, as it were. Though in truth I now know that that was not the case. My consciousness was focusing on a finer detail of the whole. Just so.

* * *

Another flash of light lit my conscious awareness, and I found myself staring at a single drop of golden light. It looked like an entire world to my sharpened vision, and only faint golden specks in the distance gave evidence of the other 'droplets' that had so recently been gathered together before me.

The thin film of gossamer light that had overlaid all the tiny drops was now a deep darkness similar to the black void that spans the gulf between worlds in the reality I know on Earth. Yet, moments before I had seen not darkness but a tissue of filmy light. Before that, a sea of golden radiance. Now I was seeing darkness—darkness in light...light in darkness. I remembered how, as a child I had often amused myself by trying to see points of light in the darkness of night and streaks of darkness in the light of day. I had noticed that the two seemed to be connected, that if I concentrated long enough on the one I could see the other. I would continue this 'game' until the entire fabric of the light or dark I stared into would seem to come apart, like key threads being rapidly pulled from a garment, revealing a network of connecting links, a lattice-work of 'threads' holding the pattern together, giving it reality. As I beheld those delicate interstices between light and dark, I would wonder which was the reality, which the illusion.

My musings came to an abrupt halt as I found myself rapidly descending to that tiny, 'world.' Like a wayward satellite, I hurled toward that rapidly growing ball of golden light. Now it had substance and a definite boundary to it. Then it seemed to swallow me up with its magnitude, and for a moment I grew dizzy and lost the sense of myself.

In what seemed but an instant I regained my bearings and found myself back on solid ground. I assumed my adventure into the body had ended and I had reawakened to my earthly self; a moment later, however, I rose to my feet and laughed with joy, for the ground all about me was solid gold in color. I knew I had not reawakened in my earthly body but had continued my journey, all the way down to the atomic structure of the brain itself! There I was...a being aware of his living in that moment on a world so tiny it stood in relation to a mote of dust the way a grain of sand does to a blazing star.

The surface of this tiny world had little irregularity, but I decided to explore it nonetheless. There was no sun in this sky, if sky it could be called; but the landscape was lit by an eerie, silver phosphorescence whose origin I could not guess. There were no birds or insects, for this was but a tiny drop of matter, perhaps too small even to be given that term. I could have hardly expected to find life there. But there *was* a mild breeze, and a sweetness in my body as it felt nourished by something akin to air.

I walked for what seemed like hours yet did not tire. The ground was soft under my feet, like sawdust, and had a spongy quality to it. I did not know why that power that had caused such profound changes in my body and mind, that mysterious force that had given me such sublime and beautiful experiences thus far, had brought me to this place; but I was determined to journey on, trusting that the answer would be revealed to me in time.

My senses were jolted as I came to a huge outcropping that overlooked a valley. I saw that what had at first appeared to be a smooth, uniform world was but an illusion created by the uniformity of color. In the valley below I saw swells of rolling hills and troughs, and in the distance small mountains with what appeared to be jagged edges. I was *astounded*, but my amazement quickly gave way to a profound sense of awe. For nestled between two of the rolling hills I saw what could only be described as houses.

* * *

It took hours, but I slowly made the descent from the smooth plateau I had found myself on to the valley below. I made my way toward the small village I had seen earlier, amazed beyond belief that even at this minute level of matter there was intelligent life. There could be no doubt those objects I had seen from the plateau were dwellings of some sort. Someone—or something—was *living* there!

As I drew near to one of the dome-shaped objects, a small opening formed in the side and a young woman emerged. I blinked in disbelief and froze in mid-step, so great was my surprise. She was human in appearance, yet like no woman I had ever seen on Earth. She appeared to be about twenty-five but no sign of age marked her face. The closest I had ever come to seeing a face like this was during my episodes with the enigmatic shadow woman—a mystery I had yet to solve.

The young woman approached me without the slightest trace of fear or amazement in her eyes. The child-like wonder and joy each of us is born with, then tends to lose as we accept the rules needed for our imagined survival in the world was present in her face. Most peoples' innocence fades over the years like a candle that flickers brightly then dies when deprived of oxygen. But it was not so with her. It was as if she were constantly expecting the miraculous by virtue of her birthright as a living being.

Her skin looked silky smooth and had a golden tint to it. The waves of tiny, silver streamers radiating from her head were a hundred times finer and more beautiful than what we know as hair. She took my hand and held it in hers for what seemed a long time. Then she spoke. She did not speak in the way we speak, however. I was not aware of her lips moving, but she did indeed speak to me. It was more that she communicated a vast range of feelings and thoughts to me in the form of images in my mind, images that picked through my knowledge of worldly things and translated them into words and impressions I could understand.

She told me her name was Radia and said that my coming had been foretold many thousands of years ago. She had known I had come by the flash of brilliance she had seen hurtling through her skies. Others would soon come to greet me.

Sensations rushed through my soul like wind through a just opened window on a stormy day. I said nothing to Radia for what seemed like several minutes, so in awe was I. I was exhilarated...and filled with a sense, a presence of what I can only describe as the sublime. In her eyes, those crystalline, argentine eyes, eyes that looked more like twin drops of pure, molten silver than eyes, was an endlessness and a peace—the peace of calm, still waters, of mountain ranges rising majestically before the light of dawn.

Finally I spoke to Radia, told her my name was William, and that I had come from a place very, very far away yet very near. I did not wait for her to reply. A torrent of words gushed from my mouth. I said that I was a stranger to this land yet willing to learn its ways, that I wished to spend my time here with her, and that I found her lovely to look upon. She smiled, and I knew by her gentle nod that she wished things to be no other way.

I asked her if there were many others on her world, for I had only seen a few dwellings from the plateau. In that unusual form of mental and emotional imaging, she responded that there were. I asked if there were cities as well; and to this she replied that there were, *for those who wished them.* I did not know at the time how important and revealing that last statement of hers was. As I came to know more of this infinitely tiny world, I saw that thought and reality were intertwined in a symbiotic way, woven like a tapestry, able to be whatever the artist chose, dependent only on his or her skill, intent, and love. The beauty of it was that the tapestry was not limited to an initial idea but evolved in time, as did the artist, so that it became a unique, shining creation, as fresh and new under the artist's willing hand as it was to the observer.

* * *

I felt no need for sleep or nourishment of any kind, and this puzzled me. A rhythmic pulsation was in the very air, if air it could be called, that bestowed energy and vitality on all that passed through its current. It was like the gentle pulsing of an electrical current, and I would later realize how close to the truth that analogy was. Responding to my curiosity, Radia said that she and her companions had no need for what my mind called food and drink. Nor did they have need for sleep. She said everything that was needed was within each person. I asked about the dwelling places, for surely someone had to have made them and out of some substance. Radia ran her fingers through the infinitely fine strands of her silver hair and told me that all structures grew from thoughts, just as her hair grew and streamed outward from her head. She said structures were not needed in the way my mind understood but were *chosen* by those who wished them. I must have looked puzzled and confused at this last statement. She told me my thoughts were strange to her. Surely this process of creating things from ones thoughts was the same on the world from which I had come? I told her it was not so where I came from, though perhaps it was meant to be.

With the innocence and excitement of a child Radia asked if my world was one of the lights flickering in the sky. I was filled with a deep sadness as I saw the vast gulf that stretched between her conception of the universe and mine. How could I explain to her that her world and a billion billion others like it could fit on the head of a pin in the world I came from? And yet, her understanding of life and her joy in it seemed much greater in their simplicity than mine. There were no dark recesses of the self she needed to unmask and release, no dragons to conquer, no hardships to endure. Words such as 'lack' or 'need' did not exist in her language, and she seemed genuinely amused and amazed when I tried to describe their meaning to her. She had a sense of humor and an innocence I came to know that had nothing of naivete in it. Her innocence was pure and unobstructed. She also had a deep wisdom that had nothing to do with age or learning. It came from the fountainhead of her being and was synonymous with the essence of her spirit.

* * *

Radia led me to one of the dome-shaped dwellings; and I saw that what had appeared to be a solid, golden structure was not solid at all in the way humans understand the word. It was made of a flexible substance, extremely thin and resilient to the touch. Its color was not solid either but was more of a changing, opalescent nature; it had an iridescent milkiness about it that was both aesthetically pleasing and somber to me. The only image from my world that seemed to come close to this structure was that of a giant soap bubble.

As if by magic an opening formed in the bubble-house, and we entered. There was no furniture or decorations of any kind inside, yet I found the interior beautiful and comfortable nonetheless. The floor was made of some half-fluid, half-sponge substance that was comfortable regardless of the position one adopted. My body seemed to merge and flow with the floor in such a way that, whether sitting, lying, or standing on it, I had a sense of great ease and relaxation. In one corner I noticed a plate with a strange blue and orange paste on it and a goblet filled with an effervescent green liquid. My lovely hostess announced that I could now eat, drink, and sleep. I was puzzled because she had said earlier there was no need for such things there. To my thought she replied that this was true, but *I* still believed in the need for such things. With a beaming smile that was part joy and part impishness she said I was not asked to change or give up my beliefs, though I could choose to do so any time I wished.

Radia left me with my thoughts. Large tears welled up in my eyes as the full impact of her presence stuck me like iron. I had never felt so completely accepted by another person in my life. There was nothing I needed to do to please her, nothing I needed to say or be. She simply loved me, purely and without a shred of judgment. A friend once told me of the time his car had broken down on a dusty back road in a rural area. After walking a couple of miles, he had come upon a New Age community of some sort. He had felt tentative about asking for help at first because he had always considered people living in communal groups as being strange and possibly dangerous, and because he had no interest in "all that New Age garbage," as he put it. But he was hungry and tired of walking, and no other houses were in sight. He told me that not only did the people in the community greet him with kindness, but they also invited him in for dinner as well. While three of the men worked on his car, he was treated to a memorable dinner, memorable not so much because the food was to his liking, which it was, but because it was what he was accustomed to. They themselves were on a strict vegetarian diet and ate sprouts and fresh vegetables; but for him, knowing what he was used to, they prepared meat. The beauty of it for him was that not once, from the children to the elderly, did he see a trace of judgment on a single face. He had never felt so accepted and nurtured in his life. His clothes were different, his ways were different, his beliefs were different. And it didn't matter. He came away with a completely changed attitude toward people who were different from himself. This was how I felt with Radia but in a deeper sense. Our differences were much more pronounced than those of my friend and his benefactors. She had such an alienness about her, yet never had I felt so comfortable with a living being—and I had barely met her.

I ate and drank and found myself bombarded by taste sensations I can't easily describe. The food and drink seemed to *assault* my taste buds, but in such a pleasant, active way that every experience of food or drink I had ever known seemed flat and passive by comparison. The blue paste electrified me with energy and humor. I felt as though I were tap-dancing while listening to the funniest jokes imaginable. The orange paste left me feeling calm and tranquil, as though I had just completed a joyful yet strenuous task and was now sinking into a peaceful, well-deserved sleep. The beverage both ignited my mind with enthusiasm and zest for life and heightened my appreciation for simple things. To say my meal was delicious would be similar to describing a mountain as tall. 'Tall' would describe only one minor aspect of the mountain. It would not begin to describe or even hint at the majesty of a snow-capped mountain reaching up to the sky with a mist like cat's feet hovering silently at its base, iridescent sun sparkles glancing and sporting off the virgin snow at its summit.

When the meal was over, I lay down on the floor, which was both liquid and solid at the same time. It was a little like being massaged while taking a luxurious bubble bath in dim lights with soft music playing in the background. I slept like a newborn baby.

* * *

I awoke from that peaceful sleep with a momentary start. Radia was next to me, staring into my eyes. I greeted her with a laugh, realizing that this gentle soul had no knowledge of such things as privacy and all the other needs we humans have invented to maintain our separation from each other. I had no idea how long she had been there staring at me like that—hours, perhaps. It didn't matter. Patience was natural to her. She was so filled with the joy of being; there was nothing to wait for. She was always enough in herself.

Radia asked if I was refreshed. I told her I was and we went outside. To my surprise a score of people was waiting for us. They looked much the same as Radia but had slightly different features and shades of coloring. The men had soft features similar to the those of the women but there was nothing effeminate about them. The men were as pure in their masculinity as the women were in their femininity; yet each had balanced elements of the other. It was easier to discern the sex of each person by the quality and nature of the energy he or she radiated than by physical features. They also wore no clothes.

* * *

My time with Radia and her companions was a joyous and fruitful one. What I learned from them is beyond what can be put into words. Let it be enough to say that, though we are literally worlds apart, a part of me will always be with them, a part of them always with me.

Yes, I fell in love with Radia, but not in the way that's generally understood in this world. My experience had been that when two people 'fall in love,' they generally do so out of need or a perceived lack in themselves. Most individuals see in the other person a mirror reflecting their own beauty, beauty they are unable or unwilling to see in themselves. Because of the peacefulness and acceptance they feel around the other, they often grow fearful that if that person should leave or change or share him or herself with others, that that place of safety and peace will vanish. Such persons grow possessive, treating love as though it were something to be jealously guarded and defended, as though it were something in scarce supply, a commodity that must be doled out carefully, like water rationed to thirsty people in the desert or a treasure of great value only the valiant few ever find, and then only after great trials and tests of endurance to prove their worthiness. Fortunately, there are those who have overcome such a limited and sad view of relationships. I had often wished to become one of those few people who know that *true* love flows as freely as a river and is worth risking everything for. With Radia that wish was eventually granted.

Radia and her companions knew only the more mature view of love. They had no sense of lack or ownership among them. Each one clearly loved all the others and was in turn loved by the rest. There was no shame in nudity or in sexuality; these elements were as natural to them as breathing the sparkling shimmers of silver air. Love in all its forms was available to everyone, was shared freely by everyone.

At first I tried to see Radia as 'my' woman, but it was such an incomprehensible concept to her and the others that I soon let go of the idea. The thought was foolishness, really, a holdover from my earlier way of thinking. The people of her world often laughed at me when I introduced a concept from our world that made no sense to them. But they did so with love, not judgment.

Sex was entered into freely by all, but again, not in the way most see such acts in our world. There was no such thing as promiscuity or perversion. These are concepts that apply only to our world. When two lovers joined on this tiny world, it truly was making love. At the first sight of this, though, I was embarrassed and tried to hide my face. Radia smiled at me with that loving, all-accepting look in her eyes, eyes that knew the shame I felt, and beckoned me to watch. She spoke to me with a voice that was even softer and gentler than before and had the quality of wind through pine trees in it. She told me there was nothing even remotely corresponding to shame on her world, for how could anything as beautiful as making love be the cause of unease?

I tried to explain how things were in our world, how the physical act could not always be called making love; but she clearly found the ideas puzzling and strangely amusing. Yet she also saw in my mind that what often passes for making love is really men having sex from anger, women having sex from guilt. In answer to my apprehensions and embarrassment, she explained, with a tone of absolute joyousness and understanding, that the people we watched were sharing their love with each other in the deepest way the Creator had provided. Those who watched got to feel the couple's love, and to offer theirs as well. And she said that of all the things I told her of my world, the idea of shame regarding the lovemaking act was the strangest and that if everyone on my world felt as I did, it must indeed be an unhappy place. I told her my world *was* an unhappy place, not at all like hers.

Radia's world didn't even have a name until I came to it. When I asked her its name, she looked puzzled. She gazed at me with those magnificent silver eyes of hers and said there was no need for names of such things but that I could call the world 'Shanti' if I wished. She had learned from my mind that the word means peace. I could think of no more appropriate name for her world. Peace pervaded that tiny world, peace from which joy and love proceeded.

When I think of the embarrassment I felt at seeing those angelic beings make love I am ashamed, ashamed of myself for such thoughts, ashamed of my world and its beliefs. Never have the words 'making love' ever meant anything more to me than 'having sex,' which in turn usually meant something unclean or forbidden or hurtful. But seeing these loving souls love playfully with the innocence of young children changed my mind at once and forever. They *showed* me what love is. I saw that not only were these gentle folk joining with each other in such a loving way that love flowed through them, they were actually *generating* love! They were literally *making* it, in the same way that bees make honey. It was the essence of their nature to begin with; yet their joining was an act of pure creation, a pure extension of that joy and love. They actually produced more love, love that would never be lost.

* * *

After what I imagine was about three weeks, I ceased eating, drinking, and sleeping. Just like that. Like one who awakens from a dream, one day I simply realized I no longer needed such things though they're considered necessities on our world.

As I said before, that which passed for air on Shanti had a living, vital quality about it that's hard to describe well. It was as though it were a living membrane, not existing outside of things but interpenetrating them. Rather than breathing the 'air' and feeling nourished by it, it was more that it was *breathing me*, supplying all my needs. When I surrendered to it I experienced great joy. No longer did I see myself as separate from my environment but as a part of it. I was still myself but was joined in a much deeper, much greater way to everything around me.

It's difficult to describe exactly how I felt. For the first time in my life, I did not feel alone or lonely. I felt at peace, and I did not care if I never saw my home world again. Earth was becoming a blur in my mind anyway. All that had happened before coming to Shanti seemed but a dream, an illusion, real only while I was in the midst of it, believing it to be true. Now I felt like a child just wakened from a bad dream, saved from the illusion of fear and loneliness and sorrow.

When I first met Radia, she had said my coming had been foretold for many thousands of years. This puzzled me, and I asked her one day to tell me more about that. I learned that prophecy for her people was not quite the same as for ours. They did not rely on words in dusty books written by ancient prophets for their knowledge. Prophecy for them was simply an inner knowing that all shared. To say such knowings were carried on the wind would not be inaccurate. In addition to giving them life and nourishment, the shimmering, silver air they breathed gave them direct knowledge of all things in their world. To say it was their god is not correct, though. It was but the messenger, the carrier wave for that presence, the intercessor between knowing and being.

There was no religion on Shanti. How could there be? Each person had a direct experience of the presence that was their god. It had always been so. Similarly, there was no need for politics or science or philosophy. No books were written; no 'work' done. There was simply *being*. The only art created was done with no other material than thought and was considered primarily an amusement, a relaxation. Though the art I beheld in some of the dwelling places was far more magnificent and alive, far more capable of evoking *awe* and wonderment in the observer than the greatest works of the masters on Earth, on Shanti it was considered only a decoration, a diversion.

But there *was* music. It seemed to come from everywhere and nowhere. In trembling strains it washed over me, lifted me to heights of intense spiritual passion. It was always in the background of my consciousness yet could be brought to full awareness with but the simple focus of intent. I first noticed it after what I guess was two months after my arrival. I asked Radia about it, and at first she didn't seem to understand what I meant. It wasn't that she didn't hear the music. It was that it was so much a part of her that she had difficulty conceiving it as something outside herself that could be discussed. It was like asking a fish about water. She 'swam' in that ocean, reveled in those crashing waves of beauty upon beauty. She and her people had never known otherwise.

The music of Radia's world came from no musician. It was an aspect of existence, of the presence. She had difficulty understanding me when I told her of my world's music, of its different types and moods. She looked into my mind and heard the music I knew, experienced it as if it were being played before her in all its passion and confusion and sorrow and grandeur. She said she saw the pain of my world in its music and that most of that music was diluted by fear and craving and broken dreams, that there were moments of beauty within it but they were not enough. She told me the music of my world was *tragic*. I had never thought of it that way, but I think she was right. She did say, though, that there were glimmers of grandeur in parts of it, that she saw moments when grand souls, raising themselves above the pettiness and separateness that characterized the lives of so many people, brought the gifts of beauty and love to my world through music. Radia spoke in a voice that did not judge or seek to persuade. Words bubbled forth from her consciousness like clear, cool water from a fountain.

* * *

One day as I was in the midst of a conversation with Radia, something like a frown crossed her face. For a moment I felt I had offended her in some way, but I knew that such a notion was alien to this tiny world. I asked her what was wrong; and she said she had seen a place in my mind where she could not go, a place all dark and hidden. She was confused that I would try to hide something from her.

I was taken aback by her words. I didn't know what to say to this lovely, pure woman. I was unaware of any part of myself I wished to hide from her, that I *could* hide from her. But when I looked inside myself, really looked, I found the answer. It had been there all the time. It was my *life* I wished to block from her thoughts. All the fears, the loneliness, the petty grievances I had developed in my thirty two years—my weaknesses, my lusts, my secret desires—all those parts of myself that I was ashamed of, all those parts I had hidden even from myself with endless distractions and outward searching I wished to hide. I had unconsciously blocked these from her mind's gentle probing. But in blocking the private world I both hated and secretly cherished I had blocked also the beauties I had experienced with the coming of the sound on that quiet evening, those thunderous inner explosions of the sublime that had been the harbinger and perhaps the giver of a greater life. These beauties I had also blocked from her, and from myself as well, so that they had become almost a dream. With the joy and peace I found with Radia and her people had come a desire to forget all I had known before, all I had been. Soon I spoke to her of my world only as a tourist who has been to a strange country and observed its ways. I could not bring myself to speak of it as my home. My shame was too great; my fear that I would have to go back was too great. I didn't want to leave this paradise. I didn't want to leave Radia. I had blocked my knowledge of the fantastic gulf between my world and hers, had let her believe my world was but a pinpoint of light in her sky and not the unfathomably large world it was compared to hers.

Now I could hide my thoughts no longer. As she held me close to her, I shared with her all that was in my heart, all the pain and fear, the thirst for love and pleasure, the feelings of abandonment and confusion I had lived with most of my life. Tears rolled down my cheeks in big droplets that splattered off her golden skin. She washed my tears of sadness and shame with the delicate fibers of her silver hair as I told her also of the joy and knowing that had come in the last two years, of the experiences and new insights that had come as a result of my metamorphosis, the shift in perception and consciousness and being that I knew was not yet complete. I grew more peaceful as I shared my past with Radia. I saw that she loved me in the midst of all my darkness, that nothing I said or did could ever remove me from the warm hold of her boundless love. I shared with her the immense journey I had undertaken to be in her world, the incalculable gulf I had crossed, the unimaginable distance and the magnitude of size that separated our worlds. I cried and cried. I knew most of what I said was strange to her and her people, unthinkable really. But it didn't matter. What her mind did not understand her *heart* did. My love for her grew so immensely grand in those last moments that I had a burning desire to give of myself to her, to share myself with her, my joy and my sorrow and my life. Nothing was more blessed for me in that moment than to *give*, not from need or emptiness, but from joy and fullness.

Her eyes shone like twin silver moons lit with radiance from an unseen sun. She took my hand and led me a to a place where a large patch of spongy vegetation grew. It had the look of thousands of tiny silver crystals and shimmered like the stars. But it was as soft to the touch as velvet.

The stars, those tiny worlds that were but infinitely small atomic particles in my world, shone through the silvery, phosphorescent airlike essence like bits of golden fairy dust. They gleamed and sparkled off Radia's fine golden skin, danced in her silver eyes. We lay down together and touched for what seemed a long time. I felt like a child, filled with innocence and wonder and the joy of discovery. I had been with many women in my world but had never viewed one the way I did this lovely woman. Every strand of her hair fascinated me, every flash of her eyes. Every movement of her body was natural and beautiful and filled with grace. I was in awe and sheer delight as we gently made love under the light of those stars. It was so completely right, so completely pure, that I was full of rapture. Never had I felt so unobstructed before. Never had I felt so filled with joy. And at the height of my ecstasy I understood that it was in this complete, unobstructed harmony in body and mind that the secret of ascension laid.

After several minutes of lovemaking I felt an immense trembling pressure building up that promised to be the greatest orgasm I had ever known. I moved toward it with joy and determination, like a man in a canoe reveling in white-water rapids charging headlong toward the waterfall just ahead. But before I took that ecstatic plunge, Radia tensed her body, stopped her flowing, rhythmical movements—so harmonious and synchronous with my own—and held me firmly next to her. There was no motion. Everything seemed to have come to an abrupt halt. The river had stopped, frozen in the space of a moment. I tried to move, but she held me still in a surprisingly strong grip. I ceased struggling but was confused. I had been experiencing great joy with her; yet it seemed I was being denied the greatest pleasure, the greatest release of all.

As we lay together for what must have been only a few moments, I became aware of an energy within myself that was swirling around, dancing within me. My body began to tingle all over. Every cell seemed alive in a refreshingly new way. Still I was confused and could not rid myself of the thought that I had somehow been denied the fruition of our lovemaking. Then we began making love again. This time it was even more natural than before; and as I approached the 'waterfall' once again, I felt her body slowing next to mine, then halting as it had done before. This time I did not fight her actions or wonder about them. This time I simply followed her lead and did as she did, for she had never done other than love me. After another interval of a few moments, we began again.

This process of making love to near orgasm, then backing away, resting in silence and stillness for a few moments, then starting again, went on for what must have been several hours. With each cycle I began to feel less pressure to complete the sexual act in the only way I had ever done in my world. Here there was no pressure, no need to 'finish' anything. In my world, if lovemaking didn't end in orgasmic release, it was usually not considered a full session; something was missing. There was a sense of incompleteness about it and of unreleased tension. In short, the whole purpose of sexual union seemed unmet. But with Radia this was not the case—not at all.

The lovemaking I had known before had never been satisfying, really. There had been a release of tension, a huge stroke of ego gratification, yes. But those sessions had lasted only a few minutes and had been overshadowed by pressure to perform in a certain way and with a certain level of expertise and prowess. After the blessed, often hard-fought struggle to find release had been won, exhaustion but not joy followed. It was more like the feeling an alcoholic has after taking a drink following a period of abstinence. Orgasm was not joy; it was relief, a relief that would not last, was not truly satisfying, and had little or nothing of love or self-respect in it. Often after lovemaking (using that word now seems almost blasphemous), I lay next to the woman like a spent flare, wondering who this person beside me was. Afterwards I felt, as I lay beside her sleeping body—a body that had been so delightfully exciting and animated and sensual only minutes earlier—that I was next to a corpse. For her body would seem like a dead, lifeless thing, an object I did not love and that I had only used for my own purposes, as *my* body had been used. All I would see before me in bed was a body that would age and die— jeering with haughty laughter at a god whose creations were imperfect and perishable—thus bearing testament to, and glaring as a living symbol of, the Creator's own imperfection. I would fall asleep confused, depressed, and often deeply ashamed—ashamed of my humanness, ashamed of *her* humanness, ashamed of being part of a world of death and decay and age, a world I could not get out of alive. But by the next morning all would be forgotten, for I would be rested once more, sexually excited once more, ready to try once more to satisfy my unquenchable thirst.

* * *

My lovemaking with Radia continued for what seemed like a long time. Having ceased to feel the pressure for orgasmic release, I began instead to pay attention to the new sensations bursting within me. One of those sensations was an overwhelming, thrilling love for this gentle woman who so freely and completely gave herself to me. So wholly feminine was she that all the women I had known before her seemed as flat and insubstantial as shadows compared to a solid, well-defined object. Radia played no games of manipulation and did not feign weakness. She was completely natural and beautiful. She had the best qualities of both sexes, yet the fathomless gentleness and compassion that clearly marked her nature as feminine.

Her eyes were two drops of quicksilver. Her gold-tinged face and skin shone like the sun. Her sensuous lips were as fresh and inviting as rose petals after a spring rain. The definition between our two bodies disappeared, dissolved, as I felt myself merging with her. No longer was there any goal. It no longer mattered if I lived or died. During those moments of ecstatic union with Radia I was complete. I was in a state of pure joy, pure being. I no longer breathed; my breath 'breathed' me. I no longer moved; the energies within me had taken over all my body's motions. Energy swirled within me in golden flashes, first in the region of my sexual organs; then it traced a circuit that rose to the top of my head and back down again. At first I was only dimly aware of this circuit but its definition increased as the speed at which the circuit was completed each time increased. I was aware of the energy racing up and down, faster and faster, until the motion grew so fast that at any given moment, the energy seemed to be in all points along the circuit simultaneously. A steadily increasing hum or vibration then began, and I felt an intensity of energy and emotion building up such as I had never known, so great in fact that I did not know if I could contain it.

As the energy continued to rise within me, I became aware of another pulsation that was going on between us. An energy seemed to be leaping from my body to hers like a spark of flame leaping the gap in a spark plug, then returning—each time with even greater energy—so that a cycle was built up between us that grew in both speed and intensity until it matched the energy and vibratory level within my own body.

In that lightning moment following the matching of those tremendous, ecstatic energies, our bodies melted in a flash of brilliant light and I heard a music such as I have never heard or imagined before. It was a music that was greater than joy, greater than love, greater even than all the worlds that hurtle through space. It was a music so grand and sublime it made the greatest music of Beethoven, Bach, Mozart, and Pachelbel seem like noisy scratchings and bangings done with nail on metal. The music I heard was loftier than a dozen angelic choirs singing praise to God. It was a music older than time, deeper than life. It *was* life—the true life, of which all else was but a dream, a symbol, a shadow. And what the sound that had heralded my transformative experiences—so long ago—was to power, this music was to beauty.

Radia and I merged with that transcendent music for what seemed an eternity. We whirled in its mystical currents through ages and distances without end. At one point I thought I was back on Earth, back in the place and time and body I had known all my life. Then the scene changed and I was on a world entirely shrouded in a light green mist. Particles of silver phosphorescence flashed continuously across the lonely, barren, mountainous landscape. Finally I saw a sky filled with golden points of light and knew I was back on Radia's world, Radia's tiny, beautiful world.

We woke in each other's arms as if from a dream. I felt no sense of discomfort or tiredness, just a residual throbbing and vibrating within my body, like the winding down of some enormous engine. The sensation was an incredibly pleasant and luxurious, like the thorough massaging of every bodily part. I *realized* then that sex had never been intended to be localized only in the generative organs, orgasm restricted to only one small, dissociated area of the body. Sex and orgasm were intended instead to be experienced throughout the body, through every fiber of one's self; the physical body was just the vehicle of expression. Oh, no! Sex was for the totality of one's being.

I realized that orgasm in our world is sometimes a mixture of pleasure and pain because it is often forced and restricted to the genital area only. Sexual energy often becomes bottled up, confined; and people become as claustrophobic as a person wedged in an uncomfortable position in the inner recesses of a cave. There's no one to call to for help, no flashlight to give a better view of the plight— just a feeling of helplessness, despair, and panic, then a bruised, forced exit from the confined space followed by exhaustion, achiness, and trembling relief. This, I realized, is what men and women often call 'good sex' in our world.

Condescension and cynicism are not my goal with these remarks. I write from what I realize are somewhat limited comments based on my own experience and observation. These views are ones I've considered true all my life—until coming to Radia's world. For the experience I had with her completely changed my life and my attitudes about sex and love and beauty at once and for all time and as irrevocably as the shifting of plates within the earth during an earthquake. I was blind. Now I see.

* * *

The love of a woman living on a golden world a billion billion times smaller than a mote of dust had placed the secret of ascension at my feet. During our lovemaking my body had become an unobstructed conduit for fantastic energies. That rapturous joining had allowed incredible energies to build up and bounce back and forth between us to the point where each cell of my body became so charged, so raised in vibratory frequency, that the light between the cells, the light which in reality my cells were, was unleashed, freed.

My body became an engine with all pistons firing properly as the circuit of energies spread from my sexual organs to my brain and back again. Over and over, faster and faster, the cycling energies had raced until my body became a perfect tuning fork, vibrating at a frequency rapid beyond description. Fueled by the dynamo formed by the arcing of energies between the polarities of male and female, that body then became light. A rare alchemy had been preformed. As a result, I experienced beauty and music and wonder without end. I was God's child in certainty and knowledge and awareness. I had crossed the edge of wonder, outstripped the margin of beauty at last. But achieving these goals no longer mattered. No unanswered questions remained for me. In that moment all questions had dissolved into knowingness in the face of pure being. In those final moments I had no body. It had been raised from the sluggishness of matter to the incredibly rapid vibratory frequency of light, and I had rested in the bosom of God.

* * *

Days passed, and I lived a peaceful, harmonious life with Radia and her companions. I would have stayed with her forever. The joy and love I knew with her was so great I would have given up my other life completely. I no longer cared about the mysterious shadow woman, no longer cared about ascension and my transformation, no longer cared about adventure. I was content just being with this lovely woman in this tiny, idyllic world. But I could not stay. The presence within me would not let me. In warm and gentle whispers it spoke to me, told me that what I had seen and felt and understood was not all there was to God, or to ascension, or to life—not all by far. To me, however, it didn't matter, for surely what I now knew was enough to satisfy the hunger in a dozen living souls. But an impression formed within my mind that there was more than my satisfaction or joy involved. The choice was not really mine to make. I did not have the luxury of deciding what my life would be any more. The presence would not let me live for my own joy alone.

I knew from these internal messages that there was even more to life than what I had encountered—something so grand and sublime that by comparison all my beauties were but dim shadows veiling a far greater sunrise. I knew that what I had seen, grand though it had been, was but a brief glimpse of the outer edge of wonder.

* * *

The greatest monuments of mankind reach toward the sky. Tall spires on countless churches point in vain toward the unfathomable sky they can never reach. The greatness of humanity is at best but a finger pointing toward the greater light of God, a light I had seen somewhat. Now I knew that just as the stars and sky are beacons drawing attention to the deeper, more radiant light of God, so light itself is but the symbol of, or a pointer toward, something still more magnificent and holy. My mind whirled with the thought; yet I knew it must be so.

The communications from that inner presence were too strong and pure to be untrue. They resonated with the strings of my heart and produced a sweet music of truth I could not deny. The voice spoke living truth. It always had, though often I had chosen not to hear it or had not heeded its message or had superimposed my own interpretation of its meaning.

I still did not know why I must pursue that endless margin of sublimity even farther. I was content to be with Radia forever on her minuscule world. I could not conceive of a greater joy and ecstasy than what I had just experienced; I was not even sure I could *survive* more.

But the promptings of that presence could not be ignored or silenced, though for a time I tried to dismiss them. I learned that with my awakening into a greater, higher life, I had also awakened to a greater responsibility, one I could not turn away from. I had *seen* and *felt* and *understood*; with these brushes with the sublime had come a responsibility to *do*. With what I now knew I could not turn my back on a humanity I knew was starving for the true bread of life.

I felt no messianic calling, no sense that I was greater than others. Oh, no. It was simply the awareness that I could no longer see myself as a separate being living a separate life, that I could no longer choose what course my life took, no matter how appealing that course appeared.

The transformative process that had begun many months earlier had been a call to awaken. Now I was feeling drawn to answer the call to serve. Welling up within my soul was a torturous desire to serve, to extend the love that filled my spirit to overflowing. It was a desire to help others know what I knew, to do what I could to heal the pain and fear and misguided thoughts in my world, to *bless*...as I had been blessed, to aid in some way the ending of the separateness and loneliness that others knew in the deepest part of themselves and that I too had felt. I wanted to somehow lessen the ache that would not go away, though it was covered over in a thousand million different ways, until we each became the child of God.

There was something more, too. It came only as a shadow of an impression, a dim foreboding, a darkness, a bleakness threatening to swallow up all the color in my life. Without understanding the blurred and disturbing image that came to me, I had a strong sense of urgency. Something was going to happen soon, and I must be ready for it. Perhaps no one else *could* be. What this something was I had not the faintest clue. But as time went on it was clear I could no longer stay with the only woman I had ever loved and the only people I had ever felt a true sense of kinship with. The thought of going back to my world was not a pleasant one.

I shared what was in my heart with Radia and her people. I told them of my need to leave, to go back to my world, to serve. I told them of the inner promptings that were drawing me toward still more adventures, more beauties. None of them, including Radia, seemed surprised or disappointed; and I was puzzled by this. I had thought that *she* at least would regret my leaving. But that was just part of my world's conditioning—the belief that distance can separate people who feel joined by love.

It was as though the people of Shanti *expected* me to leave, as though they had been patiently waiting for my announcement. Later, when I was alone with Radia, I asked her about this suspicion. She took my hand and gazed at me from the depths of her silver eyes. With a look on her face that had nothing of sorrow or loss on it she said she was grateful to the presence for the love I had made and shared with her. She told me she knew as all of her people knew, that my time with them would be what my mind called 'short;' but that for them, everything was 'forever.' I knew, however, that there was no 'short' or 'long' for them—each moment was enough in itself.

Radia reminded me that, though she had once spoken to me of an ancient prophecy that had foretold my coming, she had never fully explained what the prophecy said. I listened to the love of my heart speak, but my thoughts drifted back to those early days when I had first come to her world. It was so strange and new, so filled with wonder and strange beauty, so different from the world I had come from. Now my world seemed the alien one. I couldn't imagine leaving Shanti, leaving Radia; and yet I knew I must, in the same way a child knows it must one day leave its mother and father. As if in answer to the reluctance in my thoughts, Radia's 'voice' shifted to that gentle tone I had 'heard' before. Like wind through pine trees at evening and the sighing of leaves at dawn, she implored me to take her world—all I had known, all I had felt—back with me to my world, to the place I felt compelled to return to. She said it was right for me to go now. The presence had need of me, and all must heed its call. And she asked me to hold her and her people in my heart, to hold her *world* in my thoughts. I smiled at her. How could I *not?*

It was all so simple for her. I knew that all complexity came from my mind or, more accurately, from that part of my mind that believed in lack and limitation, from that part which resisted the guidance of the gentle presence within me. In those beautiful moments when I had experienced myself as pure love, pure joy, pure being, that negative part of my mind had not been present. It had dissolved away without a struggle, in the way that a lit candle brought into a closed room late at night dispels darkness. Where does the darkness go? The answer is simple—nowhere. There is no struggle because the darkness was never real; the darkness went nowhere because it was an illusion, real only to the mind that believed in it.

The same is true of the ego-mind. During those transcendent experiences with light, the ego-mind dissolved into the nothingness that it was; but upon return to my 'normal' state of mind, I had gathered it back around me like a familiar garment, a 'security blanket' I could not yet let go of because I thought it could still offer me something. This reluctance was because I was *afraid*, afraid to release myself completely and for all time into the boundless love of God. Like those Israelites of old who had seen great miracles but continued to fall into old, destructive ways once the miracle ended, I was too stubborn, too afraid, to completely let go and plunge headlong into God.

But I had to try. I had to offer my willingness, in spite of fear, to the presence within me. I had to release my resistances, had to recognize that the burning need to serve that had begun to course through my veins was a call I must answer. I could find no peace, even with those I loved most, until I set my feet upon the path that I knew I must follow.

Radia, like a mountain with a cloud nestled at its peak, was patient with me as I rested in silence with my thoughts, lost in reverie. She had such calmness about her, such tranquility. I took a deep breath and fully breathed in the silver-flecked 'air.' I knew I must leave, but I would truly miss this world.

When I had come fully to myself, Radia continued sending her thoughts to me. She said that the ancient prophecy foretold that someone from a world beyond all the worlds would one day come to ennoble the inhabitants of her world with light. She and her companions had never understood the saying but had trusted the gentle presence each person felt in his heart to teach them what they must know, and at the proper time. The presence now told them that *I* was that person, but it did not clarify the part about ennobling the people of her world with light.

At her words, which sounded like iron beating on my soul my mind grew giddy and spun. I wondered if I could truly be the one the prophecy spoke of. And if I were...if I *were*...what could I possibly give these pure people? What could I, with all my fears and littleness, bring to their world? How could I 'ennoble' *anyone*, much less *them?*

Questions, questions...so many unanswered questions. I knew that unless the questions were given over to the presence within, they could not be resolved. They were like vultures pecking at the naked breast of a person tied to a rock—a continual, painful distraction that took the focus of attention away from the true answer, the only answer, and led one down paths of depression and guilt and fear. I remembered how during times of stillness and peace my questions had simply dissolved into silence. It was my ego-self that demanded answers, not my true self.

I smiled a little as I realized how quickly I had forgotten the teachings each of my beauties had presented. I had been shown so much, been taught so much; yet how quickly I tossed those gems of understanding and wonder into a dusty drawer at the first sign of confusion or fear. Even with all my imagined failings, the presence within me still loved me, blessed me, taught me. All it asked was my willingness, in spite of my fear, in spite of all my confusion and doubt and gnawing, unanswered questions, simply to *listen*, to pay attention to its gentle voice.

I held Radia's hand and asked that presence to grow large within my heart. I wished to follow that internal voice and no other from that moment on. As though it were a castoff lover whose worth I now saw, I called the presence back to me. I asked its forgiveness for looking to outward things for what I could only find within my own heart and soul and felt something like a warm fluid, thick as syrup yet as light as air, rising within me. And I heard music again—sweet angel songs that seemed to rise to a high pitch, then fall in a hush. Then came a sound so mighty, yet so loving, that it could hurl entire *worlds* into existence and keep them in orbit without altering the flight of a single flake of snow. I felt myself rising, expanding. The world started to become a blur of golden light; but before it faded away, I saw Radia's face. I thought I saw a tear in her eye, but I probably just imagined it.

* * *

Shanti was a large ball of luminous, rapidly shrinking light. Then it was but a speck of golden dust, no different from all the myriad other specks that leaped into my vision—no different except that I had called it home for several months, no different except that on it lived a woman with whom I had found more love and gentle understanding than ever before in my life. But I would remember. I would remember her. The memory of Radia would not fade from my heart, would not wither with time like the petals of a rose. I would take her with me, her and all her people, all her love, all her ways. Always.

A golden mesh of brilliance leapt across the dark gap between the worlds, then engulfed them so that I once again swam in a pulsating sea of radiant light. Amid that vibrating sea of living light, I was filled once more with a sense of awe and wonder and joy. I willed that my flight through the worlds continue; and I watched as, out of that primordial golden soup, the double helix of the DNA structure began to form. Watching the structures making up life form before my eyes was glorious. I watched genes leap together to form chromosomes, and chromosomes rush in a flurry of blurred motion to become individual cells. And all the while, the music played.

A coruscating spark of golden light shocked my vision, and I knew I was witnessing the firing of information from one nerve bundle to another along the neuronal pathways. I was in my brain once more, but this time something was different. The silver radiance I had seen while going down to the atomic level had changed into a thin beam of light shining like a searchbeam into the night. Then it became a deeper, fuller ring of light that extended down into my body. I followed it down all the way to the base of my spine and saw it connect with a structure that looked like a nuclear reactor. Three circles of rapidly spinning blue light surrounded the structure, then raced back up to its point of origin. From the books I had read, I knew this to be the kundalini area—the serpent-fire, the raw, generative force that was said to rest like a sleeping dragon until its great power was unleashed.

It was clear to me that what I was witnessing was the circuit of energy that had formed when I made love to Radia. This was the unobstructed current that had unleashed the dynamo of energy stored at the base of the spine. It was also evident that this circuit of energy was part of the blueprint, part of the evolution of every human being, part of each person's divine birthright. But something had gone wrong, terribly wrong, in the evolution of mankind, and few had ever known of this energy structure. Like a spark quickly snuffed out and left smoldering, this dynamic structure connecting the subtle energies of the brain with the powerful, primeval energies housed at the base of the spine, had disappeared somewhere in the lost pages of antiquity almost the moment it came into existence and had become so rare it hadn't been missed. But the seed for its development had remained latent in all human beings, waiting only for the right combination of love, will, and surrender to spring to life. My lovemaking with Radia had kindled that latent structure into full existence. How what had happened to me on that tiny world had translated itself into the very structures of my earthly body was a mystery to me; but my life had long since given way to a mode of being in which the enigmatic was the commonplace. The exploration of this new and exciting structure promised to be a phenomenal adventure.

I allowed the final processes of becoming William Sherrill to complete themselves. I felt myself falling, grew dizzy for a moment, then was shocked to full awareness by what felt like a stab of lightning. I bolted to a sitting position, then slowly eased myself back down. I stared at the ceiling for a long time. I was back.

January 13

I've spent the last few days resting and reflecting on the great adventure that began with a journey into my body and continued on that infinitesimally small world where I met Radia, sweet Radia. I wrote the preceding account of that adventure during the two days following my return on Christmas day. I've spent the remaining time in reflection and quiet contemplation. It's strange that I could experience months of living with Radia and her people and return to find that my earthly body aged only a couple of days.

Other than needing food and water and having a little stiffness in my body, I didn't notice anything different about myself after my return—not at first, at least. But something *had* happened—I've already mentioned the curious stream of energy connecting my brain with the dynamo at the base of my spine, but there were other changes also. One change was that I started drinking enormous quantities of water, and not just water, but pure spring water. I revolted at the thought of any other beverage. I also found myself wanting to fast. My body seemed to feel heavy, whereas before it felt fine. I began to eat nothing but a few grapes and drank nothing but spring water.

The first effect of this radical change in my diet was an enormous burst of energy. I climbed hills and raced along the beach or through the brush for hours at a time. Like a well-conditioned athlete who gets his second wind, I seemed to grow stronger rather than tire the more I exerted myself. I was exhilarated. I slept little. Then for a couple of days I felt nauseated and went through a long spell of fever and chills. Never had I felt so ill in my life. My head was on fire; my body refused to respond to my commands; my eyes were filled with phantasms of color and blurred, insubstantial shapes; my mind glowed with a dim, eerie radiance. At one point I felt so weak and so ill I almost called for medical assistance, but just when I thought the call would be necessary the fever broke.

Over the next few hours the fever and blurred images faded and my strength returned. While seated outside I drank a large glass of tomato juice mixed with an equal amount of spring water. I slowly sipped it like a fine wine. The sunset was a riot of colors, each bidding for prominence. When the meal was ended, I lay down to a long sleep.

The next morning I was awakened by a gentle, whispering call. I could hardly believe my senses when I realized that I had been wakened by the *flowers* in my little garden, next to the cottage. I had not watered them for a few days. Now I heard them *call* to me!

I rose to my feet and noticed a light springiness to my actions. More noticeable was the incredible ease with which I breathed. It was as if a passageway that had been blocked all my life had suddenly come unstuck, allowing a full breath. Only on rare occasions had I felt the breath come so easily, fully, and deliciously. It was hard to imagine that I had ever been able to function with what now appeared by contrast to be a congested, cramped, confined breathing. This fuller breath seemed to be replacing the shallower one as my natural state. There was a taste to it, a sweetness; and for the first time in my life air tasted like a nourishing beverage.

I went outside and watered the flowers, those sweet, gentle beings I had heard calling to me by some unknown mode of communication. I sensed their relief and joy at being nourished and wondered at this new faculty that had developed so soon after my return from Radia's world. I did not know if it was a result of the changes I had gone through there or if it was just part of the continuing process of transformation that had given me my first beauties. Which it was didn't really matter. I was content to flow with these new experiences as they came, trusting that gentle presence within me to guide me and teach me.

* * *

A couple of days ago I began hearing sounds in my head. They were not the voices one associates with a person going through a psychotic episode. They were not even thought impressions. They were real, however; and they grew stronger the more I listened to them. The nearest thing I can relate them to is the thunderous sounds I heard at the start of my transformative episodes. But these sounds were gentle and soft, and I listened to them without the fear and panic those earlier, cataclysmic sounds had engendered.

These new sounds came as though they were surfers riding a huge wave, a new wave that had never reached the shores of my consciousness before. It was an interesting experience. The sounds varied in pitch, intensity, and clarity and generally appeared to be very distant. One of them was like the rustling of leaves by a mischievous wind on an autumn afternoon. Another reminded me of the sounds of the ocean heard through a conch shell. Still another was like the sound of crickets chirping at night in the country. The sounds were pleasant and nonintrusive. When I focused on them, they gained in clarity and volume; when I did not, they faded back into the background of my mind. But they were always there, and I wondered if they were in any way similar to the sounds I had started hearing on Radia's world. These sounds did not have the power or beauty or sublimity about them that those lovely, haunting strains had in her world; but there was something about them that was more than just pleasant and soothing. They represented a *hint*, a prelude to something more—much, much more. There was a *meaning* just beyond them. They were an echo of something in the distance; and along with that sense of unrevealed meaning came a feeling of uneasiness, a foreboding—like distant drum beats tapping out a constant rhythm in 3-4 time. This distant pounding seemed to herald some eminent danger, some mystery shrouded in a dark haze, some dark wave sweeping across the ocean soon to threaten the land.

January 20

I have experimented this past week with listening to the inner sounds that have been coming to me more and more frequently since my return from Shanti. I find that I can now pick out more tones and variations than at first. Now if I focus my attention properly, I can hear the sound of roaring waves or a tea kettle at full boil or bagpipes or flutes. Sometimes I catch the faintest echo of a sound so powerful it could rend a mountainside asunder with the sheer intensity of its glory. The sounds are beginning to resemble the haunting and beautiful tones I heard on Shanti. It is becoming apparent that what I'm experiencing is not unique to me. As I listen to these supernatural strains of music—those bits of flute and bagpipe and drum, I realize they were in existence long before such instruments were created. Somewhere in the past, certain people heard this heavenly music and sought to capture its essence with wood and string and reed. The sounds made by musical instruments on Earth are coarse and heavy compared to the hauntingly sublime tones I sometimes hear proceeding from what appears to be an interior world, a vast, strange region hidden deeply within each of us; yet sometimes those musical instruments are able to evoke remembrances and dim glimpses of that interior realm. We ordinarily screen out such remembrances and glimpses; usually we are blind to such pointers, such signals. These elements do not serve the purposes of the world of everyday life. The brain therefore screens them out in part or in whole to preserve our beliefs about the world. This screening is also done to keep us from being overwhelmed by all the impressions constantly bombarding our consciousness. But how costly! Along with impressions and sensory input not needed for the functioning of our conscious awareness, such as a host of voices in the background when a mother needs only to hear the sounds of her child in the next room, we have repressed the sights and sounds and *feelings* of that supernatural world, that world beyond our five senses. In so doing we have become prisoners in a dark, narrow cell. Humans were placed in that cell in dim antiquity by their minds' survival mechanisms to protect them from some imagined threat to their existence; but like people living for years in a bomb shelter, huddled in fear against a danger that might never come, *we* have failed to realize that it is now possible to emerge from the stuffy, limited cocoon created by our distant ancestors.

I had never thought much about this interior region my heightened awareness has begun to show me. It was a subject I thought only of concern to artists and poets, geniuses and holy men, but not to me. Now I realize it is a matter of *vital* concern for *everyone*. I now know that something is coming toward humanity, toward the entire world, that will alter life as we know it forever. I do not know *what* is coming or what shape it will take; but it *is* coming, and soon. We have little time left for the luxury of ignorance.

February 2
It's Groundhog Day. We are a lot like groundhogs, I think—living in a dark hole, only rarely poking our heads out to see if we will be greeted by light or shadow. In general, we're too easily frightened by our own shadow. We see it and usually scurry back to the comfort of the only world we've ever known—a world of fear and guilt and unmet dreams, but a comfortable one nonetheless, comfortable because of its familiarity. This has certainly been true for *me* most of my life. What I now see is that for too long people have been living in fear. They pray for miracles but would be terrified if they were to witness one, terrified because it would be obvious that there really *is* a world other than the tame, subdued world of everyday living. Most people would be terrified or would simply block the experience out, as they have blocked out the awareness of the gentle presence living

in the heart of each of us. The keys to heaven are within our grasp; but it requires courage and passion and gentleness of nature to use them.

* * *

February 3

I had dinner with Mindy last night. I hadn't seen her for several months. I knew she was worried about me, but I felt unable to call her before. So much was happening in my life. I knew she wouldn't understand. How could she? I didn't.

Before I called Mindy, a calmness had come over me, a genuine sense of peace. It was a feeling that things were right in my world, regardless of how unusual and wild they had been. Mindy and I went to a seafood place of her choice. She had Alaskan King Crab, her favorite. In the past, probably thinking my male ego needed to feel in charge of things, she would usually let me decide where to go. This time, however, I had had no preference. I have little interest in food these days anyway. She was amazed that I only had a small bowl of fruit and some spring water and asked if I was getting enough to eat. I told her I was fine, just not very hungry. That was mostly true. I *was* hungry, but it takes very little solid food these days to give me the energy I need for my body. I'm living mostly on pure water.

As the evening progressed, I noticed that though I was with Mindy, my dearest friend, I had little interest in the conversation. Too large a crack had opened up in my world in the past couple of years— a fissure that had caused a rift not only in my life and how I view the world but also in my relationships with people. I noticed, however, that even though I was bored by the content of the conversation, I was not bored by *her*. Along with the other changes in me had come a new compassion and patience for others. I knew that a vast gulf separated us because of my transformations, yet I also knew that we are all parts of the same thing. Thus, even if the content of the conversation were not of interest to me, her desire to communicate with me was. The form was unimportant; the essence and consciousness attempting to communicate was. It was evident that what had happened to me—was still happening to me—would eventually happen to all humanity.

Mindy was wonderful just being Mindy. I loved her for her sense of humor, for her kindness, and for the love she had always given me.

I yearned to speak with her about my new insights and experiences, but knew that she could not understand. I felt like a man born in a country of the blind suddenly gifted with sight. Not only did I but partially understand what had happened to me and what I was 'seeing,' but I also had no way of explaining my vision to others. I had no words to communicate what I now understood. But like the mystics and saints of old, I felt I had to try. As I spent time with Mindy, I realized that there *must* be a way to communicate experiences and changes such as I had undergone to others. There *must* be!

February 8

Last night I found myself gazing at the full moon. It has always been a favorite sight for me—so still and cold and lovely. There's a great beauty in the loneliness it evokes—not a loneliness based on need or lack or unmet wishes but an aloneness, a solitude very necessary to balance the times of being with crowds of people. As I stared at that pale, silvery orb I realized that perhaps the pendulum had swung too far to one side for me; perhaps during the past two years I had spent too much time alone. I knew that most of that solitude had been necessary because of the nature of my transformational experiences. Time was needed to allow the experiences to unfold and be properly integrated. But now the pendulum had begun to swing in the opposite direction, and a need was growing within me to reenter the world of people and in some way share what I had experienced, what I had learned.

I sensed that our lives are usually experienced as vessels holding only a drop or two of wonder and joy and love, so little of our divine heritage do we claim. Most of our time is spent trying to survive in what we often perceive as a hostile world that does not provide us with our needs and desires—a world in which we feel we must earn salvation through words or deeds. We see ourselves as prodigal children forced to live without shelter or love and to eat the scraps left by animals, all the time not seeing that we are divine children who can never be disinherited, regardless of how much we try to deny our birthright, regardless of how deserving we feel of destruction and damnation.

As I continued to stare at the moon, it was evident to me that we were never meant to spend our lives trying to 'earn' salvation. There was nothing to be 'saved' *from*! Moreover, we were not intended to give up our happiness and our joy to appease some wrathful God.

With my beauties had come the clear realization that there is a presence in the universe whose power and majesty is only matched by its love and gentleness, a presence that has no need for sacrifice or conversion. All fear, all judgment, all pain, all sorrow are the product of our own incorrect thinking. Lying latent within each of us is the power of God Himself. For we are His children, and all power and all creation is our inheritance. What a joyous thought! Because of our divine nature, our thoughts are so powerful that with our belief in them they become real for us, as real as if they were true. Yet because we have such great power and don't know it, we have turned the beauty and wonder of life into a hell of drudgery and sin. What wasted effort!

At first I thought my beauties were just unusual and sometimes wonderful experiences that had little to do with me, that I was only an observer who had for a time been privileged to lift the veil of the unknown and have visions of undreamed glory. Later it became clear that I was not separate from those experiences and their effects, that I was intimately intertwined with them, that they were a part of me. Just as the scientific community finally realized that it could not separate itself from its experiments, that the observer affected what was observed, so did I now know that my experiences were not separate events happening *to* me. They were a part of me. They had changed me. They had become me. I saw my cup overflowing with the glory of life, of God and felt a strong desire to share what I had learned and experienced. I didn't want to make the mistake of countless zealots and missionaries who sought to impose their beliefs on others. Oh, no. What I felt last night while watching the moon slowly trace an arc across the sky was not the desire for others to be like me. I felt no need for validation from the world. My experiences spoke for themselves. They were real. They needed no support from the masses to be valid. I desired to *share* with others the process that has been steadily transforming my life and the understanding that this process is destined to occur in all humanity at some time. Others, I knew, would have a different experience of transformation, but perhaps I could inspire someone to allow it to happen more quickly. Perhaps I could help someone avoid some of the pain and fear and confusion that struck me like a large hammer so many times. Perhaps I could let someone know they were not alone in what they were experiencing, that they were not going insane. I wish I had known someone like me two years ago when my transformation began.

* * *

I kept staring at the moon as the thoughts just described passed through my mind. I looked at the moon distractedly, like one looking at a hand placed six inches in front of his face but seeking to stare beyond it, for my thoughts were elsewhere. At one point I realized the moon was beginning to change. At first it seemed to lose the distinctness of its features. The dark areas began to merge with the bright ones and the disk of the moon became so undefined that what I saw was a blob of amorphous light. This fuzziness continued until it was but a smudge of yellowish white light the size of a basketball held at arms length.

I felt lost in a reverie as I allowed the strangeness that was engulfing me to continue. I felt giddy and a little nauseous for a moment, then felt something snap inside of me. In the next moment I was fully awake and alert but operating in that strange state of consciousness I had grown accustomed to over the past two years. It was not that I was less conscious than I am in 'normal' consciousness, nor was I in a dream state; but like a traveler in a new land with strange customs, things seemed very different. The differences were wonderful, though disorienting. It was as if I were operating in the normal world but with meaning and feelings magnified a thousand times. It was wonderful!

The mode of awareness that came over me last night is hard to describe because it is not a part of what can be called 'consensus reality.' The best analogy for it I can think of is that if what we call normal awareness is likened to first gear in an automobile, what I was experiencing was a shift to third or fourth gear. The car still moved down the road, the mechanism worked the same in both cases; but, oh what a difference! With the heightened speed, those petty concerns and problems and questions that were inherent in the much slower speed of first gear were left far behind and did not intrude.

Like a candle tossed into a hot flame, I felt my body melt into space. I seemed to have no substance but moved as though I were a point of light in a dazzling darkness. That part, at least, was like a dream. Then I came back to a more normal awareness of myself. Once again I had a body and no longer was just a point of awareness. I walked around and noticed a great lightness to my step. I felt good. There was an eerie radiance all around. Light and shadow played hide and seek as I looked toward the jagged mountain peaks in the distance. I felt disoriented but not uncomfortable. Then I looked up and was so startled by what I saw I almost fell to the ground. I should have known. It should have come as no surprise to me. The experiences of the past two years should have prepared me for what I saw, should have fortified my system against the shock of the unexpected. But they did not. What I saw hanging in the inky blackness above me was not the silvery-white ball of the moon but the earth with all its people. I was standing on the *moon!* I fell down and laughed and laughed. What joy I felt! I was in the midst of another beauty.

The stillness on the moon was so deep and vast I had nothing to compare it with except my experience with the meteorite. The silence was so peaceful and complete I felt I could spend many years in its healing womb. As I looked around the lunar landscape I saw a strange light that was golden in the illuminated areas and silver in the shadows. It was beautiful in all its shades and meanings, and—because of its hauntingly sublime nature, an essence which always seemed to be concealing a wealth of meaning and beauty—could only be described as mystical. That light was, in form and essence, beyond anything known to Earth. I recalled certain paintings that captured a small part of its beauty and transcendent luster, paintings by Da Vinci and Rembrandt. Had the appeal of those paintings been based on knowledge hidden in each of us of the mystical light I saw before me now?

It was not just the sublime beauty of the lunar light that gave it its profundity. That light was but the carrier wave for a *meaning* I did not know, a meaning that once again eluded my grasp, that lay just beyond the margins of my awareness. I looked up at Earth and was surprised to see that now it, too, was surrounded by that mystical light, was bathed in a shimmering, golden glow that made the planet look almost like a star burning in the heavens. I wondered if that radiance was for Earth what the aura is for the human body, if it were but the collective energy of thought or consciousness generated by all life dwelling there. It didn't matter. I was in the midst of wonder. This was no time to indulge my mind. There would be plenty of time for that later.

I stared at Earth for a long time. It was set like a beautiful jewel in the tapestry of space. I had never realized what a lovely world it is, how rare its riot of lifeforms must be in a universe filled with worlds of lifeless rock or methane-ammonia wastelands. Nostalgia came over me as I thought of all the many billions of men and women who had lived there since the dawn of time, had loved there, had struggled to raise themselves above the animals, had sought in a thousand thousand ways to overcome the loneliness of matter and be reunited with the heart of God.

As I gazed at the planet that had spawned me, seeing it with fondness and without pain, it suddenly seemed to glow brighter for a moment. It lost shape and definition, and then disappeared. I blinked in disbelief; and in that tiny fraction of time it was back as it had been, lovely and whole. A shadow momentarily crept over my eyes, leaped out of the pockets of darkness around me, and covered all that I saw with a sense of foreboding.

The shock must have been too great for me to remain in an altered state of being. When next I came to myself I was back on Earth, lying prone. I looked up at the moon and my apprehension was not lessened. A dark cloud was obscuring most of it so that only a thin sliver of white was visible. The rest was veiled in a gray mist. I spent the next two hours in a state of anxious confusion. I could not shake the belief that for a split instant the earth had ceased to exist, that for a fraction of a moment it had winked out of existence. The dark shadow that had pulled its veil over my eyes reminded me with a shudder of that sense of urgency that had brought me back from Radia and her world, back from a greater peace than I had ever known before. What the urgency was I could not say, but I knew it could not be ignored much longer.

February 14

Valentine's Day. The Day of Hearts. The day we lay aside our grievances for a moment and tell others we love them. A day of remembering the people we take so much for granted. I sent a dozen roses to Mindy this morning. Just because. I inscribed the note: "From your friend, William. I love you." I'm sure she was a little surprised and pleased. It's never been my style to be so expressive of my feelings. I've always referred to such gestures as being overly sentimental. But now it felt right; it felt right to start acknowledging in a tangible way those I felt close to. I felt I could no longer hide behind the old thought that I need not say how I felt, that others would just know. It was time to take a stand for the love I felt in my heart.

I spent all morning calling all the people I knew and telling them how much I loved them. Some people were a little surprised just to hear from me. I had kept to myself for so long, and strange stories had been circulating about me. They seemed amazed that I sounded so normal and happy. I even called my mother and father to tell them how grateful I was for having them as parents, though we had shared little in common over the years and been estranged for the past five years or so. My mother cried. My father sounded a little uncomfortable and embarrassed, but I knew he was moved.

I could stand on a big soapbox and talk of how poor our relationships are with people, even with our immediate families, but that would serve little purpose. Everybody *knows* this. The more relevant topic would be the one of trying to understand why we are so reluctant to show our feelings, why we are so afraid of dropping our world-made masks and being aligned with our truest nature, which is love, and why we'd rather exist in the limbo of separateness and private thoughts than risk joining with others and claiming our divine birthright.

* * *

A sense of clarity and peace settled over me after I made those calls. The first ones were difficult to make; the last ones were a joy. I found that my fear of having nothing to say that would be understandable was unfounded. I not only had a great deal to say, but enjoyed what was said to me. I found that I didn't have to drown people in a deluge of words about my otherworldly experiences. It was enough to say that my life had gone through many changes and that I had needed time and solitude to balance them into my life. This was certainly the truth. And when asked about those changes, I replied that I was learning about love and about God, which also was true.

I found that I received much support for the process I was going through. Most thought I was 'getting religion.' It was okay for them to think that and not entirely untrue. I *was* 'getting religion' but in a deeply personal way that went far, far beyond a simple conversion of thought. What I had experienced—and was still in the process of experiencing—was a reorganization of my entire *being*, a remaking of my entire self.

I had never been a religious person, and everyone perceived a change for the better in me from our phone conversation. No one thought I was crazy. I found myself enjoying hearing about the everyday occurrences people spoke of. There was a nostalgia in them for me, a sense of belonging. I was claiming my roots again, roots that had been shorn out from under me when my transformation began. It felt good.

But a part of me still feels very alone. I've mentioned it before. I really wish I had someone I could give full disclosure to about what my life has become, what I've seen and known and been these past two years. I want someone who can understand, someone with experiences and insights similar to my own. Perhaps that's too much to ask. But I *am* grateful to be able to move once again among others without that sense of isolation and aloneness I once felt. That's important.

February 29

There was fire on the horizon tonight. It cut through the dark clouds that covered the sky in huge layers and lit my evening with swatches of yellow and orange light. I watched the colors fade with the dying sun into somber tones of black and cobalt blue.

The past couple of weeks have been good for broadening and deepening those roots I mentioned earlier. I never realized how precious friends and family can be, how warm a feeling it is to bask in one's humanness. I have a strong feeling that this broadening of my earthly roots will be of great value to me in the near future, for that nameless sense of foreboding continues to haunt my thoughts and my dreams. I will need all my humanity to come to grips with it.

I've given a lot of thought lately to the dark foreboding I first sensed on Radia's world and again during my adventure on the moon. It's hard to know what it means. Some of the time I think it must just be some holdover of fear or littleness, some last remaining vestige of resistance to my transformation making itself known. There may be some truth to that. But more and more I sense that the foreboding has little to do with me alone, that it involves all humanity.

March 3

I woke up with a start last night to find my entire body bathed in a deep orange glow. In the darkness my body gave the appearance of being a flaming cinder, or a raging campfire. These images are not far from the truth, for that glow was not just a radiant light; it was *fire*. There was a great heat to it, yet neither my body nor my bed clothes were being burned. Somehow during the night my body had ignited, had erupted into flames. The heat from the flames was almost unbearable. And I became fearful, for even though there appeared to be no damage to my body externally, I was aware of great activity being unleashed internally. A great upheaval seemed to be taking place, eruptions and explosions I could only guess at.

It seemed as though my body were the site of enormous cataclysms, as though it were the earth rebelling against the abuses of man with earthquakes, volcanic eruptions, tornadoes, and tidal waves. I felt whole parts of me surge and expand. As this process continued, I became aware of infinitely tiny explosions going off within my body in staggering numbers. It seemed as though individual cells were unleashing their stored energy in a tremendous supernova-like explosion. As each cell flared brilliantly, then faded, I feared that that cell was spent and dead.

The supernova explosions continued and started to increase exponentially to a high-pitched sound. The thought came to me that perhaps all my supernormal episodes had finally taken a toll, had finally pushed my body past its limits. I was afraid, afraid that the 'glue' holding my body together had come undone, had been stretched too far.

As the process continued, I waited helplessly. I tried to scream, but my mouth and vocal chords were paralyzed—as indeed all my body was at this point. I saw my left hand grow brighter than the rest of my body, saw it go from the amber blaze surrounding and infusing the rest of me to a dull gold. It passed from the muted gold radiance to a brilliant gold, then finally to purest white. The rest of my body began to follow suit; each part went from orange to gold to burning white. I started to see light in the darkness, light that became more and more brilliant as the process continued.

The high-pitched sound climbed to higher and higher frequencies until it became a deafening, shrill noise. I began to see gaps in the light, gaps that were neither darkness, nor the absence of light; they were not obscuring the light either. Moreover they were not *nothing* but *something*.

My body was by now almost entirely covered with an intense, white-hot glow. The deafening scream of sound reached fever pitch, and I felt I would burst under the strain. Then it happened—an explosion like that of an entire *world* being blown apart. And my body was gone, destroyed.

* * *

Before I could feel panic, I felt love. The light I saw seemed itself to be a presence, like a warm cloud that comforted me and gave me peace. I just drifted for a time, unaware of where I was, unaware of *what* I was. I felt like a soldier caught in the explosion of a mortar. The force of the explosion had been tremendous. I didn't know what my situation was, only that I was hurt, had gone through a great shock, and must lie still. I knew beyond any doubt that I no longer had a body. The explosion had torn that precious structure of matter from me. I recalled with horror the feeling that every cell in my body was exploding like a supernova, then dying. I was a disembodied spirit—a poor, forlorn soul, adrift in a sea of light.

But the presence of the light comforted me, gave me rest. As I opened myself to it, a joy I have no words to describe rushed over me. From it an impression formed in my consciousness of what had happened to me. *I had ascended!* The goal of all my thought and hopes and dreams and transformation had been reached! All my life from its beginning had been for this one purpose. The blueprint of my destiny had been fulfilled at last! The blocks to its unfoldment had finally been overcome.

As I opened the spectrum of my awareness I saw, like a frightened child tentatively removing his hands from his eyes after a frightening incident, that I was not just a single point of consciousness in an ocean of light. I was the *light* also. My body had not been destroyed, at least not in the usual sense. It had merely accelerated its vibratory frequency to the point where it had left the world of matter and risen to light, had become light. *This* event was what all my transformative episodes had been geared toward. *This* ultimate transformation was what my changes in diet and lifestyle and thought as well as my studies of the saints and religion and the aura and psychic phenomena had been preparing me for. The Ascension.

I *was* the light. I was *all* of the light. I was everything that was or had ever been or ever would be. I was all people, all places, all thoughts. I was the tiny flower freshly risen from the seed. I was the red giant star a thousand times larger than the sun. I was the child crying in its cradle. I was the comet streaking through the darkness of the void. I was the grain of sand and the exploding star. I was the prodigal son returned home to the loving embrace of the father.

* * *

I came back to myself as a separate being sometime early this morning. I don't know how long I existed in that state of joy and transcendence. Time had no meaning there. I was delighted and surprised to find myself back in a physical body for when the translation into light occurred, I was certain my body had been destroyed. And that is apparently what *did*, in fact, happen. There was no body *waiting* for me to return to as there had been in my other beauties. My physical body simply reformed itself from my thoughts.

Everything was exactly as it had been, right down to the atomic structure. Always before I had feared some harm might befall my body as I journeyed into other realities. Now I had a greater freedom than ever before for through the process that had led to my ascension, I had gained the capability to go wherever I wished without concern for my body. I was free, free as the wind that moves and blows yet cannot be seen or captured, free as the flame flickering on a candle stick or raging from a burning building. Wild and free. Wild and free.

It was not just the sense of freedom that exhilarated me. It was also the remembrance of the state of being I had experienced in those moments of eternity, moments beyond time, beyond worlds. I was a universal consciousness; yet a part of me was aware of myself as an individual awareness also—not an awareness of myself as William Sherrill, at least not completely, but as a much larger, much grander William.

My soul was filled with beauty and joy during that ecstatic moment of ascension. But the way we understand those words is in terms of a body and its ability to experience sensation. I had no body in that transcendent state, nor had I any mind in the usual sense. I had no ego, no thoughts; I simply *was*. I had lived in the heart of God. Joy was not an attribute that a part of me experienced; I *was* joy. And I *was* beauty...and I *was* love...love so great it created all the worlds— love that was not born of light but had given birth to light, love that was beyond light.

That part of me that knew me as a separate awareness had been in the ascension also, but like a tiny spark amid a forest fire it had been beneath notice. Just as Plato had postulated that all things of Earth are but imperfect shadows of a perfect form, I had been the perfected form of that imperfect shadow which on Earth was known as William Sherrill.

* * *

I rose from my bed intending to get all that had happened down on paper while the clarity of the experience was at its height; but as I looked back at the bed, I received another great shock. On the sheet on which I had slept was an imprint of my body lying in the position it had been in during my translation into light. At first I thought the brownish blotches were singe marks from the heat generated; but upon closer inspection I saw beyond a doubt that it was an image of me, or at least the part of me that had touched the sheet. The surprise was not so much that a side effect such as that had occurred; it was the resemblance the effect bore to the Shroud of Turin, said to be the burial clothes of Jesus. If I had ever been able to convince myself my experiences were just fantasies or mad delusions in my mind, that time had ended. There could be no further doubt. My experiences were *real*; I *had* ascended.

With this awareness came also a great humility. I had no wish to compare myself to Jesus, but I felt a great, onrushing understanding of him and a great love for what he had given the world. It was obvious that if he lived eternally in the state I had but briefly known, unbounded by the world of time and space and bodies, he was still giving his love, still giving his peace. He was accessible to all and in all ways. For us to experience his love and peace all that was required was the simple willingness to let him in.

The secrets of religion rained down upon me like gentle drops. A veil was lifted from my eyes. Oh, what a joy to know, really *know* these secrets of life. They were so simple! So simple, yet so powerful, so beautiful. I laughed uncontrollably, tears running down my cheeks. I ran outside, naked. It was raining hard. I didn't care. I ran along the beach yelling, yelling. I was alive! I was exhilarated! No time existed but each moment, each holy instant. I felt the energy of life coursing through my body, the body I had thought lost to me. I claimed my divine birthright, threw off all chains of limitation. I cared nothing for what others might think. Life moved through me like lightning through a stormy sky. The rain, the cold, the darkness were precious to me. The sheet of gray clouds that cast a dim light on my path was a miracle. I ran screaming, screaming into life.

* * *

Now it is evening. The rain has stopped except for an occasional splash on my windows. A few stars have poked their heads through the dim, gray-white clouds. I have never known such peace. I have never known such fulfillment. Never will I be so lonely again.

March 6
Oh, my God! Oh, my God! Radia! The prophecy! Oh, my God! The *ascension!* All those cells bursting into supernova explosions of light.... How could I have been so blind? In the wake of my joy at having ascended I missed the connection between that powerful process and the prophecy on Radia's world of Shanti, the tiny world that was but an atom making up one the cells of my own brain. Radia and her people—they're gone...*gone!*

March 8
My greatest fear has been realized. The sense of peace I reveled in a few days ago has vanished like a cool summer breeze that whistles by, then is gone without a trace. Radia and her people—her entire *world*—are gone...transformed into light through the power of the ascension process I underwent. After the connection between the prophecy and the energy released by the ascension process finally dawned on me on the morning of March 6th, I willed my consciousness back into my body. I went down to its cellular, then atomic levels. I searched and searched for Radia's world. But it was all in vain. I knew her world would be gone...knew it had been given to the fires of ascension; but I had to *try*...had to see for myself.

Deep feelings of sadness roll over me like tidal waves of emotion buffeting the island of my heart. I remember how scars and imperfections were healed when my transformation began, with each episode with the light. Now I know that Radia's world was located in a damaged or diseased cell in my brain, one that was purified and made new by the holy, cleansing fires of ascension. Other cells returned exactly as they had been after their explosion into pure light.

But why did Radia, sweet Radia, and her people—her world— have to be given to the fire so that *my* transformation could continue? Why? And how did the dissolution of her world into light 'ennoble' anyone? Certainly I don't feel ennobled. I feel empty...and sad. Too sad even for tears.

March 12

A calmness has finally settled over me when I think of Radia and her tiny world. I know that nothing ever dies—nothing is ever truly lost. Life always moves forward in an ever-ascending spiral toward perfection and freedom. I believe Radia and her people are now part of all that is; that they are experiencing the freedom and joy of unlimited being that I felt during the moments following my ascension. Perhaps they truly *have* been ennobled by being released from the confines of a limited, individual existence. No matter how gracefully they lived, it was still a limited bodily existence. Perhaps it was right for them to go beyond physical life into a state of unity with all things.

Perhaps Radia would have been gone by now anyway. The time sequence in her world ran much faster than it does in mine. Perhaps she had already lived the full measure of her life in the months I've lived since my visit to her world. I don't know. I've been too preoccupied the past few months, too caught up in my own transformation and the dim forebodings I've felt recently to have considered Radia's fate.

When I left Radia and her world I knew I could not live my life with her. I knew that I had to serve the larger sense of purpose growing within me. But knowing that she was *there*, inside of me—literally—made all the difference in the world. She was a lifeline for me, one that reached all the way down into that tiny, tiny sea.

And now Radia's gone. Radia...sweet, beautiful, gentle Radia. The only woman I've ever truly loved...and been loved by. Gone.

March 16

Gray clouds plying their way across a sky of cerulean blue. Birds singing plaintively from the branches of distant trees. The sun sinking, without a fuss, into the embrace of the darkening sea. Shades of peach and violet and lavender exploding on the horizon, then giving way to deep gray, going down to dark. Shapes and sounds of night leaping into form. A gentle wind whistling by.... Nightfall.

In the wake of all my wondrous experiences, I had almost forgotten the mysterious Shadow Woman. I knew nothing about her from the first time her image appeared several months ago except that she was alive and real, not just an image conjured by my mind, or the psychic shell of some departed soul. Last night she appeared to me again. I was in a peaceful state, having finally come to grips with the loss of Radia and her people. I was casually watching the evening come and go by stages to twilight, then the fullness of night. Shadows were all around me as I sat on my porch, but they did not alarm me, did not give my mind cause for fright or imagined terrors. Then out of the darkness came a shape, a form. Before me, forming in the dim shadows of night, the image of a woman appeared. I knew her. She had appeared before. She was the Shadow Woman. I had for many years been comfortable in the dark; it held no fears for me, and such wonders and changes had come to my life of late that I welcomed the mysterious woman's coming as part of that marvelous process. Her arrival was like images formed in the air from heat off a paved highway on a hot summer day—a shimmer, a blur, an invisible movement catching the eye. Then her form leaped into view all at once, distinct from all the surrounding darkness, like a penciled outline and a depth without substance. This time she was not merely a face hanging in the air like a wisp or a face forming itself in the wood grain of a door as she had been when she first appeared several months ago. This time she was a full woman. She walked toward me and, though there was no chair for her, she sat beside me. Since she had no physical interaction in this world, the lack of a chair did not matter. Whether she had actually sat in a chair or not would have been the same for her. But to give some measure of familiarity to her visit she adopted that position, across from me. Since her form was distinguishable from the surrounding darkness by just a faint outline, I was hardly aware of the incongruousness and, perhaps, humor of the situation.

For a long time we just stared at each other. There was a look in her eyes, a freshness about her essence that had nothing of death or dreams about it; and there was an ancientness and an alienness about her also. Her eyes held a fascination and curiosity that told me I was as much an enigma to her as she was to me. I wondered what place, what time, what dimension of being she had come from, for surely one such as her had not come from Earth. I had never experienced such alienness, even on Radia's world. Had this woman's arrival been a fluke, a rare accident that had occurred without her wish? Was she here seeking help to get back to her world or had she come purposely?

These questions and others flooded my mind as I looked at her. I reached my hand out to hers; and though I felt no physical contact, I did feel *something*. There was a slight coldness mixed with a mild electric charge as my hand passed through hers. From the look on her face, I knew she also felt something from my touch. I wondered if in her reality *I* was the shadow and *she* the one with substance.

Then she spoke. Her mode of speech was very different even from the way Radia had communicated with me. Radia's 'words' were a rich tapestry of images I 'heard' and 'felt.' The Shadow Woman spoke with actual words; but when her lips moved, no sound came from them. I heard the words in my head; but they did not correspond properly to the movements of her lips so that watching her speak was much like watching a poorly dubbed foreign film, the English words not matching the movements of the actors' lips either in timing or word formation. They also seemed to come from a great distance, even though she was directly before me.

She said her name was Iripan and that she was one of only a few currently able to enter my world. I told her my name, said that I had seen her before, and asked why she had come. As she continued staring at me with the dark eyes of her shadowy form, Iripan told me that our worlds are bound tightly together, closer even than hand in glove, and that what affects one affects the other. She then said that there is little time before both Earth and her world of Iltar *transit to light*. My heart sank to my stomach; my mind started spinning. The impact of those last few words was greater than if she had told me the oceans of the world were about to engulf the lands. She paused for a moment and seemed to sigh. A heaviness settled over her. She said our twin worlds are unprepared for such a change but that there are those on both Earth and Iltar who can help prepare for its coming, beings such as she and I. I asked if there could be a mistake, if she could be wrong about the approaching change, but she said there is no doubt such a change is coming—and soon. She asked if I had seen the signs, for surely they must have appeared. With a tingle of fear I recalled my view of Earth from the moon, of how the planet had glowed brightly with a strange light, had lost shape and definition, then disappeared for a moment. I wondered if this was what she meant by 'transit to light.'

Iripan said she had come to me because I had found the gap separating our two worlds and knew the secret of traveling between them though I had not yet done so. She further said that this knowledge only comes to those who have gone beyond their body's limitations, only to those who know the body is not just a pleasure-thing, but an instrument of service. She had come to help forge a bridge between the two worlds so that together we might assist in the mighty transition to come; she and I were to be midwives of a grand, new birth.

Her words burned into my soul. I now knew what she meant. That winking out effect I had seen on the moon was not a vague imagining but part of a process I had had no understanding of. The sense of dark foreboding I had felt on more than one occasion had not been some dark, fleeting fancy. Each experience of it had been a signal heralding a change that was to come soon to Earth and to Iripan's world of Iltar as well.

The atmosphere was filled with a sense of impending doom on a scale vaster than anything I could imagine. This was not just a portent of physical destruction to the point of the entire *world* being destroyed, it was also a portent of the destruction of dreams and souls. The latter part I did not understand, but I knew that her statement about our being midwives ready to assist in a grand, new birth also carried with it the possibility that the birth was not certain, that we might instead stand by helplessly while the infant was stillborn or born grotesquely malformed.

Iripan noticed the effect her words had on me. My eyes must have blazed like twin question marks before my shadowy guest, betraying my concern. After a short silence she spoke again. She said the questions in my mind were rising like locusts toward the sun. She told me she understood my confusion and concern, for they were hers also—that there were many things about the times to come she did not know either. She said she *did* know, however, that our worlds are joined like light with dark, that they could be called parallel worlds, that all that is in this world is mirrored in hers. She further explained that the universe is vibrating at an incredible rate and that just as a fluorescent light oscillates between light and dark many times a second so does the universe pulse, but many billions of times each second. She said people in this world see only one half of the cycle of light; those in hers seeing the other half. Her world is not a world of darkness except when seen from my perspective; her 'Earth,' Iltar, is on *the other side of light.*

I took a deep breath in an attempt to digest her words. They represented such a new and different view of the universe that it was not easy to blend them with my own. They carried such a ring of truth and forboding that I felt I needed time alone to ponder them. Since the experience of ascension my mind had been deluged with new thoughts and possibilities, new shifts in my picture of the universe and life and God; and now, only a few days later, a new bombshell had been hurled into my world view. I needed time to rest, to let things sink in. I felt overloaded with new information.

I told Iripan I needed time to think, time to weigh her words, time to sift through the events of the past few days, time to let her words and the astonishing nature of her coming be absorbed into my heart and spirit. She said it was well that I should do so, that my desire to serve must be complete—my will and strength unobstructed—if I were to be of use. She said that I should let my heart guide my thoughts and actions, that there was little time and much to do be done. She then told me it was a great strain to be in my world and that she had to leave. Her final words were that I should come to her when I was ready and that I could find her in the gap between the worlds.

With that last statement barely from her mouth, her outline began to grow dim. There was a quivering in the darkness, and I could see only the shadows on my porch cast by the pale moon.

March 22

The first few days after Iripan's visit were not happy ones for me. That I was in great need of rest is borne out by the fact that I slept at least twelve hours each of those days. A very human part of me has for several months been having very God-like experiences. Though most of the obstructions to the full flow of those marvelous, divine energies have been released, I am still a human being living in a physical body in a world where time and space *seem* real, even if they're not.

I have felt it important to forgive myself my limitations in thought, experience, and understanding. I will, of course, help Iripan in any way that I can; I understand the need. What has concerned me is the thousand ways my consciousness has been racing. I look back on all my experiences of the past two years or so, all the states of consciousness and emotion I've experienced, and each one seems to have been valid; each one seems to have been real. I'm confused. Which is the truest state of consciousness? I've experienced several states of being I thought were the ultimate only to see each one fall away before a still greater one. Where will it all end? What is the purpose of it all? Will I ever truly know?

That mysterious *something* that lies beyond the margin of beauty and wonder still eludes me, still dances out of sight. I see that beauty is a heady drink; it must be sipped slowly rather than gulped if one is to avoid being lost in its myriad eddies. Some moments of beauty serve as pointers toward potential *lifetimes* of fulfillment. It is too easy to get drawn into those powerful currents, to spend time upon time in vain though pleasurable pursuits.

At the beginning of my transformation I was buffeted by the currents, thrashed against the rocks, drawn into whirlpools of wonder; and along with the sense of awe and unspeakable joy I felt fear and pain. I have been fortunate enough to sail down that river of wonder without being lost in those fierce currents. The inner presence has guided me, has steered me toward the center of the river, even when I didn't choose to listen to it. The presence has taught me and loved me. It has led me away from the painful blend of joy and anguish so that my more recent experiences have been mostly joyful ones touched with the sublime. It has kept me from losing sight of my purpose in life.

I've often asked myself what the purpose of my transcendent experiences is. I am learning that a more important question is: how can they be used to serve the purpose of life and to extend God's love? If they are used only to serve the ego, the little self's goals and needs, they will be of little value. They will remain words and images divested of meaning, mere shells, hollow husks of glory. Given to God, the sublime source of my life, these experiences and all I've learned from them have a chance to go beyond being separate beauties and become something more glorious than I can even imagine.

The more I reflect on my beauties, the more certain I become of myself and my purpose. For a few days I felt like a person put behind the steering wheel of a car for the first time and expected to drive expertly at a hundred miles per hour. The territory covered was unfamiliar, the movements and reflexes untested and shaky. I feel much calmer now. Most of the initial apprehensions from Iripan's urgent warning have subsided. I'm still uncertain what I can do to help, but I'm willing to try.

I'm becoming more and more grateful to the inner presence that has been guiding me. In the early days of my metamorphosis I discovered that when I listened to my mind there was often fear and confusion, but when I listened to the presence, inevitably there was peace. That is how I learned to distinguish the two. Also, the chatter from my ego always involved events or patterns from the past or concerns or projections of the future based on the past.

When the voice of the presence speaks to me, it is always in the present. This is an important distinction. I now realize that when I used past experience as a guide for present action, the present disappeared and became merely an extension of that past. The present became an imprisoned, frozen moment, unable to be what it was; a stillborn child trapped by my demands that it be a certain way.

Through all my experiences, through all the fear, the pain, the joy, the love, and the splendor, that presence, that inner voice, has been with me. It is somehow connected with the inner sound that has come to me in so many different variations, though I don't know how. Now I will let it guide me in the adventures and struggles that must surely come if the words of Iripan and the ominous portents I have felt are true.

March 26

I've gone over Iripan's words in my mind again and again, weighing each word against the promptings of my heart. Her coming was clearly sincere and well-intentioned. She said she had come because I had found the gap between our two worlds and knew the secret of traveling between them. That statement still puzzled me. I could imagine that somehow, when I ascended, the intensity of the energies involved sent a signal she had been able to receive. Just as an enormous, thunderous sound is produced when the sound barrier is broken, perhaps a similar kind of signal is produced when a higher matrix of consciousness and being is achieved. Certainly, the culmination of all those transformative episodes, that joyous moment of bodily ascension into light, might have sent forth a flare signifying its occurrence. That I had generated enough energy through the ascension process to bridge the gap between our worlds was understandable—what was unclear to me was how I could harness that energy to enter Iripan's world.

As I reflected on that ascension experience, I remembered that there had come a moment when the surrounding darkness had been replaced by light. It was as if the darkness were but an illusion of my slow-moving mind and that when the energies of my self were revved up, I was able to see the true reality—light. Just as water is always enclosed in ice, so the light was always enclosed in darkness.

Even more curious had been the experience of observing that the light began to pulse more and more slowly. This, of course, was only how it looked to me. A similar effect can be achieved if a person looks at a fan through a spinning gyroscope; he or she will eventually 'catch up' with and see the individual blades either moving slowly or standing completely still. This is called a stroboscopic effect. The truth was that *I* was vibrating faster and faster and 'catching up' to the *light's* frequency. *I* was the gyroscope. And I was able to 'see' at incredibly high frequencies.

I remembered there came a time when the light itself flashed on and off like a strobe light, then slowed down even more so that what I saw in the gaps between light flashes was neither darkness nor void. It was not the absence of light or the negation of light. It was *something* but nothing I could name. Then my curiosity vanished for my body exploded into light. The explosion was like the energy of matter being released from an atomic bomb; yet even that is a tame analogy. It is probably more accurate to compare that transformation to the explosion of a star outward as a supernova. Indeed every cell and every atom of my body underwent such an explosion.

From my readings about ascension, I had gotten the idea that it was a gentle process, a smooth transition into a higher matrix of being. I now knew that it was anything but gentle. It was the violent unleashing of energies so great they had not even been dreamed of by Earth's scientists. If that explosion had happened in the physical world rather than on a higher plane of being it would have ripped the entire solar system apart, leaving nothing but debris in its wake. Suddenly, I saw the key to Iripan's message, really understood the meaning of her words. Whereas my world has its being in the 'on' aspect of light, hers has its life in the 'off' cycle. Both worlds have light, but from two different perspectives, two different foci. I wondered if the aspect of light which gave birth to her world was similar to the Buddhist idea of Nirvana and the Void. Had I seen what the Buddha had seen? Had the Buddha slipped between the worlds and lived for periods of time in that vast void which was but the sister to our reality? Had he seen it as nothing when it was really something?

I now knew what must be done. That evening, when the moon was high and a sprinkling of fairy-dust stars lit the night, I would attempt to go to Iripan.

March 30

I want to be fully a part of the process that's going on in me and not just an observer clinically reporting what he sees. Once it was enough to hear about the exciting episodes of other peoples' lives—to vicariously experience the adventures they had had. Now the time for secondhand experience is over. The adventure is waiting for each of us. Mine is unfolding. All the dreams and hopes and joys of my youth—and much, much more—are bursting forth in me. I don't need to hear about another's adventure to be thrilled. I don't need to invent fantasies about my own life. Adventure is not something that lives only in fertile imaginations or dreamy-eyed malcontents. It's real. I'm living it.

I spent the rest of the day outside after writing the previous entry. I needed to be outside—to feel the cool wind against my face, to hear the distant chattering of birds and the drone of insects, to smell the scent of salt from the crashing sea-spray, to see the sun sparkles dancing among the swaying leaves. I know it's important to keep an account of my transformational process for those that will come later, but writing sometimes wearies me.

After a relaxing afternoon of doing nothing I watched the evening, with the soft padding footfalls of a kitten, begin to gently creep up and replace the light of day. Sunset's riot of colors bursting through the gray-white scales of a mackerel sky slowly faded into darker hues as twilight hushed the vaulted heavens, heralding the dark of night.

As the last remnant of sun prepared to ease itself into the ocean, I let my gaze rest once more on the wide swatch of golden light draped across the ocean. The color was a darker gold that was almost brown, but there was nothing drab or plain about it. It was still lit with the sun's magical glow. Once again I felt that the fiery blaze was not just the sun's reflection off the water but a pathway to some undreamed of world of wonder.

With the sun's passing I watched the sky change rapidly from a deep blue to an inky blackness, punctuated by silvery stars. With such an enchanting, peaceful scene unfolding before me, I could not imagine needing to be entertained or otherwise distracted. A supremely engaging show was there for all to see and at no cost. The idea of being able to hold on to anger or fear or depression while this magnificent panorama unfolded before me was beyond belief and brought a faint smile to my lips.

But those stars—still and white and lovely—evoked a loneliness in me, a loneliness I could not describe, a longing I could not name. It was not a negative quality or an aspect of myself that needed to be released, like a petty jealousy or unfounded fear. It was not an obstruction to the marvelous energies I could feel coursing through me, filling me with abundant life. Oh, no. It was something else. It was a feeling of—yes—of *homesickness*. Somehow I felt I belonged in that starry expanse, that Earth was not my true home.

As a small child I had felt I didn't belong here, didn't come from this world. It's a common enough fantasy in children, perhaps brought on by an inability or unwillingness to adjust to their environment. In my case it was simply a feeling that, though I loved and was loved by the members of my family, only blood-ties joined us as family. The aloneness, the feeling that I could not share the ideas and feelings bursting in my young mind was great. It was not so much that those around me would not have sincerely *tried* to understand my strange fancies and ideas, it was that I learned early on they could *not*. I therefore invented the idea that I had come from another place, another world, that I had been left behind on Earth by accident or as some special emissary but had lost that knowledge through some accident of amnesia.

A childish fantasy, really. Yet as I looked into those twinkling points of light, floating like tiny islands adrift in the ocean of space, they called out to me, beckoned me. I felt like a sailor removed from the sea for many years—living in a dim cellar, the only reminder of the sea, his true home, the occasional scent of salt air; but that fragrance is enough to evoke a distant memory in him, a vague recollection of a life that was infinitely more fulfilling to him—more in keeping with his nature—though now it seems but a dream, a far off echo.

Perhaps my experience with the star stone was brought on by this nameless yearning. Or maybe remembering the star stone episode has elicited this yearning in me now. I don't know. Probably it is a little of both. But even as a child, though I had a solid anchor of friends and family keeping my place in this world intact and bearable, I felt my true roots had been planted elsewhere...somewhere in all that dark immensity. I felt I had been washed ashore on this island Earth—this world that was not my home but a temporary dwelling place.

***

I did not want these musings, pleasant though they were, to distract me from my purpose. I went back into the house and prepared for bed. After drinking a large glass of spring water, I lay down and began a process of deep breathing—all the time focusing my attention on the inner sounds that were always in the background of my awareness. The sounds began to grow louder and more distinct as I focused on them. There were several distinct variations, but as I placed my intention on those with the highest vibratory frequency, the others faded into silence.

I saw in my mind's eye the silvery ribbon of light connecting the coiled serpent of energy at the base of my spine with the radiant globe of light at the top of my head; and it became not a fanciful visual image but a living reality that was fresh, and changed before my sight. I noticed that this time, however, as the energy cycled between the two poles to form a closed circuit of energy, several other energy spheres were also enclosed by the loop. My readings of psychic sciences and Eastern mysticism had taught me that these warps and swirls of energy were called chakras. I hadn't paid much attention to them before—the explanations of them had seemed dry and distant; but now they came alive before my heightened vision. They were part of the dynamo of energy that accelerated the vibratory frequency of my body as surely as a cyclotron accelerates the speed of atomic particles. They were not distinct globes of colored light with definite boundaries but warps of rapidly vibrating energy that merged at the edges with the systems they were part of. Each warp was of a pastel color that had a brilliant center, and that rapidly diffused into a fuzzy edge with the surrounding light; each warp thus gave the impression of being separate. I saw as I watched these whorls of energy that they were transformers of higher energies, acting as relays connecting with lower energies. They were also like spark plugs, firing in sequence each time the pulse racing through the silver ribbon of energy passed by.

This internal mechanism was clearly an engine of some sort, as I had discovered during my lovemaking with Radia. The understanding had enveloped my mind like morning mist over an open meadow that when this engine's individual parts were cleansed and joined in proper alignment with each other, a magnificent energy was produced—a power that could pale the force of atomics. Of all the billions of people who had inhabited Earth, only a scant few had ever truly known this. Even fewer had learned to harness that energy and reclaim their God-like heritage.

As I continued to watch this marvelous process grow in intensity and speed, the frequency and pitch of the internal sound raised accordingly. I don't know which influenced the other more, but it was clear there was an intimate relationship between the sound and this internal engine. I began to see light in the darkness and felt an upward oscillating movement forming in my consciousness. Then I saw the light pulse on and off and was once more aware of the void between light flickers—the void that was not nothing but *something*.

The sense of movement and activity within my body increased. The silver ribbon of light forming the elliptical circuit—along with the chakras, glowing like a string a beautiful jewels—began to blur until all I could see was a kaleidoscopic shimmer of light and color. The collage of colors blended and merged until it became a shifting blob of formless, golden light. The dynamo of energy my body and mind had become was reaching higher and higher levels of intensity, and an internal strain was building up.

I could sense that the depth of activity and change was reaching all the way to the cellular level and beyond to the atomic structure itself, preparing to translate everything to light. This transmutation of matter to light was what had been prophesied on Radia's world for thousands of her years. T*his* was the way in which I, as a new Prometheus, had brought fire to them. Remembrance of the fate of Radia and her people still brought a twinge of sadness with it.

I withdrew my attention from the 'soft' vision of my internal eye and looked at my body with physical eyes. What I saw was a blaze of golden light encapsulating my entire body. That it was not the amber glow of my earlier experience did not concern me. Perhaps amber was but the final coloring of an impurity still within me that had now been purified.

At this point my body felt like a tuning fork vibrating at an unthinkably high frequency. The high pitched sound flooding my consciousness was far beyond what physical ears could withstand. The sense of wildness and primeval cataclysm continued as the tiny supernova explosions began to occur in ever increasing numbers. When the flicker between light pulses reached a point where the off cycle was equal to the on cycle, I knew that I was looking at the gap between the worlds, the bridge between my universe and Iripan's. I also knew that the intense level of activity in my body was building up a pressure that would result in my body's exploding violently into light.

As the sound and intensity reached a peak, I braced myself for the impending cataclysmic shock. Amid this cyclonic energy, I focused my intent on the gap between the worlds and with a strength that surprised me willed that I enter Iripan's world.

When the shock of translation came it was much less explosive than the first time. There was a thunderous sound like that of a volcanic eruption, and I felt I was being blown about like a leaf in a huge wind. The shock to my consciousness was much less traumatic also. Perhaps that initial experience of ascension had prepared me for the ones to come. I had no sense that any less energy had been released or with any less violence within my body. No words can describe the sheer, naked *power* summoned up as this process reached its height.

I felt I was bursting through an ancient barrier, and then I was free. My body was no more. Every cell and every atom of that body had exploded into light. The freedom and joy I felt was beyond description. Let it be enough to say that I was a genie freed from its bottle.

My last thought had been of Iripan and her world on the other side of light. At that moment of translation I had focused all my will on going through that margin, that window, that connected the two realities. I gently avoided the temptation to let the process proceed naturally into an ascension experience similar to the previous one; as marvelous as that experience would be, I could no longer think only of my own desires. Now was the time to take the love within me and turn it outward in the form of service. The peril that was coming to both worlds must be my focus now. I had no time for the luxury of private beauties, though the adventure I was embarking on was certainly profound.

I remember there being an instant in which I had a choice. I could either let the process of ascension continue along its natural course, could expand outward to embrace the entire universe, or I could maintain a pin point focus and slip into Iripan's world. In that moment I willed the awakened genie to return to his bottle.

Like an atomic explosion that turns inward the moment the fantastic energies are released, I channeled the energies released by ascension into the one goal of piercing the gap between the two worlds. The energy required to accomplish such a transition was beyond belief. It was no simple effort of the will. For a creature of light to enter a world of 'unlight' was more difficult than traversing the entire universe. My journey into Iripan's universe was to be an entry into a region of existence more alien and remote by far than anything I had encountered in the worlds of light.

As only a point of awareness propelled by the raw energy of ascension, I launched myself through the off cycle of light into that alien place. For a time I felt giddy and disoriented, as though I were caught in some vast whirlpool of energy. My consciousness experienced the equivalent of a 'pins and needles' effect as the vortex spun me around and around, buffeting me.

After what seemed like hours, the movement ceased and I was still and alone. I was aware of nothing but a vast void, but it was a void that was not nothing. There was *substance* to it, fullness. I know that a full void sounds contradictory, and perhaps it is. But there is a place in the higher realms of consciousness where paradox is the rule, where things can be both true and not true at the same time, where light can have an opposite that is not light and not dark, not substance in the usual sense and not shadow but *something*. Words, crude tools that they are, know nothing of paradox. I can't communicate what is not in my repertoire to describe.

I drifted in this realm of unlight for several moments, focusing all my thought on Iripan. Then the void just disappeared, dissolved into form and shape. And before me I saw a lady. She was tall and lovely. Her hair and eyes were dark, but her face was very fair. On her sensuous lips was a faint smile. It was Iripan.

For a while Iripan just looked at me, as one might look at some novelty of nature. Then she took a deep breath and closed her eyes for a few moments in a gesture that could only have been one of giving thanks. This beautiful woman had an aura about her, an aura of strength and wisdom. I had never been so impressed by the striking beauty of a woman as I was by hers. Even Radia, precious Radia, had not possessed beauty like that which I saw before me now. While Radia's beauty came from innocence and child-like simplicity, Iripan's came from maturity and inner knowing. While Radia possessed a strong sense of compassion and acceptance, Iripan had a great strength of purpose fired by a phenomenal desire to serve. Radia had chosen to *be*, Iripan had willed to *do*. She had clearly taken her place as an instrument of God. She was the truly mature woman who sees beyond her own needs and operates at a global level of consciousness. At the same time, I later found out, coupled with that high sense of integrity and responsibility, was an impish, playful side. This side of her was obvious by the way she occasionally cocked her head or flashed her eyes.

I tried to speak with Iripan, but words were difficult at first. In this shadowy form, which I would later realize was not a shadow at all but a warping in the fabric of her universe, it seemed that my words were traveling through a long tunnel and being garbled into a mass of echoes. This feeling passed, however; and like the static that is eliminated from a radio station as soon as it is tuned in properly, soon we were conversing easily. The words I heard in my mind from her did not correspond exactly to the movements of her lips, but I had grown used to this anomaly during her visit to my world and scarcely noticed it.

Able to voice nothing more than the obvious, I announced, in this slightly awkward way of conversing, that I had come. Her eyes, green as emeralds, flashed her excitement and joy. She said she *knew* I would come to Iltar. I asked her if she had entered my world the same way I entered hers—through the energy of ascension. She nodded and said that she and a few others on Iltar had learned to ascend their bodies while still alive. She explained that she had accomplished this process many times before she came to my world, my reality. She had grown curious about the other cycle of light she observed when the energies neared the height needed for the ascension process to complete itself and one day had simply willed herself through the gap. She said that she was drawn to me because I, too, was undergoing the powerful bodily transformation that leads to ascension and that the energy of my process drew her to me like a beacon in the night. When she first saw me, she had been so filled with awe and curiosity regarding me and my world that she had only observed. After I fully ascended, however, she knew it was important to make contact with me; she knew that if I had the requisite strength, will, and understanding to *ascend*, I could perhaps be of help in the challenging days to come. I was curious how she knew I had ascended. To this she replied that the energy released by the ascension process is so great it leaves a faint trail that others may follow, just as a jet leaves a vapor-trail if it flies high enough.

We were outside a large house similar in style to an early American mansion. Trees graced a lawn of blue-green grass. The leaves were bell shaped and the branches were generally reddish in color and had a sharpness to them; the trunks were less rounded than those of trees on Earth. I was very disoriented when I tried to walk because I could not feel the ground beneath my feet or the gentle breeze against my face. In time I adjusted to this lack of physical sensation, for I knew that, in Iripan's world, *she* was the person with substance; *I* was the shadow.

Iripan led me into her house and into a huge drawing room. I followed at her side; but though my feet were moving, they touched nothing, felt nothing. I simply willed to follow her and did—in a drifting, dreamy manner like a disembodied spirit. She motioned to a white, wicker chair, inviting me to sit. At first my shadowy body slipped right though the wooden seat. My lovely hostess erupted with laughter at this sudden, unexpected action. She then covered her mouth with her hand in a gesture of slight embarrassment, concerned that I might take offense. I found myself laughing at both the absurdity of my situation with the chair and her reaction to it. She roared with laughter once more, her eyes dancing with humor and liveliness. Her sense of humor was not unlike that of Radia. Iripan regained her composure and I mastered the technique for 'sitting' in the chair—I had only to visualize myself in it. She showed me a large book with numerous entries in it. It was a journal similar to the one I'd been keeping, chronicling her transformative process. Hers was thicker than mine, however, for her process had been going on for twelve years to my two. She said she knew that I, too, was keeping such a record and emphasized that I must continue it "for those who will come after you." She said it would be a code, a signal, a key whose worth would be without measure for others in the future.

I knew it was important to chronicle my transformation but had never seen it as vital. Originally I had viewed it as therapy for keeping what little sanity I had left. Later, when I gained a partial understanding of the process that was occurring, I recognized its value to others who might at some time go through the same transformative process. The look of seriousness on Iripan's face, the piercing quality of her eyes as she spoke, told me it was far more important than I knew. I did not understand at this point why it was so vital, but I promised I would do as she asked.

We talked for over an hour. I told her about the experiences and thoughts and feelings I'd had the past two years. I told her what an enigma—what a curiosity—she had been to me. I told her of Radia and the completion of the circuit needed to power the engine of ascension that had formed after our lovemaking. Then I told her of the other beauties I'd seen and experienced up until my translation into light and of the confusion and fear and loneliness and pain I had felt in those early days when I had no one to confide in, no one to guide me.

Iripan listened intently, marveling at the uniqueness of the winding path I had trod to achieve ascension. She told me that she, too, had experienced great fear and confusion when her process began but that her initial experiences had not been so explosive. She had had more time to integrate and balance them within her because they had not occurred as frequently. I was glad for her. Her process had taken longer to complete, though she had first achieved ascension three years ago.

We felt such rapport with each other we could have talked for days, but a type of strain I can't describe started building up in me. I knew I had to leave soon. She understood this and asked that I return as soon as possible, remembering, as I journeyed back to Earth, that I was as unique a being on my world as she was on hers. She bade me go with the knowledge that I was no longer alone in my transformation and that there was indeed a purpose to it.

I gave in to the strain that was building up within me and allowed my focus to expand. Iripan's world began to shimmer and fade, and then I was alone once more in a void that was neither light nor dark. The last thing I remembered was Iripan's face. I moved through the void of unlight, that connecting bridge between the worlds, for a few moments, then saw the pulsing of light. I willed myself through as the light pulsed 'on;' and after an endless feeling of falling and the rushing of hot winds, I was back in my room.

* * *

I rested for a few minutes after my return, then got up to get some water. For some reason I was incredibly thirsty, and the spring water tasted like ambrosia. It trickled through my body like a nourishing rain through a parched cornfield. I went outside and sat on my porch, where I could reflect on my trip to Iripan's world under the starry sea of night. Saturn was high in the sky and shone like a tiny smudge of gold. Scorpio blazed in the heavens, upraised tail poised as if to strike. It was a marvelous sight.

I just sat there for a long time staring at those stars, wondering if the same ones shone in Iripan's night. As I continued to gaze I thought I saw her face forming in those stars—a new constellation, a new image forming in my night, Iripan.

The thought of that lovely woman, a universe and more away, made my heart sing with joy. Her beauty, her strength, her wisdom soothed my spirit like a mother rocking her new born babe to sleep. Not even Radia had given me such peace. Iripan *knew* what my life had been like, had lived a similar life herself. With her I felt I had found a true friend in spirit and mind. How different my life and my transformation might have been had I known her before! But even if I *had*, a vast gulf separated us, a gulf that stretched farther than all the worlds adrift in that endless sea above me. Moreover, neither of us could remain in the other's reality for long.

April 9

For several days I have let the previous journey to Iripan's world sink in, mellowing like a fine wine in my consciousness. My body needed to rest both from the unleashing of those fantastic energies and the pressure of existing in that world on the other side of light that was Iripan's home. Filled with delightful thoughts about Iripan, filled with wonder and joy and the budding shoots of love, those days have flown by like clouds across an unblemished sky. Iripan has certainly touched my heart and soul though, of course, a relationship with her is impossible on several counts. Not only can neither of us exist for long as a solid being in the other's reality, but the emergency which has drawn us together overshadows any individual desires. There is little time for the luxury of dreams.

* * *

As I reflect on those brushes with the infinite called ascension, it is now absolutely clear that matter is but compressed light, light but unleashed matter. Just as ice and water are different states of the same thing, so are light and matter just different states of the same essence. Einstein in his brilliance knew this. Light and matter differ only by the vibrational energy each has. But Einstein failed to grasp an equally important understanding: a consciousness present at the time of this great release of energy from matter will become too scattered, too diffuse, to remain aware *unless the will is powerfully focused.* And unless this powerful focus is used to harness the tremendous energies involved, the expansion will force a break in awareness; and the experience will be remembered only as a vague imagining or a dream soon forgotten. Many wondrous beauties have been no doubt been lost or forgotten by souls who could not maintain the necessary focus of the will and passed the experiences off as dreams.

The problem is that sometime in our history as people, the blueprint set to unfold our consciousness, to unravel it in time all the way to God-like illumination in the same way puberty is set to unfold at about age twelve, was greatly damaged. Because of this damage, unknown and unmissed by humanity through our ignorance and apathy, we have settled for an engine that has grown rusty and broken, and largely unknown; one that will not ignite. A tiny cell of the battery still functions, and it is this we draw our energy from; this we call life.

Ascension is the process by which the matter of the body is released to light. It involves releasing all the blockages to the body's energies and the building or restoration of the circuit of energy that ignites the bodily engine once it is in readiness. This readiness involves a purity of purpose, unblocked by fear and anger and guilt. All those who have had the resplendent experience of ascension have gone through the purification process in one of a thousand ways. I never took on the discipline of a spiritual or religious life. Perhaps that is why my initial experiences with the light were so disorienting and fearful; but a purification process *has* taken place in me. If this had not been so, I am certain that my translation could not have occurred.

I've always liked getting down to the nuts and bolts of why things work. I feel a great personal joy in knowing that even in spiritual matters there are understandable working systems that induce or allow knowledge and experience. Great joy comes for me in the knowledge that ascension is not some arcane topic exclusive to a few monastic initiates, not a subject unknown or unknowable to others but is instead as precise in its workings as the workings of a Swiss watch or a finely tuned automobile engine. For the body *is* an engine, an engine for utilizing energy and translating that energy into other forms for its use.

Ascension is no forbidden, arcane trick of magic and the devil; it is an outpouring of unspeakable love. It is not an evil journey through madness brought on by illness or derangement or fanaticism but a process of healing and joy available to all of God's children as part of their divine heritage, a testament of wonder that cries out in ever-resounding tones that though we are *in* the world of time and space we need not be *of* it.

April 12

I went back to Iripan's world last night. Under the stars I again willed the process of ascension to occur. The Great Bear was high in the sky; on the horizon Orion blazed with sword in hand. This time the translation happened more quickly and with still less shock to my system than the time before. It was becoming much easier for the substance of my body to give itself up to light. The sound came like the great hot, rushing wind of a sudden storm in the desert sweeping through me. The frequencies of both sound and light grew as the cataclysmic explosions fired in huge numbers throughout my body. But I was not afraid. I had learned no damage was being done to those atoms and cells that make up my precious body, though certainly these explosions seemed violent beyond belief. I had learned that when my body was reconstituted at the end of the process, it was better than ever before. The chronic stiffness I had in various joints has disappeared completely. Small scars and abrasions had vanished each time I returned.

I once again resisted the powerful temptation to expand into full ascension and choose the path between light pulses that led to Iripan's world. I rested in the quiet strangeness of unlight for a time. I was unceasingly awed by it; it was such an *alien* experience. I then moved through it as through a dream, focusing all my thoughts on Iripan. Then I stepped through its shadowy curtain into the world of form, into Iltar.

Iripan saw me amid the shadows of a large tree outside her stately home. She was sitting on her porch with a slender young man when her eyes leaped up in recognition. The man noticed her sudden start and quickly looked in my direction but saw nothing. After a moment more of conversation the friend left, no doubt at her request. When she and I were alone, I drew near her and held out my hand in greeting. She put her hand to the shadowy one I offered; and I felt a mild, electric coldness that could almost have been dismissed as my imagination had I not felt the same sensation when she last came to my world. I wondered if she, too, felt that pleasant charge. When I asked her about this later, she said that she had but that others probably would not, just as she felt certain others could not see me, would only see shadows where I stood.

Clearly, an affinity of natures was growing between us, a communion of spirits, a love. If only she belonged to my world and not to this mysterious world on the other side of light! For a time we just stared at each other, captivated by the alienness each held for the other, though that alienness had nothing to do with differences in form or manner. That we came from such different realities yet shared such affinity was remarkable and joyful. I felt great strength of self and purpose in her presence, and I know she felt strengthened by me as well.

Iripan led me into a small room and ushered me to a chair which I sat in but could not, of course, feel. The room appeared to be some kind of small chapel with an altar set up on its far side. It was dimly lit by candles, and there was a smell of incense in the air. A small mat was on the simple hardwood floor. It was obvious this room was her private place, her inner sanctum. It had an air of sanctity and reverence about it.

On one side was a small bookcase. I looked at the titles and was thrilled by what I saw. There were books on religions that had never taken root in my world—books of philosophy, music, mathematics, and the spiritual nature of life. I could have spent weeks, months, studying these books. What impressed me most about them was the sense of *power* that came from them. From each one an energy emanated, a faint radiance I could just barely perceive. They were like living things. What new worlds might they open for me if I but had the time to explore them?

I realized with a profound sense of awe that, though our worlds had followed similar paths in their upward spiralling of evolvement, they were different enough to allow a great richness of cross-pollination. Each world could offer endless fascination and knowledge to the other. What a mighty tool it would be for each to have benefit of the knowledge and history of the other, the successes and failures, the accumulated knowledge and beauty, the whole evolution of thought and being that had made each planet what it was. And now a measure of that was possible, for Iripan and I had crossed that incredible gulf separating our two worlds. We were emissaries for our two planets.

But even in this private sanctuary, the shadow of impending disaster hung like a thick black mist. Clearly, we didn't have the luxury of creating an exchange of knowledge between our worlds—not now. Perhaps there would come a brighter day when that would be possible.

Iripan gently drew my attention from the bookcase and began to speak, not in greeting, for her eyes had already done that, but of things that needed to be known, of work that needed to be done. With a heaviness in her voice she said the shadows of destruction were growing longer each day, that each day brought with it further evidence of pressure building up among nations and peoples of her world. She said further that it was *fear* causing this dark blot on Iltar—fear of change, fear of transformation. This fear, she said, was causing panic in the lands. I told her the same was true on Earth, though I had never associated the building pressure between nations and peoples with fear of transformation. I asked if she thought the reason for such fear and mistrust and evil doings in our worlds could be the unconscious knowledge in each person that the blueprint of evolution had been damaged.

Iripan ran her fingers through her coal black hair and looked at me intently with her cat-like dark green eyes before she responded to my question. She then nodded in assent, saying she believed that life moves each being along the evolutionary path by means of a blueprint set to unfold in the way the petals of a rose are set to unfold from the bud at the proper time. If there is damage to the blueprint, however, there must be conflict because the individual cannot achieve its purpose and potential. She said life will then push that being onward toward a matrix of evolution it cannot achieve; and the stress thus created will necessarily engender great fear and resistance, for that person will not be living in rhythm with his or her inner self. She further explained that this stress creates a great division between the outward reality and the inner pattern of growth for that person, which is why we must always be understanding and forgiving toward those who act from fear and limitation rather than from their unlimited, divine nature. And, she added, with a deep humility in her voice, we were no different from others before our transformation.

Iripan smiled, then sighed as does one for whom a great weight has been lifted. She said she and I were rare and blessed for we had been privileged to see beyond the limits imposed by the damaged blueprint which had been passed on for countless generations in our worlds; we had been gifted with experience that had transported us beyond those imposed limits and which had allowed the energy of life to repair or remake that impaired blueprint. Then she said that we must always keep in mind that when much is given, much is expected; with power and knowledge come responsibility and the need for clear judgment. She said she and I must act as stewards of our worlds, of our realities, during the coming crisis. She added that though this crisis was grim, we had the wisdom, the power, and the love to meet its challenge, to do our part. With a measure of concern and doubt in my voice I asked what would happen if the impending crisis were not resolved.

All signs of joy seemed to drain out of Iripan's face at that question. She was clearly concerned. She took a moment to compose herself, then said that perhaps the worlds would end and those not ready for that transition might be forced to start the rise to Godhood from the first rung of the evolutionary ladder—a ladder which might not be available again for billions of years. She said that perhaps the life force would have to try again to accomplish what it failed to do during the current cycle of time; but that even if this were so—even if we could not stop the transit to light coming to both worlds—we must *try*.

I drew tremendous strength from this noble woman. She had a sparkle of joy in her dark eyes—a joy born of her love of life. Here was a woman who had struggled and learned and loved. Here was a woman who had risen above the lot marked out for her in life, who had gone beyond the limits her world had set, had made a definite choice to settle for nothing less in her life than a complete unfoldment of her God-like nature. For her there was no compromise.

I told Iripan that the joy and personal fulfillment experienced in the past couple of years had filled me with such a great desire to give back something to life for the beauty and love it had given me that I would do all I could to help. I told her I had found that experiences, even ones of great beauty and wonder, could not be fully satisfying with that dark shadow—the knowledge that while I sought personal understanding and adventure, others were in need of my help—hanging over me. I could no longer see myself as separate, could no longer maintain the illusion that my life, however exciting and beautiful it was becoming, could be lived without extending myself to others. The recognition of the kinship I shared with all people was a greater beauty than all those I'd experienced during my transformation, for that recognition had given *meaning* to those experiences, had given me a sense of worth so great it could not be shattered. I told her I was ready to take my place in life, to do what I must—what I could.

I was a little surprised at the conviction I heard in my words. Iripan listened intently, a smile gently playing across her lips. Then she said we were most certainly meant to meet though a universe separated us. She said joy raced up and down her spine when she heard my feelings for they we hers also.

April 27

I've been back to Iripan's world four times since my last entry. Each time I saw new wonders, felt new feelings. It's hard to describe what her world is like. Chairs, houses, and trees all *seem* very similar to what I've always known; but there is an incredible *remoteness* to them, as if, though they exist in the space before me, they are actually on the other side of the universe. And I know this is not far from the truth.

Maintaining my awareness of Iripan's world creates a great strain similar to that which would be encountered if a person tried to force tired, out-of-focus eyes to continually focus on an object that was already obscure. But this analogy is a poor one. The sense of alienness I felt in Iltar simply can't be described in earthly terms; and I know Iripan felt something similar when she came to Earth.

I was able, however, to adapt somewhat to the strain and extend my stays in her world to about two hours each time. It was like learning to walk or ski or ride a bicycle. At first it was awkward and very difficult; then it grew easier. But the limits were still there, though I wished with all my heart I could have stayed with her for longer periods of time.

As I have grown more accustomed to being in Iripan's world of Iltar, I have noticed more and more the differences between it and Earth. The people I observed there are taller and slightly thinner and more graceful in their movements and gestures than those of Earth. Iripan herself is very nearly six feet tall, which is my height, and is considered only moderately above average. Science and technology are roughly as advanced there as they are on Earth, though I did find out that colonies have already been established on the moon and Donamor—the planet in Iripan's parallel universe equivalent to Mars. The same political problems exist on Iltar that plague Earth. Officials are elected because of promises they make to specific groups of people. These groups base their votes on what that candidate can do for *them* rather than looking at the broad picture of greatest possible good for all. Once again problems arise because of unwillingness to look beyond personal needs and desires to what best serves the greatest number of people.

From what I gathered in my short visits there, problems of pollution, overcrowding, starvation, and a thousand other ills that plague us here exist there in the same measure; and wars are raging in several parts of that globe. The sense of separation and lack that is the basis of individual problems here is mirrored on Iltar. That debilitating state of mind is projected outward at the societal level *there* just as it is *here*. Clearly, there can be no peace in a nation or a world as a whole when there is no peace in its individuals. This seems so simple; yet a shift in perception must come in order for people to see themselves as worthwhile parts of a whole, not as separate, lonely, autonomous pieces struggling for survival, trying to snatch by force or trickery the little pleasure or love they see available in the world.

Iripan and I both know that we can effect no changes through speech alone. We can only teach by example, by the personal testament of our lives or by parable, as Jesus the Christ so beautifully demonstrated. We are all like lonely, solitary islands adrift in a sea of sorrow—aimlessly floating, endlessly drifting, reacting with fear and hurt to anything that crosses our separate lives. That is why the practice of judging and seeking to correct others never works no matter how noble and righteous we convince ourselves our intent is. *No one* listens when his or her life is being judged even if the truth *is* being spoken. And as the Bible so beautifully illustrates, there is an arrogance in pointing out the splinter in our brother's eye when there is an even larger one in our own.

As I have said, the world of Iripan is similar to our own in most ways; but one way it is strikingly different is in its colors. Not only are there more colors than can be seen on Earth, but they are of a quality and essence far beyond ours. The primary colors are the same for their sun is also yellow. But while in our world colors usually seem flat and passive, on Iltar they appear vibrant and active. There is a richness to them that any poet or artist would glory in seeing. They are not passive *qualities* waiting to be perceived; they are active *entities* collaborating with the perceiver in the act of perception itself.

Another aspect of the Iltaran colors is their depth. They make images appear like holograms, so rich and full are they.

Everything on Iltar *glows* with colors. Our world is one of lifeless shades of gray and black by comparison. Iripan's world is much more beautiful than Earth. Even a common rock shines with a brilliance unmatched here. But beyond the heightened beauty of the colors is the depth of emotion they evoke. They elicit *meaning* from objects rather than simply covering them with shades and pigments. While looking at a chair, for example, I was overcome by a sense of its unique beauty and meaning. It would have appeared as only a commonplace item in my world; it took on a sense of wonder in Iripan's. Yet this magical quality seemed to go as unnoticed or taken for granted by Iltar's inhabitants as the beauty of sunsets and starry skies are by Earth's. On one of my visits to Iltar, Iripan and I stepped outside and saw a delicate pink and violet haze hanging over the city heralding twilight and the coming of night. The colors were so beautiful and light and soft that they seemed hardly to be colors at all; yet there was an aliveness to them I'd never seen in colors before. Such depth of color is rarely or never seen in our world. They were not merely shades of blue or red or green but living colors—entities in themselves that interacted with my consciousness almost like a lover. They were full of life and substance and meaning.

The almost white, delicate blue that signaled the coming of twilight Iripan called 'uln;' the deep, passionate, pinkish-red of twilight going down to night she called 'patto;' the wisp of pale greenish light we saw hanging low in the evening sky she called 'morille.' At one point these colors moved me to tears, at another to excitement, at yet another to awe, wonder, and then stillness.

* * *

After many conversations, our task has unfolded into two parts. First, Iripan and I must gain a better understanding of the damage done to the blueprint of perfection she and I have overcome through our individual efforts. This understanding will give us a better direction for considering how we may best serve our worlds. Second, we must either find a way to delay the transit to light that is coming or accelerate the transformational process on both worlds so that our people are ready for the change. Iripan has chosen to focus her attention on the second task, I on the first. She will come to Earth in a few days, and we will share what we have learned.

The Edge of Wonder

April 30

fine sheen of sun is sparkling in the trees today. Like impish pixies playing amid the leaves, the sun-flickers dance and sport before my eyes. With a purity that reminds me of ice floes adrift in arctic seas, unblemished white cloud bits drift across the deep blue sky.

I spoke with Mindy this morning. I've spent so much time focused on the onrushing wave of cataclysmic changes that I've once again felt unconnected with life in the world, have felt untethered in a sky of uncertainty and hard choices. It was good to touch base with her, to reassure her I was all right, just very busy.

I've spent a great deal of time during the past couple of days searching my mind for some clue to the mystery of humanity's damaged blueprints. When did the damage occur and why? What caused it? Can the damage be corrected? These and other related questions kept buzzing around my mind like annoying mosquitoes—eluding my mental swipes at them, irritating my senses, demanding attention but giving no answers. The questions arising in my mind could only generate answers from the same source. I knew I must therefore go beneath that stormy region of mind and gently sink into a peaceful, calm place of rest—that haven from the storm within the roseate glow of my heart.

May 2

Yesterday I did as I knew I must. I let go of the questions nagging me. I let go of my mind's control and sank into a peace in which I had no need to know, no need to be right or in control. As I was resting in that state beyond the turbulence of the world, my questions began to dissolve, began to melt away like fresh snow under a warm sun. And in their place was a presence—one I knew well. It was to this presence I turned for guidance in this time of questions and far-reaching concern.

At first there was nothing but silence. Then a wave of sound gushed into my spirit. After a few moments I felt slightly giddy. Then I heard what sounded like a snap or an electrical crackle inside my head. I felt myself rising in consciousness as energy began cycling up and down my spine. There was no fear or thunderous noises; I had learned not to resist the alchemy taking place within me. I was aware of my body as an instrument that was ready to serve at my beck and call. No longer would I be taken by surprise by episodes I could neither control nor understand. I was in charge of my body and all its systems. I had taken command of my life.

Pictures began to flash through my mind like the fluttering frames of an old, silent movie. As I watched these frames race before me, I knew that the answer to my question had its origins not a few thousand years in the past, as Iripan and I had thought, but in an immensely ancient time I could only guess at. What I was shown were flashes of history, each glimmer representing a thousand years or more. The flashes came slowly at first, then sped up until they seemed to blur together and I could barely distinguish individual pulses.

I floated free of my physical body in an ether of golden pinpoints of light. As I stared at the tiny points as a whole, they formed themselves into a screen on which the pictures of the past continued to flash but now as images with great clarity. I saw life pass before me like the waters of a receding flood. I saw civilizations rise and fall in the blink of an eye, watched whole races and cultures develop and then die.

Each flicker was an image containing a millennium of the world's history; and though each flash reflected a time earlier than the one before, each revealed itself in a forward direction—but that's not exactly accurate. It was more that with the passing of each frame, I *knew* in a single instant all that had happened during that entire period of time. My mind simply interpreted the events of each flicker as occurring in a forward sequence. How it was I could see and know so much in such a short time I don't know; but I am learning that the whole can be contained in the part, eternity in a single moment. This makes no sense in the physical world; but it is so, nonetheless.

What a joy it was to witness the path humanity had taken to achieve its present level of development and being! But as I watched time scroll back a hundred thousand years, five hundred thousand years, I could see no evidence pointing to the time when the damage to mankind's blueprint of unfoldment had occurred. I began to wonder if Iripan and I had been mistaken. Surely the warping of that basic life program could not have happened *this* far back in the past—when men and women were little more than intelligent animals.

Before an answer came to my query, I was thrown off balance by a feeling of violent upheaval. I felt as though a huge chasm had opened up beneath me, all at once. I had the sensation of plunging into a dark, bottomless abyss. I was completely disoriented by this movement. When I regained my composure, I found that the flickers of time now contained not a thousand years but a *million* years, then *tens of millions* of years each, so that I took in an immense span of history every moment.

As I witnessed tremendous stretches of time parading before me man became an unborn dream. I saw the dinosaurs become extinct when an errant moon, smaller than the current one, plunged into the earth, creating a cycle of cataclysms and covering the planet with a dark ash that, by letting in little sunlight, plunged the planet into an ice age. I watched the dinosaurs' evolution proceed over millions of years as the frames of time ran backward like the rewinding of a film.

The land and seas changed form continuously. Continents rose and sank; creatures evolved and became extinct. All the while I saw no answer to the question that had led me on this wonder-filled journey into the past. Finally, I saw the beginnings of life itself on this planet—billions of years ago from single cells. But amid the primeval violence and upheavals hammering the planet into form still I had no answer, no clue. Earth was but a mass of seething rock and gases, bilious vapors and scalding seas—an unshaped mass of flowing, formless chaos. Then it was gone. Nothing remained of it but a fiery swirl of gases extending in all directions and merging with other cloud masses to form one vast network of blazing vapor that extended for billions of miles—an immense cloud punctuated only by a smudge of bright light at its center, a blotch I knew was the hot young star that would eventually become our sun. Then even that was gone. And I was alone, alone in a darkness older than time.

I felt an enormous pressure building up in my consciousness—a tension like that of a rubber band stretched to its limits and ready to snap. The thought struck me that perhaps I had gone too far, had taxed my consciousness too much. Perhaps the pressure of witnessing so much had vastly overloaded my unfettered soul. I feared I could not get back. But to what? There were no more images to guide me. I could not remember who I was or where I was from, what *time* I was from. I felt completely overwhelmed by what I had just witnessed.

All attempts to remember my purpose and my life and my time were futile. I could evoke nothing—no memories, no feelings—nothing I could hold on to. I feared I had gone so far back in consciousness that I could not reel myself in. There were no more pictures, no more sounds. Emptiness. Nothingness. I was adrift in a void more complete than anything I'd ever known. There was no thought, no desire, no purpose—nothing but a dim awareness of myself, an awareness that was rapidly fading into the void I had stumbled into. There was nothing I could do as consciousness drained from me like life from the eyes of a dying creature.

Suddenly a movement, a stirring. *Something* was in that void with me, a void I thought was nothing but endless darkness and infinite silence. There came a creaking, as of some immense creature moving after just being born or waking after being lost in hibernation for eons. But I was too spent to care. Life was drifting away from me like an untethered balloon.

In the midst of that terrible emptiness, I saw a dim blur, a blur that became a smudge of light and color forming a face. The image filled the emptiness of the void I floated in with color and meaning and song. It was Iripan!

Like a hospital patient lost to death until an electric shock restarts a failed heart, so my spirit sprang into life once more. Iripan was with me, touching me, holding me, healing me. Her presence nourished me, gave me strength, brought my consciousness back from the terrible shock it had sustained in the journey back to the beginning of my universe.

The pressure of that awe inspiring knowledge I had exposed myself to lessened as Iripan and I floated in an endless sea of nothing. I felt like a small child frightened out of his wits by a terrible nightmare made real upon waking by the creaking roof, the shadowy shapes, and the moaning wind, relieved to have his loving mother turn on the light, hold him close, and sing him a soothing lullaby. Iripan was that mother for me in that critical moment—and more, so much more. The energy of her spirit not only kindled mine back to life and restored its movement but joined with my spirit to form a circuit—an enclosed loop of light many times stronger than either of our individual circuits. The energy between us bounced back and forth, gaining force each time, as we made love with essences far beyond the capabilites of bodies. We made love with our *spirits*, and I knew that this divine joining was the union which bodies of flesh blindly and unconsciously seek to emulate.

The energy between Iripan and me was much as it had been with Radia on her tiny world. The loop of light pulsed ever brighter between us; and like a sailboat tacking against a powerful current, we were able to exist in this place before existence began, this place from which time and space would one day spring. We chose to go back still farther, to explore the mystery and wonder of existence still more, to unravel the mystery of its origins and answer the last remaining questions. For we knew that that immense presence that had stirred when I arrived in this dark *nothing* that existed before time and the physical universe, held the key to the unmaking of the separateness embedded in us all.

Iripan and I merged into one mind, one spirit. The two halves of existence were reunited, man and woman, light and unlight, were rejoined into one essence. That essence moved toward the immense being that floated in the void, that perhaps *was* the void. We thought it was God, so terrible was its magnitude and the majesty of its being. But as we drew nearer we heard a voice inside give rise to a gentle "no."

The voice continued to speak to us, to teach us. It told us the true plan for male and female was the joining of individual energy circuits into a dynamo of far greater consciousness and power and love than the sum of its parts, such as Iripan and I had accomplished. It said that, like adjacent fruit trees that bear far more fruit than those that stand in solitude without the chance of being cross-fertilized, the spirits of male and female were intended to join, to bear more 'fruit.' The voice further revealed that when the physical worlds were still but a dream, a split had occurred in the source of all being—a split into the two archetypal energy forms, male and female. This split occurred so that from the male-female union would spring forth meaning and joy and the wonder of diversity. This union would bring forth abundance and would foster creative expression and unlimited freedom.

I held Iripan close to me—closer than life, closer than light—and listened further to the voice in the void. From it I knew that *the fall into matter* was the true fall, not the story of Adam and Eve in the Garden. I knew that Lucifer the Light Bearer *was* that fall from spirit, *was* the universe of time and space and bodies.

The voice said the fall of spirit into matter was the birth of the universe and that this fall was the seed from which all creation had sprung. It was also the origin of the damaged blueprint in all beings. "How could it *not* be so?" the voice asked. "How could the blueprint that unfolded transcendence of time and space and the physical worlds *not* have been damaged from the start?" That which saw itself as separate could not but damage its chances of returning to that which it chose to separate itself from in the first place. It was a double bind. But as I listened to the gentle whispers of the voice, I knew there *was* a way back to the source. Iripan and I had found it within ourselves. There *was* a way of healing the damaged blueprint that led to transcendence. And perhaps it was just this vision beyond the body and beyond the worlds of matter that healed the damage in us. Perhaps with this knowledge of the fall of spirit into matter one could merge back again with God and awaken from the dream of separation as though it had been but a nightmare revealed to be unreal the moment lights were turned on.

That such gentleness could come from such an immense being surprised us; but though the tone the words were spoken in was infinitely gentle and soothing, there was nothing of weakness in it. The voice of this monstrous entity floating with us in the void had a power greater than both of our universes in it, yet it was gentle enough to caress the fibers of a tiny milkweed seed floating in a soft summer breeze. The voice was neither masculine or feminine but had qualities of both. Indeed, the voice seemed the source from which all masculine and feminine qualities had sprung—or would spring. It had the power of flashing lightning and violent eruptions of fire in it; but it also had the beauty of resounding bells and sparkling crystals, the power of a father's will, and the softness of a mother's touch.

Then it came to us that this immense being was none other than the voice that had guided and loved us during our transformations, the presence called by many names, among them the Holy Spirit. But it was *so* large...so powerful...so magnificent! We had had *no sense* of this being's magnitude before! We were swept away by its sheer size. As immense in proportion as I in reality had been to the people on

Radia's world, so was this presence to Iripan and me. For it was no less than *God Himself* in the aspect of Guiding Presence for the worlds of time and space and bodies; it was no less than that divine principle whose purpose was to guide the fallen Lucifer back to the oneness of God.

The images of the story from Norse mythology of Thor's journey to Jotunheim, Land of the Giants, with his companions, flashed through my awareness. The giants made sport of Thor's prowess and asked for a show of his strength. He was to wrestle with one of them; but because of their enormous size, they felt he would be unworthy. It was therefore suggested that he demonstrate his strength by lifting their cat off the ground. For a mere human that would have been an amazing feat because the cat was as large as an elephant, but for mighty Thor it should have been child's play. To his surprise he could barely lift the huge cat from the floor though he tried with all his strength. After a series of defeats, he felt he had failed, so he and his companions thought it best to leave. Each god felt ashamed of the way his homeland, Asgard, home of the gods, had been represented; but before the young gods left, one of the giants said he would tell them what had *really* happened in each case of apparent defeat if they promised never to return. To this the Asgardian companions agreed. The giant then proceeded to say that none of the tests was what it had seemed; that each of the Asgardians had shown great ability and strength in his trials. Loki, for example, had failed to out-eat his opponent; but the truth was that his foe was the embodiment of fire and had beaten Loki only because of fire's ability to consume things instantly.

When the giant spoke of Thor and his trials, there was a trembling in his monstrous voice. For as with Thor's other challenges, things had not been as they seemed. The cat he had tried in vain to lift, for example, was not really a cat but was the last tip of a tail belonging to a serpent so large it encircled the entire *world*; therefore, when Thor managed to lift it—even a small amount off the floor—he was moving the *entire* serpent! Such strength as that required was beyond belief and had the giants shivering in fear that it would turned against them.

The 'cat' from this Norse myth was how I now saw that mighty presence floating in the void. Though it had been such a gentle, soothing voice of instruction within me, it was in truth a monstrous being, immense and powerful beyond all description. It was a large tornado used to provide a gentle breeze to cool a child's face.

I understood as I listened to the voice further that it was this presence that would enable the damaged blueprint for transcendence to be restored and properly unfolded. After the fall of Lucifer into matter, the presence had come—with love and power and direction to aid that fallen Lucifer back to his true home, back to God. But it would not—could not—intrude. It would force neither the awareness of each being's natural state of transcendence nor the overcoming of the damaged blueprint. The choice had to be an *individual* one, a choice made by each being. The damaged blueprint was a carrot dangling in front of our eyes. It was what kept us striving to overcome our limitations so that ultimately we could ascend the physical universe and return to the heart of God.

If the blueprint unfolded in individuals merely as a function of time, the overcoming of the physical body through the process of ascension would not occur because the *consciousness* of those individuals would not have been transformed. They might still be living in the blissful innocence and ignorance of Eden.

At last I understood why we were forced out of Eden. How could we have stayed? To rejoin God as his children we need *maturity* coupled with innocence. We need *will* and *courage* along with simplicity. Our only fall from grace was our collective belief that we could be separate from God. This belief arose in the beginning and gave rise to the worlds. It caused not only the fall of man but the fall of universal awareness into individual consciousness, the fall of spirit into matter as well. That collective fall of spirit into matter was the fall of Lucifer from heaven into hell. I now understood that beneath even the blueprint of unfoldment that should have led present day mankind as a whole to illumination and ascension was another program, one still more deeply embedded—the belief that we could be separate from God. From that deeply imprinted belief had come the damage to the true blueprint of unfoldment. In actuality, however, the blueprint was not damaged at all—just masked and distorted by the deeper program of separation which had given rise to the physical universe in the first place.

The impression came to our awareness as we rested within that immense being that God was the first cause, the essence itself, not the creator of all the worlds. God's entire nature was spirit—beyond time and space and matter, existing in a state of pure being. Because of that nature, God was unaware of that which was other than God;

indeed God was unaware of *how* anything could be other; thus God *saw* nothing other.

God rested in a sea of eternal spirit, which was God. And when, in some incomprehensible way, the insane idea crept into being that there could be separateness from the One, God knew nothing of it. The physical universe—both my 'on' cycle universe and Iripan's 'off' cycle one—was, therefore, but a bubble of froth that one moment appeared on the surface of that vast ocean of being. Lucifer was that insane idea; Lucifer *was* the fall from spirit to matter. Lucifer, was, therefore, the embodiment of the physical universe, the building blocks out of which all the worlds were made. The presence, the Holy Spirit, came into existence the moment the 'bubble' appeared. Its role was to be an intercessor between the two states of existence—spirit and matter. Because the presence had the ability to see both worlds simultaneously and the ability to interact within both, it was not a separate being, but God in the *aspect* of intercessor, of redeemer, just as Lucifer was the aspect of God—of The One—that had for one fleeting moment seen itself as other that God, as separate from God, and fallen into matter.

The voice of the presence was the way back to God as pure spirit, but it had gone unheeded throughout eons. As a result, progression toward a transcendence which it could not force, had proceeded very slowly, too slowly. And now the time for that transcendence to occur was almost up. The thought that it was not just our two worlds that were in danger of losing themselves to nothingness when the transit to light occurred but that it might be *all worlds everywhere* shook Iripan and me like a thunderclap. Because the fall into matter, which was the myth of Lucifer, had brought forth the entire universe and not just a part of it, the *entire universe* might be in danger. The Holy Spirit's purpose had always been the redemption of that fall, but its voice had gone unheeded too long.

Iripan and I rested in the essence of that mighty presence known as the Holy Spirit for what could have been a moment or a billion years. We were beyond time, Iripan and I—beyond time, beyond space—beyond all the worlds. We were blessed beyond measure with a glimpse of that which was before creation.

We felt a pull and had the feeling of being sucked backwards at a fantastic speed. But just before we entered that mighty current we had a glimpse of something grand and wondrous beyond anything we had ever seen—a brief image of something so sublime that nothing we had experienced so far could compare with it. All of my beauties had been but the flickering of candlelight compared with the blinding radiance of the sun I now beheld. It was an image, a vision, of something as far beyond light as light is beyond matter. Though Iripan and I had both come to the realization that matter is but compressed light and light but unfettered matter, we sensed that what we beheld for that glimmer of an instant was that of which light itself was but a sluggish, crystallized form of. As our minds whirled with the thought that there could be something as far beyond light as light is beyond matter, Iripan and I were hurled from the void toward physical creation. At one point Iripan and I split from each other and became separate entities again. In that instant light was born, and from it the stars and worlds began to form. Iripan became a shadow once more, then was gone, back into the spaces between pulses of light, back to her universe, which was but the flip side of mine, gone to retrace the steps her mirror-image universe had taken in its spiraling ascent as Lucifer seeking to climb back to God.

Again I watched the history of the universe unfold before my eyes in rapid-fire flickers. This time, however, it proceeded in a forward manner, so that events unfolded before me like the string-by-string weaving of a tapestry rather than its unravelling. I knew in advance the outcome of each event I witnessed on my world. All the wars, all the rising and falling of kingdoms, all the striving the world had ever known were based on the sense of separation that had given rise to the physical worlds.

Like the rapid forward playing of a film, the history of the world raced before me, frame by frame. The speed at which it flashed was so great that I was as unaware of individual frames passing by as a person watching a movie is unaware of the movement of each frame. As the eons rolled before me I was caught up in the great drama of life, with its joys and sorrows, its loves and fears. Then suddenly, with an electrical crackle, I felt myself gently enter my body. I was back.

I lay in my bed for hours—exhausted mentally, emotionally, and spiritually. I got up after a couple of hours and drank a quart and a half of cool spring water, which seemed to nourish and relax me. I wondered if Iripan had arrived safely in her world. My last thoughts before drifting off into a dreamless sleep were once more of Iripan, my saviour from the carelessness of extending myself too far back in time, Iripan—my mother, my teacher, my lover, my friend. Iripan....

May 5

I slept for three days after that ordeal at time's beginning—at life's beginning—waking only to drink water or take care of bodily needs. I did not dream. No broken images haunted my sleep. I existed in a state that was not waking consciousness, not heightened awareness, and not a dream but something else—something *other*. Like a vast computer system that had been overloaded, I simply shut down and existed in a state of limbo. I thought no thoughts—not even of Iripan. The stress of the experiences had been too much.

When I spoke with Iripan later I learned that she, too, had needed time to recover from that journey. I knew that if she had not come, I would have surely been lost forever; she had risked herself for me. For I had gone beyond time—beyond even the worlds—into an ancient antiquity that had given birth to all the gods, a place sacred beyond words, the holiest of holies. All that had saved us from being destroyed by the sheer force of that raw, primeval glory had been the powerful energy generated by the two of us together. That was all that had kept us from buckling under that soul-crushing force not meant to be looked upon by mortal eyes.

After my recovery, color once again flooded my life and love welled up inside me for the one who had risked all to save me from my blunder. What greater love could there be than to risk one's very *soul* that another might be saved?

I reflected for a while on what I had seen in those brief gleams of life's journey through time and space and bodies. I knew those images were the same for Iripan's parallel universe. The birth of the physical worlds came about because of the thought that separation from God was possible. The author of that mad thought was Lucifer, who fell from the glory of spirit into the lower state of time and space and bodies. The moment Lucifer fell, the Holy Spirit, the gigantic being we had briefly touched in its pure, unfiltered majesty, had come into being that it might lead Lucifer back once more to the glory of God.

Lucifer, then, is all that makes up the physical universes—but without a guiding principle. He is the raw material formed from that one tiny thought of separation from God and is of himself chaos. The Holy Spirit is the guiding principle aware of both God as spirit and Lucifer as light and sound and matter; thus the Holy Spirit is able to bridge the gap between the two states of being and lead the one back to the other. But this bridging can only be done at the *request* of individuals living in the lower state; the decision cannot be forced. The Holy Spirit, for all its magnificence and unfathomable power, can only pose a little question, can only suggest and nudge. Thus, the return to grace of Lucifer cannot occur until that freely willed *choice* is made by each of us to return to God as God's child.

Just as puberty is encoded to unfold in humans at a particular age, the blueprint for transcendence was set to fire in all beings at a certain stage of development; but the blueprint was damaged—or at least masked—by the subconscious decision to be separate, which was Lucifer. Paradoxically, if that decision had not been made, the physical universe would never have existed in the first place. For some reason, however, my blueprint, my encoded signals, *had* fired—as had the blueprint of Iripan and others. These exceptions prove that it *is* possible to overcome the damage or masking effect—to outstrip the programming itself—and reach back all the way to God. The need for all people to overcome their impaired blueprints was what my apprehensions had been prelude to. *This* was what my meeting with Iripan had been for. *This* was what was implicit in the presentiment that Earth would transit to light soon.

But it was not just Earth and Iltar that would undergo that translation to light, two entire *universes* would—mine *and* Iripan's! *All* the physical worlds in the two parallel universes would face the same transformation. The journey back to God had been set in time and thus been given a span of time for its completion. The Holy Spirit had done its mighty and gentle work; but its voice had fallen on unreceptive ears, had gone unheard and unacknowledged for so long, for *too* long. And now Lucifer's time for redemption had come. All those who consciously have chosen God will undergo the mysterious and wondrous process of ascension, as have I and Iripan. But those who have not, those still under the veil of Lucifer—will be left behind.

Lucifer is stirring. His time has come. The voice has been denied for too long, and Lucifer must either return to his source *now* or be cast into another bottomless pit for an eternity.

May 9

Iripan came to me last night as the final vestiges of light quietly faded into the blue, then pitch-black gloss of late evening. A kiln of ivory stars dotted the heavens; a cool breeze brushed my face and hands in a loving caress.

I was sitting on my porch, enjoying the change of color and feeling which the coming of night brings. There was a shimmer in the shadows, then a slightly jerky movement in the darkness. And then Iripan was standing before me, as beautiful and elegant in her shadowy form as ever I had seen her, even when fully embodied and splashed with living colors in her world.

There were no words for several minutes; then we met in an embrace that was not the meeting of flesh with flesh but of spirit with spirit—a mild charge of electrical coldness along with a pins-and-needles effect was all I felt physically. But, oh, the feelings I had! She evoked such a heightened sense of power and beauty and strength in me! Like an engine being started, I felt the circuits of energy igniting within me, revving up. I felt so very *alive* with Iripan.

I shared all that I had felt and understood on that perilous journey back to the beginning, shared all the realizations and insights that had come as a result of it. She had come to the same understanding about the Holy Spirit, its role in the evolution of the physical universe, and of the true nature of Lucifer.

I told Iripan how much I loved her and how unspeakably grateful I was to her for risking herself for me. Nothing needed to be said about it, of course, for true hearts always beat in sympathy with each other; but it felt good to say it anyway. I asked how she had known I was in trouble and how she had been able to come to me in that far-flung place beyond time and the worlds. She said we had grown so close in spirit that though we were physically very far apart, her heart felt what mine felt, her mind knew what mine knew. And she said, with joy in her eyes, that love is beyond time and space—even beyond all the worlds. She said that the love we share was born eons ago, before our worlds—our universes—were born, and that we were now merely awakening to a love that has existed since the beginning of life. She said it was this love that enabled her to know of my plight; and this love combined with her will that empowered her to find me in that distant void.

Tears seemed to fill Iripan's shadowy eyes. She said if I had been lost, she would have been lost also; and our worlds have been lost along with us, for we two are the key to saving them. We two bear the burden of preparing the way for the transition that must come soon.

Before my soul reached out to Iripan's, she had given all her thoughts to the plight of our two worlds and the question of whether or not it was possible to delay or in some way prevent the transformation to light from occurring. While reflecting on that predicament, she had gazed out her window and seen a number of people walking along the narrow road that winds its way along the edge of her property. She said there was nothing special in this; they were just ordinary people enjoying an evening stroll. But then came a moment when she had almost shrieked in terror for as she watched, their forms became indistinct, amorphous, luminous blobs. She said not only were the people thus affected but the trees and houses and the distant hills as well—all became lit by a dull, yellowish light; all became formless smudges, then vanished. For a tiny fraction of a second there was nothing—no form, no life—just the lingering shadow of that formless, dingy, yellow light that had nothing of beauty to it. She said it was horrible. Then everything was back exactly as it had been—trees, people, hills—all back, all restored. It was as if nothing had happened; the people had not even missed a single stride. But something *had* happened; of this she was certain. She said that for the briefest of moments her world had ceased to exist, had come unglued, had literally winked out of existence, and that all that was left was the dull, yellow light—a light that looked wrong, distorted, a grotesque caricature of true light, a distortion of light akin to what a grossly malformed child would be to a healthy normal one. Iripan then said she *knew* she had just witnessed a tiny tremor heralding the monstrous quake to come, knew she had just seen a small preview of the final impending change. She said she knew her world was clearly unready for that catastrophe.

Iripan told me that after pondering for a few minutes the frightening change she had just witnessed, she willed, as she had done many times, the true translation into light to occur within herself. She then saw the true beauty of light—pure, holy light—and felt the joy and wonder I also had felt. She said this pure light stood out in stark contrast to the lifeless, barren glow that had for a moment swept over her world. It was the light of truth and beauty and harmony, the divine birthright of all beings, to be claimed when the holy blueprint is fulfilled, the damage overcome. She further remarked that she knew in those moments of pure rapture and pure love that our worlds are beginning to wink out—to become unglued—because they are losing *love*. Though my dismay at the last statement was obvious, she continued, saying that love is the glue binding all things together and that this glue has grown weak and diluted over the eons. She said I should know this myself given, what I've observed recently on Earth. What usually passes for love, she said, in most cases is but a watered down mockery of true love. She further stated that true love is so rarely seen that people have few examples from which to learn.

Iripan recalled that I had once spoken to her of Jesus, who came to Earth to show that it was possible to overcome the beliefs of the world and rise to God through love of others. She said that on Iltar, the God-woman Shebar brought the same message and that, as it was with Jesus, her focus was on love—love of oneself, love of others *as* oneself, and love of God. She reminded me that love is the vital energy that holds form together and keeps it from sinking back into the chaos of Lucifer. She said that the Holy Spirit, which in her world is known simply as the Breath, is that guiding principle; but it cannot maintain its integrity if its voice is ignored. She said that the voice cannot be heard through fear and that each being must overcome fear on his or her own, though that mighty presence will surely come at the slightest request.

Iripan told me that the guiding principle of our worlds has grown weak because people have left the Holy Spirit's call unheeded. She did say, however, that it was inaccurate to say that love has grown weak; it has merely been obscured in the way the light of the sun is obscured by dark clouds. She said *fear* is that dark cloud; and people from both our worlds have bowed down to it, have made graven images to it, have worshipped at its altar. She said love has become like a myth or a long-forgotten dream; and because love has become obscured, it has become a distorted, weakened force in our lives. She explained that just as a weakened strain of a virus is used to protect the body again a powerful strain that could cause great illness or death, we have accepted love in a weakened, sluggish version, thereby establishing a barrier against true love. We have, in a sense, become inoculated against the 'disease' of love.

Iripan looked sad as she told me it may be too late for our worlds. She explained that in a state of joy and rapture she had seen the truth, that the transit to light is already beginning, that it can be neither halted nor delayed. All we can do is hope that with our combined strength and knowledge, we will accelerate the growth of others before that mighty change occurs so that it will be seen as a joyous and rightful end to life's journey, not a bleak defeat.

Iripan continued and I listened intently as she told me that it was not just our two worlds that were to go through the transit to light but both physical *universes*—hers *and* mine—since they were cut from the same cloth and born of the same reason—the fall of Lucifer. The magnitude of the problem we faced, therefore was magnified *many*, many times. She thought I must know this, and must also know that our work will, therefore be more difficult as well as more important, and more glorious. Our work was a glorious opportunity to serve God, and give back to God in full measure our joy and our love for the sublime gifts of grace and beauty the two of us have been given.

I asked Iripan what we must do first to prepare for the cataclysmic change to come. She said we must find others like ourselves who are ready or nearly ready for the change, teach them what we know, then send them out into our respective worlds as teachers. Next we must reach out to beings from other stars, other systems, that either already know what we have to teach or are ready to hear our message. We must contact and teach all beings everywhere who are willing to listen; throughout our two universes we must send a ripple that spreads and grows like wildfire as others begin to reach beyond their damaged blueprints.

After this long speech Iripan left, faded back to Iltar. She left me to ponder her words and her love, left me to begin the task of reaching those on Earth with the ability and willingness to heed what I had to say. She would begin the same task on Iltar.

We both could have left—left our bodies, our worlds, and ascended into the formless love of God, the pure light of ascension. We were ready for the change to come. We could have spent eternity engaged in a wondrous voyage of discovery, moving from insight to insight, wonder to wonder, beauty to beauty, joy to joy—forever.

But with that ability to transcend the body and the world had come the knowledge that our needs and interests are not separate from those of the people around us. Though we have grown far away from most others in our consciousness, have far outstripped the evolutionary track the masses move along, we still feel a great kinship with them. It is clear that though we have unfolded ourselves far beyond most others, we really have done nothing out of the ordinary. We have only claimed our divine birthright as others are free to do at any time. In fact, that's all that time is *for*. With true humility has come the realization that at any moment, anyone can become as Iripan and I have become. The distance separating our consciousness from that of others is but another illusion for there are no levels to reality. All is One. With that understanding comes also the responsibility to help others attain the heightened states of freedom and awareness we have been blessed to discover within ourselves. The paradox is that the beauties that came to me gave me a wonderful sense of personal adventure and meaning and served ultimately to lead me away from mere personal experience into a sense of unity with others. The separate part of myself has been gradually led back to an awareness of its place in the whole. Now I can no longer experience those beauties as before; I have no more time for the luxury of personal adventures, no matter how beautiful and transcendent they might be. That is why I couldn't stay with Radia on her tiny, peaceful world, why I cannot explore all the worlds with Iripan.

My beauties were the catalyst, the driving force, that prepared me for my entry into union and wholeness. I now see that wholeness is not a loss of self or individuality, as it first appeared; it only seems so to the limited, finite ego-self, the part that fears letting itself go down to dust. I now know that when we release ourselves from the bondage of the ego-self we become like a Phoenix emerging from the flames into a second, grander birth. From those purifying flames a true self can be born—one that is uniquely itself yet part of all, the separate cell reuniting itself in the body of God. From this glorious vantage point questions of loss of self or individuality dissolve into the formless love of God.

My destiny called to me and led me not away from the masses of humanity I had grown apart from but *toward* them into their hearts. Perhaps my greatest lesson through all my adventures has been that in the heart of humanity lies the heart of love. Now my path seems laid out before me; my destiny is set. No respect, no appreciation, and no support will be needed from those I come in contact with. My strength comes not from a source outside myself; my source of gratitude lies within me as that magnificent presence. I will give of myself fully, proclaiming in heart-struck tones my joy in existence, my love of life, my supreme pleasure in giving back to life some measure of what it has given to me.

Beyond the Margin

May 12

The world is losing love. Over the ages it has been steadily leaking out of our consciousness like air from a poorly tied balloon so slowly that people have not noticed the change. Caught up in our separate lives with its attendant focus on personal survival, we too often view love as a luxury we have little or no time to cultivate. I understand this. I remember the William that let the fluid play of colors he knew as a child fade into the often harsh, crystalline edges of adulthood—until that day of unspeakable grace when his feet were placed on the path of wonder.

When I think of how I was during that time I feel sad yet compassionate. My heart opens to that other part of me—that part that cried out for love in a thousand different ways, that part that sought love in material comforts, in sex, in status, in security, and in creativity.

The heart of the world is bleeding, crying out for love and redemption; it is a wounded organ, hardened, bereft of feeling and movement and hope. But now there *is* hope. The course of humanity *can* be changed. The attainment of the goal lies not in continuing on the present course or steering onto another course but in shifting individual consciousness *above* the course—in going above *all* courses, beyond the damaged blueprint, beyond the evolutionary track humanity is hurtling down like a runaway train. That track will end soon, forcing that train to either crash and go down to dust or to rise with silvery wings above the track—above the *need* for tracks—into that unfathomably glorious destiny in God we are being called to.

I was overcome yesterday with thoughts of love that is waning, like a parched flower dying in the desert, and the compassion that is welling up strong within me for myself, for Iripan, for all humanity, all life. Tears grew thick in my eyes and as the sadness and sorrow of compassion mixed with the stalwart love in my heart, I began to feel a pain, a physical pain not very different from the pain of a heart attack. It *was* a heart attack, but one of a different kind. It was an attack of love, a reminder of the overwhelmingly personal love I've begun to feel for all my brothers and sisters everywhere. I felt the delicate tissues of my heart ripping, but I would not—could not—stop the process, though I felt my heart might burst. The ripping and tearing went unabated as my heart continued to expand, struggling against its physical boundaries.

The love I felt could no longer be contained in the small space it occupied. The walls of my heart burst like the walls of a dam no longer able to withstand the pressure of the water pushing against it. I felt the blood flowing within my chest, then spreading throughout my entire body until I was nothing more than one vast, bleeding heart; and that's all I wanted to be in that moment—one compassionate heart, large enough to hold the love for others that was growing inside me.

The painful expansion continued until all I could see was a living, bleeding heart rolling outward, covering all it touched. On and on my heart rolled, across mountains and plains, through deserts and verdant valleys. Seas grew red with my heart's blood and mountains were covered with throbbing, blood-stained tissues until the entire *world* was enfolded in my heart's bleeding embrace. I wished for nothing more in that moment than to offer myself to this dying, wounded world—to give of myself, my love, and my life—to give, to give, to give—to rise with eagle wings beating praise to God through compassion and love for God's creation.

Then the moment was gone, and I was as I had been—a man with a healthy heart in a healthy body. That painful tearing and expanding had happened not to my physical heart but to that spiritual orb corresponding to it, that pulsing globe of energy that entwined my heart and vibrated with the energy of love.

August 12

I had no idea how to begin the teachings, so I relied on that mighty, interior presence to guide me. A few nights after I wrote my last entry—after much thought and inward meditation—I sent my mind and heart throughout the world to touch those sensitive enough to hear my call. It is clear that as time grows shorter the need for teachers to serve as divine midwives for the birth that is to come becomes correspondingly greater.

For a few days I heard nothing and wondered if my call had been improperly sent or had been left unheeded. Then I began to receive telephone calls and letters from people I had never heard of, from people who felt guided to call for a reason they could not name, felt guided to dial a certain sequence of numbers on the telephone. I heard from others through the mail, through the newspapers, through my mind as mental impressions. Most were uncertain why they were contacting me; others knew.

I began speaking at public lectures at few weeks ago; from these talks private gatherings were formed, at which I was requested to speak. The message was—and is—always the same: The love within us is weak; we are blocked by fear in a thousand guises. By removing the blocks to the love which is our natural heritage, we can go beyond the conditioning of the world and become more than mere flies stuck to fly-paper. We can soar to unknown heights, can outstrip the entire evolutionary track, and reach beyond time, beyond space, beyond the worlds. The way to remove those blocks and to strengthen the love already within us is to forgive, forgive, forgive.

The message is given almost nightly. There is no fee. The meetings are offered on a love offering basis; all gifts are graciously received. What is offered is always enough to meet our needs. I ask only that those who hear and understand tell others.

The specifics of what I say is always geared toward the audience I am addressing. Sometimes I speak of the damaged evolutionary blueprint; sometimes not. In more advanced—more hungry—gatherings I speak of the power of sexual energy and of the energy circuits that, when unencumbered, allow the creation and maintenance of a spiritual engine powerful beyond their wildest dreams; and I give the members of such audiences the basic mechanics for creating this engine so that it becomes more than just interesting theory and can be applied as practical experience.

I permit those who take part in accelerating the unfolding process to teach either in the manner I teach or in one of a thousand other ways. They may teach another method of enlightenment, another technique for unfoldment. They are low profile, and others may not know they are teaching under my direction.

technique for unfoldment. They are low profile, and others may not know they are teaching under my direction.

As others begin to experience the first signs of the ascension process, I give them a complete understanding of why it is so important that they unfold quickly and assist others in doing likewise. I base the thrust of my teaching techniques on the theory of morphogenic fields postulated by the eminent biologist Rupert Sheldrake. The idea borrowed from this theory is that each person on Earth need not understand the process of ascension for it to be attained by all. Just as only a small percentage of the ingredients of a mixture enable the entire solution to gel, if a relatively small percentage of people learn what Iripan and I have, they will enable a global awakening to the ascension process.

So this is our plan—to enable enough people to learn the techniques for unfolding themselves to the level of ascension so that the knowledge will be spread to all, or almost all, as a global, human understanding, as a global opportunity. Just as the discovery and harnessing of fire brought a leap of consciousness and evolution and possibility to mankind, so too will the discovery and harnessing of the energies of ascension bring an equally great leap into the divine. And, as Teilhard de Chardin said, "...for the second time in the history of the world man will have discovered fire." This time, however, it will be the spiritual fire of transmutation.

Iripan is doing the same work in her world. She and I communicate almost daily with each other. We no longer need to traverse that awful distance between our worlds to be together. We are so much a part of each other, that even that immense gulf cannot separate us. About once a week, however, one of us does make that journey between the worlds; it is always better to be present in body rather than just mind.

Iripan, too, is teaching others and encouraging them to go out into the world and teach many more. At first she met with resistance, just as I did. But the resistance was just the fear of those who felt their way of life was being threatened. It *is* being threatened but in a way that it must. The resistance we each felt is only the backwash of a humanity afraid to go beyond itself and become divine. This backlash is the rising wave of those who wish to go backward rather than forward, of those who wish to cling fearfully to the side of a mountain rather than scale its heights, of those who wish things to be the same rather than risk moving onward to some glorious destiny.

not with fire and brimstone but with its translation into beauty—into light. It will be a new Eden, a new mode of being. Those ready for that transition will consciously become the children of God; those not ready will be left behind.

November 29

The plan is going well, both on Earth and on Iltar. Several thousand people have already answered the call. Many, of course, are only curious or are looking for something, *anything*, to help make their lives easier; they will not be of much help at present. But the majority are sincere truth seekers drawn to the teachings because of the chord of truth and beauty they strike within their hearts and souls. Many are leaving their old traditions to follow the call; others are enhancing their old ways with the new ones.

I have personally instructed several hundred seekers regarding the actual techniques for ascension of the physical body. I have had to be rather secretive because this knowledge requires a thirst, a hunger, a burning in one's heart for truth, for God. Just as it would not be wise to teach a child how to drive a car, so, too, it would be unwise to teach the techniques Iripan and I have learned through our own transformative experiences to those without the proper desire and maturity.

I hope this record of my transformative experiences will be useful. I hope that through this personal chronicle I have shown that an unfoldment such as mine is one to be cherished and at the same time respected and approached with the utmost sincerity. My experiences almost killed me more than once; if anyone reading this journal is seeking to also become God's child, know that you may die in the desert of transformation. But a great effort is now in progress to give direction and help so that many of the pitfalls and dead end paths can be avoided. The voyage of transfiguration is one that is taken alone; no one can do it for you. One need not undertake the journey *alone*, however. Many others are making the same voyage; and the number doing so is beginning to ignite like a forest fire spreading from a single spark. From these others, strength and courage can be drawn as each takes his or her part in the final salvation of the world.

December 3

The winking out effect has happened twice since I began the teachings. The dull, yellowish light is still present. I'm hopeful that when the final quake that signals the translation of the world to light occurs, Earth and all its people will be ready; and the light's color will be purest white or silver.

December 8

The teachings are consuming most of my time. I have little time left for anything else, even the writing of this journal. In the beginning the journal was to be a record of the process I was undergoing. It was mainly for me, for my sanity. Then it became a guide for others who might be having similar kinds of experiences. It was kept as evidence for them that they are not crazy but are instead going through a transformative process that has been happening to individuals throughout the entire history of mankind. Now my time is spent *living* those experiences, those beauties. They have become my natural state; consequently, less time has been available for recording the experiences.

Many of those rare individuals who underwent a metamorphosis similar to mine tried to tell others of their experiences and to lead them to the same kind of transformation they had undergone. Unfortunately, those harbingers of the glorious destiny of our race were either martyred or set on tall pedestals and silenced by deaf ears. When those rare and beautiful beacons of our race knocked holes in the walls of human possibility, rather than step through those holes, mankind quickly covered them over with stained glass.

In light of its importance with regard to the teachings and the changes I hope will come from them, this journal's purpose has become global in scope. I no longer need to keep this chronicle for my own sanity for I have entered into a chamber of being and knowing beyond the need for such reassurances. It's purpose now is to *awaken* as many people as possible, as *quickly* as possible. Time is a precious commodity now. I must use it wisely and for the only purpose for which it was truly meant—to bring others to a full awareness of who they truly are. That awareness is not a sterile, cerebral understanding of identity—not some parroted, lifeless mumblings on arrogant lips but the full and deeply known experience of the divine.

December 16

Nostalgic images from the past are flooding my mind—the final clinging effort by my human self for a life that cannot be. Though time is in short supply, I feel I must indulge that human part of me once more, must fully embrace the roots of my life on Earth by giving rein to such feelings one last time...one last time.

I smile as I remember driving through an affluent part of town many years ago and seeing elaborately designed houses with their well-manicured lawns and flower beds and two well-maintained new cars in the garage. The smell of spring was in the air along with the sounds of happy, rosy-cheeked children playing in the yard and the playful bark of a dog in the background. I loved the feelings that experience evoked and thought I'd like nothing better than to have a life like that—all apple blossoms and rosy cheeks, a sweet life. But something inside me told me even then that that life was not for me, that my life lay in another direction, one that would take me away from such an idyllic existence. During that time I wrote a poem I have not thought of until this day—a tiny cry for life to be other than it was to be for me, a thin smile for the joy which that life might become. I found it this morning, and it was this:

> When,
> on crested wings I fly
> toward heights you cannot know,
> think no sad thoughts for me.
> My vision is yours no longer.
> Weep not for me in fear
> I'll be lost
> or struck down
> by some wild current
> sweeping through the night.
> My dreams have no room
> for safety or calm.
> The plains and valleys
> hold peace and comfort;
> yet, oh, my friend
> I cannot stay.
> For such a life
> is not, and never can be,
> my way.
> Should I be swept

against mountainous crags
while seeking the Height,
or clipped of wing
by some dark force
I'll go on still.
On hands and knees
I'll climb
if that I must to reach the sky.
Icy winds
howling through
corridors of my mind
cannot freeze my heart
or chill my spirit.
And though sunny skies
and rosy cheeks
fill my thoughts
and press me,
as if to steal me
safely away
I'll smile...
and think of you...
and how life might have been.
And on I'll go,
though bones may splinter
and skin peel away
from fingers
grasping for light.
For my way lies
through silver skyways;
and on crested wings
I fly, my friend—
to Him Who gave me life,
and taught me how to live.

    The poem was written on a whim, an expression of both sadness and fierce pride. Now with fondness—and without pain—I see how that path has unfolded for me, has led me toward a greater destiny than ever I could have imagined. With the understanding that has led all the way to my ability to ascend, I *have* flown on crested wings beyond all separateness, beyond all fear and all sorrow, back to the source of my life in God *as* God. Now I have the privilege to serve the source of my life, to give back something in gratitude for my joy in existence.

Iripan and I cannot afford the luxury of that house with the well-trimmed yard and all it implies. She and I can't have that kind of life, just as I could not have that life with Radia. Perhaps Iripan and I can be together some day in that new Eden that is to come, some day when our work is done. Perhaps some day.

December 19

A short time ago, in an effort to expand the range of the teachings, Iripan and I sent forth the message of urgency like a laser beam in all directions into the far reaches of our respective universes. Last week the answers began to come.

From the Pleiades came the first responses to my psychic sendings. In my living room one afternoon a shimmer in the air appeared, then a dull glow like blue flame that congealed into the forms of several beings. They were blue-skinned with long, pendulous bodies, approximately eight feet in height. Their faces were bright and ancient, with dark black eyes set deep in rounded sockets. Their thin, one-piece garments were white splashed with blotches of purple. The garments flowed like gossamer webbing in the gentle breeze and seemed to change colors and hues to reflect the wearer's ever-changing emotional state. The most beautiful iridescent and opalescent colors I had ever seen were present in these clothes. I learned that these gentle people had elevated their emotional nature to a very high degree; everything for them was based on feelings. They had developed a great science and had occasionally traveled to other worlds in faster-than-light crafts. It had all been in the name of feelings. They had no interest in conquest of other peoples, other worlds. They felt no need to colonize or categorize other places in the universe. They left each world to its own making, allowing their presence to be known only in cases wherein their intervention might help that world avoid great suffering. Their explorations were all in the name of *feelings*; science and the other mind-disciplines were far in the background and were only considered useful to the extent to which they served the grand emotional nature. Their musical sense, I discovered, was also very highly evolved and closely linked with their emotional nature. Only music that was in harmony with their emotional, spiritual, and physical natures was permitted on their world. Anything that went against the natural rhythms of the heart or other organs was unthinkable.

On the Pleiadeans' world, many had learned to ascend, so little was the resistance their bodies and minds offered to the process. Yet many had become fearful when the imminent translation of their world—and all others—became known to them a few years ago. So great was their feeling nature that a lofty balance had to be maintained. If feeling was directed toward a negative thought or fear, it became many times more powerful than the same thought in our world would be.

These angelic beings had come to help us for clearly Earth had more work ahead of it than did their home world, Radistar. They had come to seek my help as well because the level of fear on their world had become great and they had little experience dealing with fear. I knew that all worlds must become linked in a cosmic network so that each could assist the others along the way. Each could offer wisdom and strength when possible; each could ask for help in areas of weakness or ignorance. Alone, a world might not be prepared for the transition to light; united with other worlds the great work would be accomplished in time—all beings would rise to the level of awareness in mind and heart and body needed for the great leap in evolution that was to come.

The joy I felt with the gentle Pleiadeans was overwhelming. I felt at home, as though I were with my true family at last. To my amazement, they explained that my feeling was not far from the truth. Many, many years ago, they said, I had lived on their planet, been born to their people. From an early age I, along with other promising children, had been trained for a great mission to the stars. My task had been to give up my Pleiadean body and enter the womb of a woman on Earth so that I might learn from my experience on Earth what I could not learn on Radistar. I would learn and love, unfolding myself and my feeling nature to such a high degree that those around me would learn to unfold theirs more and more.

I was sent to teach through *feelings* more than words to help bridge the gap between the two worlds. Earth was clearly crusted over with the hardened energy of mind and heading for destruction because of the reckless unleashing of powerful forces. I and many, many others had been sent to help soften and balance that hardened, single-minded energy so that a return to the simpler, more meaningful feeling nature might be effected. In this way the maturity that would allow humankind to properly handle the great and terrible energies it was now able to unleash might be gained.

But something had gone wrong in my case, and I had not made the adjustment properly. The program embedded in my nature—the one that gave me full remembrance of my home world identity and purpose in a time-release fashion—had been damaged, had not fired at the proper time. All that was left to me from my home planet was a great sense of loneliness, homesickness, and a highly developed feeling nature. By feeling nature I mean not merely the capacity to feel things deeply, but the ability to enter into true communion with another person, to function virtually as an empath, to feel things so deeply—so profoundly—that if another feels pain, I feel pain also. If someone is angry with me, I feel a sword plunging into my heart. If another truly loves me, I feel a joy so great the gentle caress of angel wings is felt by all around.

I would have been but one of the many whose program had not properly fired had not a greater program activated within me during that period of unspeakable grace this journal has recorded. I felt full with the joyous reunion of my true family. I now understood all the problems I had growing up—trying to fit in with others when the fitting in was against my nature, when I did not understand the motivations others were driven by. I breathed in several joyous breaths and released the lingering vestiges of the loneliness I had known. Loneliness was totally behind me now, and there was much work to be done.

I taught the Pleiadeans all I knew. In exchange I learned what they knew. It was a pleasure to share with them what I had learned. There were no words used or needed. I simply *thought* and *felt* an experience, idea, or technique and they immediately integrated it into their beings. Much of what I had to share they knew already, but many of the techniques for accelerating the process of ascension were new to them and filled gaps in their own knowledge. Human bodies are very different from theirs in many ways. Their bodies would not have been able to withstand the atmosphere and gravity of Earth had they not come in a more subtle form; that they could travel without their physical bodies demonstrated an already high degree of mastery. The Pleiadeans left with joy in their large, round eyes and with the promise that they would seed the knowledge of ascension in all the worlds they were in contact with; those beings in turn would seed it farther and farther into our universe until all beings everywhere were aware of the changes coming and of how to prepare for them.

* * *

Two nights after the Pleiadean left I received a host of other beings from the stars. These beings came from much nearer than the Pleiades, from one of the planets encircling the double star Arcturus, only a few light years distant from Earth. They came in a silent, translucent craft that looked much like a soap bubble.

The Arcturans were not gentle people. They were wild, harsh and rough, with immensely powerful orange bodies equipped with four rough-hewn arms. Their craggy faces had non-smiling mouths and tiny slits forming triune eyes. I learned that despite their frightful appearance they were completely consistent in thought and deed; their sense of duty and honor was unswerving. An Arcturan would die without hesitation rather than tell the smallest lie.

This race of fearsome beings had risen to superiority through intelligence and a war like nature that made the most militant human traits seem the height of pacifism or cowardice by comparison. Arcturan wars were more brutal and bloody by far than any waged on Earth, and there had been many. Their need to be right far exceeded that of humans, and a simple disagreement was often grounds for a bloody fight to the death. Because the women were built as powerfully as the men and had the same need to be right, they participated equally in the warring nature of life.

Because of their sense of honor and duty, the Arcturans employed no weapons that killed at a distance or that did not require their own strength of arm and mind. They firmly believed in fighting their enemies eye to eye; all other forms of war or combat were unthinkable. They had therefore used nuclear energy only for constructive purposes and explosives only for celebrations. The devastation that had occurred on their world of Golfar had been so gruesome that life there was being threatened as surely as life on Earth was being threatened by nuclear weapons.

The threat of nuclear warfare brings a smile to my face now, for compared to the sheer power that will soon be unleashed when the world rises from matter to light—the sheer magnitude of violence that translation will entail—nuclear weapons are but the front-leg kick of a grasshopper.

Many of the Arcturans had attained an understanding of the energies contained within their own bodies and of the blueprint of evolution and unfoldment present in all beings. But they knew nothing of the damage to the blueprint or the method of its repair, and that was why they had come. They had come to learn so that they could now be a part of a greater duty, could now wage a different kind of war. I welcomed their sincerity and began teaching them what I knew.

December 29
After the experiences with the two groups of space beings, I began to extend my mind more and more out into the universe. I no longer need to sleep. I rest to replenish my energies, but I no longer need the break in awareness sleep brings. Instead I shift my mind to a more subtle level of consciousness and continue the work. The message I send out is a beacon of light radiating in all directions, transmitting that all the worlds will soon be transiting from matter to light and that unless all beings everywhere are prepared for that great holocaust, the new Eden being ushered in will pass them by.

The beacon is a plea to awaken and a plea for help. In it I put my heart and my soul so that those receptive to the message will feel my sincerity and realize the severity of the crisis looming in everyone's sky. Whenever I feel the subtle brush of energy that signals the response of some conscious entity in that vast expanse, I send forth my awareness and my subtle body to that point.

A group of intelligent arachnids living on the planet Mordeb, a world encircling a star in a galaxy a billion light years from Earth recently answered my call and I sent myself to them. Up until this time I had only been in contact with humanoid life, and though alien, that life had always been understandable to me; but this group of arachnids looked like monstrous, hairy tarantulas three feet in height.

After a moment of tentativeness born of my acquired fear and loathing for what my ego-mind considered a grotesque and frightening appearance, I used my feeling nature to merge with them, to understand the incredible beauty and utter strangeness of their lives and their culture. Merging with them was a joy. Smiling, I remembered how great my fear of spiders was when I was a child; and now I was in the midst of half a dozen tarantulas, each a hundred times larger than its earthly counterparts! But the distorted sense of fear I had known as a child for the different and the unknown no longer touched me. After that initial twinge, I felt no fear or repulsion toward these creatures. I had learned to allow only love in my heart. The Mordebians proved more gentle and compassionate than any other beings I had known, except perhaps Radia's people. I imparted the message to them as best I could. I felt such a kinship with them, such love for them, that I no longer saw them as alien and frightening creatures but as brothers and sisters with interests and needs not separate from my own. I bade them good-bye and left that distant world with a smile on my face and love in my heart.

Last night I received an answer from a group of small, tan colored humanoids from a small planet circling Sirius. They told me they had long been observing our world with their advanced technology and had visited Earth many times in the distant past in an effort to assist mankind on its journey toward maturity. Their minds were given primarily to mental and scientific workings; they had only a rudimentary religious nature, though some had formed societies of their own for the purpose of gaining meaning from all the technological advancement. Those I was now in contact with belonged to just such a group. The concept of ascension was fairly new to them, but they believed the message I sent and were willing to learn—were willing to let the seed they had nurtured for many thousands of years become the gardeners of their own growth.

January 17

Since my last entry I have been in contact with several dozen groups of beings throughout the universe—some humanoid, some not even remotely human. In all of them is a spark of life and of God that lets me see them as brothers and sisters. Before, I was concerned with the fate of humanity and its reunion with the source of its being. That goal has not changed; but now I see humanity not just in the narrow, limited way I did before but in a much higher spectrum of vision. I see humanity as all beings everywhere, throughout both universes.

In nightly sojourns I visited worlds much larger and smaller than mine, saw wonders that cannot be told in earthly words. I saw planets with green atmospheres and immense silver craters pock-marking the smooth, grayish landscape. I saw ringed worlds and worlds a thousand times larger than our own. I saw cold and barren asteroids where even the *air* was frozen—but even *there* intelligent life existed, though it was in the form of crude-looking, crystalline daggers.

I met with beings of all shapes and types and was constantly amazed at the sport and play of life and the joy of diversity it constantly interacted with. All these life forms had the spark of God within them; each was hallowed and holy in itself. The forms life took on these distant worlds, which were so different from our own, was unimportant. The vehicle of expression was inconsequential, just as the shape and size of a goblet holding wine is unimportant; all that has meaning is the *content* of the glass. And these glasses always held but one thing—God. In the shining, black, insect eyes of a race from the Denebian system I saw God; in the gossamer wings of the sublimely beautiful elven race from a double star system in Andromeda I saw the savior—and on and on with a hundred other species.

It was the same for Iripan in her parallel universe. Her thoughts, her experiences, her joy and awe and wonder at the beauty of life mirrored my own. Though we were always separate, we were never apart in spirit. We were two hearts beating as one. We nourished each other, acknowledged each other, assisted each other. Had there not been such a pressing need to give ourselves to the great work that was before us, we might have roamed all the worlds together...forever. But as great as our love for each other was, we had a still greater, still higher love for God and the magnificent life that expressed itself *through* us, *as* us, and through a million million different forms and faces.

January 24

My days are filled with phone calls and speaking engagements. Books of the teachings will be written soon by those with the gift of words. Several of my first students have appeared on television and radio programs. The message is being seeded in many ways and clothed in many robes. I am hopeful enough people will heed the call in time and take the necessary steps toward unfoldment.

I look at the process of unfoldment that has occurred in me during the past three years and am amazed that I was able to learn and grow as well as I did. Others with an open heart and mind will learn and unfold far more quickly than I. Just as a person is able to walk with bare feet over a bed of coals hot enough to melt aluminum upon seeing another do so without injury, so will others learn more quickly and easily because of the examples I, Iripan, and others are providing. I and the other transformed individuals are paving the way, are showing that it *is* possible to transcend the limitations of the world and of the body, that this transcendence is not just a dream but a living reality.

Iripan has three students on Iltar already able to translate their physical bodies to light; I have two. Already having that many students able to ascend sounds phenomenal, and it is. But learning to ascend is, in truth, incredibly simple—child's play really. When we give up our investment in fear in all its forms and turn our hearts into vessels of love, we go through a cleansing process that need not be fearful. When we know that even though our personal process of transformation appears frightening or confusing to us, that we have mighty friends who love us and will help us along the way, we no longer feel alone or frightened or hopeless and can rise up with the strength of God within us. We can *choose* to reclaim our divine heritage. In that process miracles such as ascension occur.

As each person rises above his life as a caterpillar into that rare alchemy of consciousness and being that is symbolized by the butterfly, he contributes his consciousness to the field of energy called by Sheldrake the morphogenic field. With each addition to that field, a greater knowledge than before is available. It thus becomes easier and easier for other people to realize the same truths. As Newton said, "If I appear to see farther, it is because I stand on the shoulders of giants." All those who are learning the teachings are becoming 'giants' for those who will follow.

February 12

Last night I was visited by an angel of the Lord. I was lying in my bed, preparing for sleep, when she came. Hearing a sound like ancient Viking horns, I propped myself up abruptly, then fell immediately back. I was struck in the chest by what felt like a bolt of lightning. When I recovered myself, I saw a form materializing in the darkness before me.

She was tall and beautiful in a way that makes our ordinary concept of beauty seem pale and shallow. Her hair shone like the sun, and sparkles of light constantly fell from it in a dazzling fireworks display of energy. Her face was young in the way the ancient earth seems young when spring comes and trees that have borne the icy and barren harshness of winter send forth new shoots of growth and life. Such a face was hers.

Her body had the innocence and purity of a girl's coupled with the stately grace of a true queen. She wore a thin garment that looked like spun snow. When she spoke, she used not words or even thoughts, but *music*. I smiled to myself. How else could an angel speak other than with music? Music—God's language, of which earthly music is but a shadow. And her name was Aurien.

Aurien sang to me in the trembling ethers her presence had created in my bedroom, there in the night. Her words touched my heart in a way no earthly music ever had or could. It was clear she knew of the onrushing destruction of the physical universe and its translation to light and how I and others were striving to prepare the way for that impending event. She knew also, as she sang to my heart, the hidden fears I had experienced regarding that greatest of all changes, knew I feared life was not ready for it, that it would arrive too soon and would leave the universe stillborn, barren.

Moving across the ground like a song through the air, Aurien led me outside. She bade me look up at the moon. I gazed at the silvery orb and saw it as a magnificent pearl floating free in the dark sea of night. For a moment I saw the moon pulse and lose form and shape, as I had seen Earth do those many months ago. I feared I was being shown the beginning of the end time, that Aurien was the harbinger of the end of the worlds.

What followed is difficult to describe. The moon began to lose its quality of form, and I saw it not in three dimensions but as something other. It began to fold itself into a shape I cannot describe. It started to move *into* itself in a manner similar to how a blossom might fold its petals into itself in a reversal of its growth process until it is a seed again. The moon was enfolding itself in such a way; but the process seemed not to be toward its beginning but rather toward its ending—as though it were *completing* a process rather than winding back to the start of that process. Strange.

Then not just the moon but the whole sky began the process. The entire universe started folding itself back to what it had been before we had chosen to see it in three dimensions, before we had chosen to perceive life as having an outer, external reality clearly defined and delineated from the inner one. The universe was winding back in those dizzying moments to what it must have been like before the existence of time and space and bodies; yet it was inexplicably moving *forward* rather than *backward*, just as the moon had done.

It would be more accurate to say the universe was becoming what it would be like *after* existence in the physical worlds ended. The process was different from the one I saw on my journey back to the ancient beginning of things. That journey had had little love or awe or joy to it. This vision, if vision it was, was filled with joy and song. There was a glorious overlay of brilliant light that went from brightest gold to purest white, then to most dazzling silver. Embodied in these living hues was a sense of meaning and joy too great for the conscious mind to contain. The quality of that silver light was pure and sublime, unlike the dingy, yellowish glow that made a mockery of light—that malformed light Iripan and I had both seen in our respective worlds.

Watching the entire universe become a magnificent, formless, silver essence was glorious beyond words or thoughts. As I gazed at Aurien, the music of her soul sang me the rightness of what I had seen. I was filled with something too grand to be called wonder. Aurien was an angel come straight from heaven. She *lived* and *moved* through states of being such as she was showing me now. All my beauties paled beside the sheer splendor of her sublime and mighty soul.

What Aurien showed me was not life going back to its beginnings. She showed me the end of things, the way the physical universe must end. I understood that it was not to be a true ending any more than the caterpillar's metamorphosis was an ending. It would be a new birth into a grand life, just as the caterpillar would emerge into a new life as a butterfly. As Aurien's music poured into my soul, I felt that what I had just witnessed was the resplendent ending of the universe and its translation into light. It was not death that was being shown me but life. This was not a tragic ending of things but a glorious new beginning.

I asked Aurien through my heart if what I had seen was truly how the impending change would be. She replied it was how things were *intended* to be, not how they *must* be. She said the preview I had just witnessed was being given to all awakened beings throughout both universes to help it be so. I asked what would happen to those who hardened their hearts and refused to hear the message. Was there no hope for them? In my heart I knew that if even one of my brothers or sisters was barred from heaven's gates, I could not enter either. She lifted her golden voice up and sang my heart to peace. There was always hope for those who did not hear the call to awaken. There would be other universes, other bubbles on the ocean of God, other inbreaths and outbreaths of Brahma, though in terms of earthly years, another such fall into matter might not happen for a stretch of time so great my mind could not hold the concept of it. But when it did happen, those who did not make the voyage this time to the new Eden would have another chance to enter the heart of God.

I knew then that God waits with patient arms outstretched for *all* 'prodigal sons' to return. And those arms do not tire; they are open forever. Though delay is meaningless in eternity, it *is* tragic in time. Those who do not make the journey this time will lose all they knew during their current existence and must start anew from the bottom rung of the ladder. But when they, too, return—as they must—there will be a great rejoicing, for the lost children will have finally found their way home.

I felt a great weight lifted from my heart as I breathed in the music of Aurien's soul. I had feared that what was being done to accelerate the growth and awakening of others was perhaps not enough or was too late. Now I rested in the peaceful knowledge that nothing is ever truly lost, that delay is *our* choice, part of our divine birthright. I knew also that it *is* possible for all beings to be ready for the journey to the new Eden. *No one* need be left behind. I dedicated myself anew to the task of awakening all the others before it is too late.

The vision of the universe's ending drew to a close, and I rested in the gentle haven of Aurien's music. I was like a vessel filled to overflowing with what I had felt and what I had seen. Though Aurien spoke not, there was music, nonetheless; music was part of her being in the same way that light is a part of the sun.

Aurien looked at me with a gaze of pure acceptance and joy—or at least I so interpreted it for she was something more than human, more even than light. She was beyond expressing emotions in the way we understand them. I met her gaze and stared for a moment into the swirling pools of her majestic eyes.

It was hard to maintain eye contact with Aurien for long, however. I felt uncomfortable. Though there was only love and joy and music beaming forth from her, there was also a very great sense of the holy. I felt unworthy to be in the presence of such a high being for a long period of time. She seemed too pure for this world, for this universe—a creature of pure spirit come straight from the heart of God—a being so pure even *light* must be difficult for her to bear, so far beneath her essence was it.

Aurien's essence was the answer to the image that had puzzled me since that journey back to life's beginning. As Iripan and I had left that vast presence known as the Holy Spirit, the true guiding principle of the physical universes, I had caught a glimpse of something still more magnificent than purest light. Now, after witnessing Aurien, I know what it was. It was *spirit*—pure spirit, the essence of 'God I Am.' I reflected with joy and awe on this thought—that there was something as far beyond light as light is beyond matter; and a new thought took hold of me. If this were truly so, then there might also be experiences as well that are so grand, so sublime, that all my beauties, wonderful as they were, might be but dim shadows by comparison. Could this be so? My mind grew dizzy with the notion.

All these thoughts flooded my mind with purest light while I gazed at the holy presence before me, sparkles continually bursting from her golden hair and spewing on the ground. I was going to say something; but just as my mouth opened to speak, Aurien's eyes flashed lightning and a sound like thunder boomed all around me. Then she began to fade away. First her body grew transparent; then it burst into light. Then I saw another flash. This time the light was silver rather than gold, and she was gone.

The force of Aurien's departure was so great it knocked me off my feet. I lost consciousness as she faded away into the moonlight, a ghostly figure draped in glistening silver. When I came to myself, the first light of morning was breaking. Like a line on a piece of paper erasing itself, a small airplane was flying across the horizon in the distance.

July 25

The work goes well. Many are awakening all over this world, on Iltar, and many other worlds as well. The guises that awakening takes are many, the vessels that hold the wine are many; but the wine, the message, is essentially the same, and it is pouring like vitalized water into the minds and hearts and spirits of many.

I have gone into seclusion permanently. All my time is now devoted to assisting the beings on other worlds with this mighty work of preparing all of life for the transit to light. The metaphorical ship that will sail to the new Eden will be arriving soon. My deepest hope is that everyone will be ready.

I am in almost constant contact with beings from other star systems, other galaxies. The message is spreading like wildfire throughout the universes—both mine and Iripan's. Consciousness is igniting; the ability to ascend the body and the worlds is increasing proportionately. I am more encouraged and optimistic than ever that the work Iripan and I and so many others have been doing for the past several months has been effective, has been in time. And though there will always be those who refuse to hear the call to awaken, I am content in knowing that the call was issued and that there will be another chance to enter the new Eden, though it may not occur for a time distant beyond imagination.

"Whither Goest the Wind?"

August 3

I have always loved to watch the ever changing ocean rush toward the shore—rolling and scrambling over itself like many people fearfully rushing away from some danger, oblivious to the injury they may be causing those unable to move as quickly. I've loved watching it rush in, seeking to break its anger against the silent, compassionate land, then rush away again like a flirtatious woman who kisses playfully and withdraws when the man seeks to deepen the embrace. Such is the ocean.

I love watching the sun gently lower its fiery head to the edge of the waters as a riot of rich colors explodes in the sky around it. Tonight I saw brilliant golds and violets and flashing reds turn the underside of the darkening clouds into the hulls of fierce war-galleons swiftly sailing into glorious battle with enemy vessels. So great were the feelings evoked that amid the beautiful splash of colors I thought I saw patches of Uln, Patto, and Morille. But perhaps I just imagined it.

Finally, the sun became a small slice of light above the waters. As twilight pulled a mantle of deep blue darkness over the scene, Once more I saw a path of golden light forming on the ocean's surface. Sparks of gold and silver light sported there, dancing in the moonlight. The scene was a magical one. But it was not a fantasy world, an unreal world, that had replaced the one of time and deadlines and the struggle to survive. It was a truer one by far I now witnessed, one that had been overlaid with the other. As I gazed at that path of golden light, that path of wonder extending to the world's end, I wondered once again if I could walk it; and if I could, where it would lead.

August 13

Soon I must leave this world. I've known that for a while now. I can best do the work that still remains while in a higher state of being. The ascension process calls to me daily; but I've been ignoring those promptings so that I can complete my work here. Part of that work has been to leave a record of what has happened to me. As I have said before, I leave this chronicle in the hopes that it will quicken the evolutionary process in those not reached or moved by the teachings in its myriad forms during the next few years.

Iripan and I met two days ago in the space between our worlds, that place that is not light and not darkness. What a joy it was to be with her! I love her with all my heart and soul. At times I still wish there was a place, a little corner in one of our universes that was not in need of us, a place where we could live our lives together forever. But I know this cannot be—not now. She and I must each be married to God before we are married to each other.

Iripan feels drawn to a higher state also, for a person can see much more from the top of a mountain than from a valley far below. Soon both Iripan and I will leave our worlds and carry on the work from that higher place reached by ascension. She, too, has been working tirelessly with beings throughout her universe, and the process of its evolutionary acceleration is proceeding at the same rate that it is in this universe. The fuse has been lit in both universes; she and I have done our part. There is little more we can do in our present embodiment.

August 26

The time has come for me to leave. I've said my good-byes to those I am closest to and to the sky, the sea, the mountains, and the stars. I think of all the things of this plane, I shall miss the stars most. As a child, they beckoned to me and evoked a nameless sense of wonder and awe and loneliness in me. They still do.

This is such a beautiful world, such a beautiful life. I shall miss it, for I may never pass this way again. The old way is ended for me; it is finished. I am so very blessed to have had this precious, shining moment in time—in this embodiment. What a sublime joy it has been to be human! Of all the possible states of being and consciousness, this may prove to be the most wonderful and precious of all. My only regret is that I did not know how to appreciate it most of my life, that I saw it as a punishment and a drudgery.

Last night the final beauty of this life came to me. The sun had set and the stars had lit up the velvety black dome of night. A sweeping wind was whistling through the trees behind me as the ocean waves broke in the distance. Then a soft voice came to me, then another, and another. Soon I was immersed in the sound of countless voices uniting to form an angelic chorus singing joyfully. The voices became intertwined with glorious strains of music. Then, there was a moment when all sounds ceased and a hush of silence as deep as the tomb fell over my soul. A strain of music similar to what I had heard with Aurien then started. And once more I saw the world lose substance and turn into a formless blob of golden light.

In the wink of an eye the world vanished. In its place was a sheen of endless, formless, golden light. This time the light was of a more brilliant hue than I'd ever seen before in that heightened state. Only thin streaks of darkness striated the beautiful glow, which was not the mottled, dirty color I had seen before. This time it had a sweet beauty to it; and I knew it signified that others *were* learning, others *were* hearing the message to awaken. I knew also that it was now time for me to complete the last part of my work from a higher, more sublime place of being, time to ascend once more, time to go beyond the edge of wonder and that elusive margin of beauty. This time I will go beyond even pure light into what can only be called spirit—of which light itself is only the shadow. And this time the change will be forever.

Tonight, when the sun sinks low and the stars begin to appear in the gathering dusk, I will walk that golden path of light the sun lays down across the sea. And I will never return. Before doing so, I will send this journal to Mindy with the hope that she can find the right person to ensure its publication. The time is right to make a full revelation to the world of the process that led to the eventual formulation of the teachings.

I love this life. And I love you, dear reader. Weep no sad tears for me. Rejoice instead! The hopes and dreams of all humanity are coming to everyone, and very soon. And more, so much more.... Read this journal carefully, over and over. Let it teach you what it can. Let it aid you in your process of unfoldment and awakening. The time grows very short. Live love. Love life.

We will meet again.

EPILOGUE

Here the journal ends. I cannot say with certainty that all it sets forth is true; but the sincerity and urgency of it should cause the serious reader to pause and consider.

Shortly after I finished reading the manuscript, I contacted a friend who is a dabbler in the unseen and a traveler in mystical circles. I had always regarded him as something of an eccentric for his interest in what cannot be seen or cut up into little pieces in a laboratory. I no longer do. I asked him if he had ever heard of William Sherrill. He said he had not but that something very close to what I described as the teachings had recently found its way into numerous trainings, seminars, and secret societies he had had contact with.

William Sherrill was never seen or heard from again. For a time the local papers and news programs talked of foul play, but the sensationalism of his disappearance died down and nothing ever came of the investigation. It is my belief that Sherrill did exactly as he said he would—walked that magical band of golden light formed by the setting sun across the ocean, and left this world, this life, that he might continue to serve elsewhere.

Last night I drove to Sherrill's seaside cottage and watched the sun set on the waters. It was a beautiful sight, but there was nothing extraordinary about it—at first. As the sun dipped into the waters, however, and the silvery stars began to poke their heads out of the cobalt blue canopy of the night sky, the spectacle changed until it was nothing short of magical. The golden light formed its path across the ocean, and there came a moment when I felt I could almost see Sherrill as he walked that ribbon of golden light stretching all the way to the sun. In the tiny sliver of the crescent moon, I imagined I saw his smile, the same smile I had seen during our brief meeting almost four years ago. And I *knew* his final words were true. Perhaps all his words are.

V. H.

Journeys to the Edge of Wonder
A Novel of Spiritual Adventure

Jack Byrd

To order gift copies, fill in the coupon and mail it to:

Heartsinger Press
2021 Guadalupe St., Suite 100-56
Austin, Texas 78705

For each copy please enclose a check or money order for $9.95 (sales tax included) plus $2.00 shipping & handling for the first copy and $0.50 shipping & handling for each additional copy. *If 5 or more copies are ordered, all postage & handling is free!*

✂ ✂ ✂ ✂ ✂ ✂ ✂ ✂ ✂ ✂ ✂

Yes! Please send me
Journeys to the Edge of Wonder
A Novel of Spiritual Adventure

_____ copies @ $9.95 $_____

Shipping & handling @ $2.00 $_____

Shipping & handling @ $0.50 $_____

☞ *if 5 or more copies are ordered, all postage & handling is free!* 👈

Total Amount Enclosed $_____

NAME _____

ADDRESS _____

CITY _____

signature and phone # including area code
(Allow 3-4 weeks for delivery)